THE UNITED STATES OF AIR

ALSO BY J.M. PORUP

NOVELS

The Judas Syndrome
The Second Bat Guano War
Death on Taurus
The United States of Air

PLAYS

Very Skinny People
Ariadne's Lament and Two Other Shorts
Thy Fearful Symmetry

TRAVEL GUIDEBOOKS

Lonely Planet Colombia
Lonely Planet Venezuela
Lonely Planet Dominican Republic & Haiti
Lonely Planet South America on a Shoestring
Lonely Planet Caribbean Islands

NONFICTION

Colombia's Diversity Problem: a Speech on Tourism

DIET/SELF-HELP

Food-Free At Last: How I Learned To Eat Air*

* with Dr. Robert Jones, MD, PhD, DDS, ODD

THE UNITED STATES OF AIR

BY

J.M. PORUP

For the fools who still believe

ONE

LOOK AT HOW FAT I AM. ISN'T IT DISGUSTING? Here. Let me pull up my shirt. See? Zoom in that camera. Can all of you see? How much fat I can pinch? And don't you go telling me that's loose skin. Just because I have an eighteen-inch waist doesn't mean I'm not fat. I know what fat looks like. It's my job. Or used to be. Before I became ambassador to France, I was plain old Jason Frolick, Special Agent for the ATFF.

That's the Bureau of Alcohol, Tobacco, Firearms and Food, for all you ferrners out there watching. It was my job to put food terrists in Fat Camp. And the kinds of fat I saw! A reminder every day why the Global War on Fat is so important. Thank the Prophet for the Amendment. No, not *that* Prophet. I mean President Jones. We all call him the Prophet. If it weren't for him, our country would still be enslaved to addictive caloric substances, otherwise known in ghetto street lingo as "food."

What's he saying? Come on. Translate for me, already. By the Prophet's empty belly, you'd think an advanced country like France would have learned how to speak English by now, and how to eat air.

Fat Camp. He wants to know more about Fat Camp. Is that it?

And no, I'm not irritable because I'm hungry. That's French propaganda and you know it. That's what this news show is, right? A thinly disguised propaganda machine? Next you'll be telling me that food is not a drug, and that no one can eat air.

Oh, for eating out loud. You mean that so-called undercover documentary? By whatzizface, the BBC journalist? Or should I say, French *saboteur.* Just listen to the guy.

"People are starving to death. Hoarding food, eating in secret, denouncing their neighbors. Selling everything they own to buy precious calories on the black market. Corpses whisked away at dawn by special cleanup crews."

I mean, come on! Those dead bodies are obviously fake. Probably filmed on some movie lot right here in Paris. It's lies like this that have forced us to censor the Internet, so that you ferrners cannot infect our people's faith with doubt.

Now where was I... Fat Camp. Thank you. Our finest achievement. I am so proud of our network of re-education facilities. From coast to coast, dedicated military personnel help citizens, free of charge, get the monkey off their backs. Our trainers teach the air-eating technique pioneered by the Prophet and set forth in his ground-breaking book *Food-Free At Last.* But even more important, Fat Camps offer sanctuary from temptation. A place where you can go to reinforce your faith. Because even the slightest doubt will destroy your ability to digest air— and on an air-only diet, that can be fatal. Nowhere else I know is so conducive to breaking the shackles of addiction and setting yourself free.

Because that's what it's all about. Freedom. Abraham Lincoln freed the blacks from slavery. The Prophet freed us from the Tyranny of Food. No longer must we be slaves to our appetites.

We are free to become pure spirit, undiluted intelligence. Souls unstained by orange cheese puff smears, stray dollops of pizza sauce or mashed-up French fries.

In doing so, he set us all free. The entire human race. That is why I've come here, to France, as your ambassador, to bring you a message of hope—glad tidings of great joy—that you too can be free. I call on all of you, everyone out there watching now, in every country round the world: rise up! Rise up, and break the chains that bind you to your dinner plate. Eat air. Drink water. Have faith. That is all you need.

You are laughing, sir. You claim to be, what? France's most venerated and distinguished newscaster, whatever your unpronounceable name is? I remind you, sir, of Gandhi's words: "First they ignore you, then they laugh at you, then they fight you, then you win."

Not laughing anymore, are we?

Let us be clear. I am here today with a message. From the Prophet himself to the people of France. The rest of you ferrners out there too. The Prophet is the Leader of the Food-Free World. And France, I am sorry to say, is stuck in her oldey-worldey, food-addicted, pleasure-loving past. A time is coming when you will have to choose. You are either with us, or you are against us. Which is it going to be?

Don't bother to translate that, whatever he's saying. I'm not interested. I'm not asking for an answer now. I will say only this: attempts to depose the Prophet and reinstate the Tyranny of Food in our country, as the French Secret Service tried to do last month, can only result in war. Because of you French, we almost lost everything.

But I forgive you. It's not your fault. It's the food talking. All these baguettes and cheeses and wines I see you people eating. My heart aches to think how you must suffer. That's why I agreed to come on this news show. I understand, from painful personal experience, how hard it is to break the cycle of addiction. At the Prophet's personal request, I am going to share with you my own struggle against food.

If you've tried to lose weight, if you've tried to free yourself from the seemingly inescapable vicelike grip of appetite masquerading as hunger—come closer. Yes, you. Here. Huddle around the television and learn that you are not alone. Because I used to be just like you. Eating every day. Unable to stop putting food in my mouth. Dancing to my stomach's tune.

Nor is my struggle over. Even now, three years since the Prophet came to power, and the Amendment passed, my faith is not complete. I still suffer from—but how can I say this? I must. The Prophet has ordered me to tell you. Of my secret shame. It is only with your help, all of you out there watching, that I hope to finally be able to hold my head up high.

How can you help me, you ask? You shall see. But first, let me tell you of my own journey. How I came to know and love the Prophet's words, to embrace the path of eating air, and from my humble beginnings as an ATFF agent, became the ambassador to France, and the Prophet's spokesman to the world.

TWO

I WASN'T ALWAYS THIS FAT. I USED TO BE A TUB OF lard. In fact, lard was my favorite food. I'd use an ice cream scoop to make lard sundaes, smothered in hot bacon drippings, crunchy chunks of pork rind, with a pickle on top. To cut the grease a bit, you know. Even now, just thinking about it makes my mouth water.

Sometimes I'd go on a diet. I'd buy half a dozen pallets of the world's best diet food: Twinkies. The diet was simple: all the Twinkies I wanted. But only Twinkies. Nothing else. After a week of this grueling diet, I'd put myself up on the scale. Since it was impossible to see my feet at that time, much less read the scale, I had to guess my weight. It usually seemed like I'd lost a few pounds, so I'd celebrate with a hot lard sundae, extra pork rind. Man, that crunch used to drive me wild.

This was before the Prophet came to power. I was working as a D.C. cop, and when I wasn't patiently explaining to criminals their constitutional rights, or reminding them that the American justice system was the fairest in the world, I was eating. On a typical shift, my partner Harry Green and I would each consume three dozen doughnuts, two large pizzas, seven or eight Big Macs, depending on our appetites, and, for dessert, hidden in the trunk of our cruiser against all regulations, our secret ice box of chilled butter and lard. I confess I never could understand his preference for butter. We'd cut off thick wedges, let them melt on our tongues. For a time, it seemed like heaven.

Looking back, I know that it was hell.

I will never forget the first time I heard the Prophet speak. I had finished my shift and grabbed a bucket of fried chicken on the way home. A light snack before bed. Crashed out on the sofa, the bucket between my gargantuan thighs. Flicked on the news. And there he was. Running for President.

"Food is a drug!" he thundered at an arena full of blubber. People just like me. "You don't need to eat! That's a myth! All you need is air!"

Then he proceeded to do something extraordinary. He showed us his teeth, opened his mouth wide and chomped down on something invisible. He chewed, jaws working up and down, then swallowed loudly and patted his stomach with a satisfied grin.

"If I can do it," he shouted, to cheers from the crowd, "you can do it too!"

He railed against the agro-business special interests that had brainwashed us into thinking that food was harmless, had corrupted our youth with their addictive caloric substances, and filled our hospitals with patients suffering from heart disease, diabetes and cancer.

Global warming. Crowded jails. Nuclear weapons. Drivers who forget to signal. All our social ills are caused by one thing only: the stuff we put in our mouths that we don't need. By food. By calories. And by eliminating the source of all these evils, and enforcing a zero-calorie air-only diet, we turn our country into a city on a hill, a light in the darkness, a beacon that other nations may follow on their own journeys down the Superhighway of Purity and Air.

"There is hope!" the Prophet declared to a sea of worshipful faces, their double and triple chins quivering with joy under the stadium lights. "Hope for a Food-Free World! Ask yourself: Whose fault is it that you're fat?" And his face went grim and the crowd fell silent. "It's *their* fault!" he roared. "Them! The fat people!" He pounded the podium with his fist. "How can you be thin if you're surrounded by fat?"

As if on cue, the crowd began to chant, "Down with fat! Down with fat! Down with fat!"

"Don't blame yourself!" he shouted, to cries of swooning adulation. "You must see the change you wish to be in the world!"

I threw my half-eaten chicken wing back into the bucket, and kicked it across the room. "See the change you wish to be." My God, he was right! Those evil fatties would pay. The Prophet continued to speak, but I don't remember his exact words anymore, just the realization that this was my last chance.

Because, you see, I didn't eat because I wanted to. I never *wanted* to. I didn't even enjoy it. I ate because I had to. If my jaws weren't moving, I wasn't happy. If one of my hands didn't hold the next mouthful in readiness, primed for the moment my mouth became vacant, I'd get panic attacks. I'd have to stop whatever I was doing and find something, anything to eat—a dozen hot dogs cold out of the package, ten-pound bags of year-old liquorice, boxes of melted chocolate abandoned in a supermarket dumpster—it didn't matter. Being a D.C. cop is stressful, especially when you let criminals go if they promise not to do it again and you wind up arresting them the very next day for the exact same crime. This happened to me all the time, and it was so disappointing. All I wanted to do was plunge both hands full of food into my mouth at once. Eating calmed me down. Nothing else worked.

Of course you know the election results. It's a matter of history. The Prophet campaigned on the slogan "Let's Put America On A Diet!"—and won. By a landslide. Within six months the Amendment passed by unanimous consent of all fifty states, except for Vermont. A real disgrace, that. Apparently some quack doctor, a member of that state's General Assembly, probably high on barley or wheat or whatever the food users pop up there, abstained from the vote in protest, making the absurd claim that consuming food is necessary to life. You might as well say that drinking a bottle of gin every day is necessary to life. Or snorting cocaine. Shooting up heroin. I mean, come on, you know? Anyway, he got his due. A group of Vermont's leading citizens, enraged at this blot on their state's reputation, burned the man's house down, raped his wife and shot his dog. I'm sorry? It's a traditional American way of showing disapproval. Don't worry, though. The dog survived.

I see you shaking your head. Now, I know it's hard for some of you ferrners out there to understand the innovative ideas coming out of the New World. Backward Old World types like yourself—no offense—well, you've been addicted to food for thousands of years. In America, or "Air," as I should say, the name got changed by the Amendment, we've got the chance to do things differently. To do things *right*. Make a better life for ourselves and our children.

The Prophet rode a mandate into office, and he wasted no time in spending his political capital. In making that better life come true for all Airitarians. He declared a Global War on Fat.

As soon as he moved into the Thin House, he ordered all supermarkets bulldozed, all restaurants demolished, all farmers forbidden to cultivate under penalty of death. By the time the Amendment passed, the Prophet's crop-dusting program was well under way. The entire Air Force, stealth bomber and all, was equipped with aerial spraying equipment and billions of tons of the most potent herbicide available. Twelve months ago today he celebrated the sterilization of the last square inch of arable land in the country: a tiny crack in a sidewalk in Baltimore, where grass had sprouted between the concrete slabs. And don't think he kept anything aside for himself, either. The Prophet has always led by example. He personally put on a space suit and sprayed the Thin House lawn, making sure that every last flower in the Rose Garden was dead.

I told you, I'm not going to take any questions until the— what? Excuse me? People starving in Africa... Why don't we send our food to Africa? If we don't want it, they'll eat it. You know, it's questions like this that piss me off. I'm sorry to use the p-word like that, but it makes me so mad. What's happening in Africa is a tragedy, but it's not our fault. We sent them missionaries. To show them a new way of life. Air-eating is sustainable regardless of drought. It doesn't matter if it rains or not.

And what did they do? What did those ungrateful Africans do? Strapped down our young men and women and force-fed them cornmeal mixed with soybean oil and sugar. You understand? They tortured our missionaries. So forgive me when I say, if people are starving in Africa, it's their own goddamn fault. There, I used the g-d-word, see what you made me do.

No, I don't want any water. I am calm.

9

Listen, I'll tell you what is a problem that worries me. Illegal emigration. These people are slowly destroying our country. It's like they *want* to be slaves to their digestive systems. I feel sorry for them. This is why we've sealed our borders. Why sentries patrol the no-man's-land with Mexico, with orders to shoot to kill anyone trying to escape over that wall or wade the Rio Grande. These people must not be allowed to reach the taco and burrito stands that line the Mexican side of the river.

This may seem extreme to some of you, but I assure you it's a question of freedom. Every citizen of the US of Air is born with the inalienable right to be free. Free from addiction to food. But some people, hardened food terrists, most of them, reject freedom. They refuse to be free. I tell you now, the Prophet will not rest until everyone is free, no matter what the cost in blood or treasure.

Take our decision to ground all civilian air traffic. The economic impact was huge, but it was necessary to combat food terrism. Shortly after the Prophet took office, food terrists hijacked hundreds of 747s and forced the pilots to fly to Cuba at the business end of a corn dog. Dangerous thing, a corn dog, especially to a pilot suffering food withdrawal.

Of course, we demanded these terrists be extradited, to be tried for their crimes in Food Court. But the freedom-hating regime of that island nation refused.

In fact, not a month went by before Cuba rebranded itself the "Fat Capital of the World." Trying to lure our tender young minds away from the Path of Righteousness and Air to the soul-destroying corruption of their beachside "restaurants." Food labs is what they are. And they invite thousands of French chefs to come and practice their disgusting and illegal craft in these food labs. "Cooking," I believe the dealers call it. You know, when they mix different caloric substances together in precise measurements in a metal container, and then hold the container over a high heat. Kind of like a meth lab, except none of the ingredients are available over the counter.

It gets worse. It's not enough that Cuba supports these manufacturers of suffering and addiction. Our intelligence sources indicate the presence of joint Cuban-French training camps—don't bother to deny it, we've got satellite photos, we've even got the recipes—where Cuban guerrillas train French chefs with at least three Michelin stars to infiltrate our borders, prepare addictive caloric substances to tempt senior government officials, and then blackmail them.

Cuba is, as it has always been, one of our greatest enemies.

And you know, if Cuba wasn't such a threat to our freedom, the Flotilla would never have happened. That's what you vultures in the media called it, right? Cuba sets itself up as a beacon of food for the so-called hungry, and soon thousands of our citizens are risking their lives to paddle across the Florida Straits, many on improvised rafts made out of driftwood and lashed together with old shoelaces. The Coast Guard turned back boat after boat, raft after raft, until the yachties organized the Flotilla. Six months ago, it was. You remember. Twenty thousand boats left Miami in one great pack, yachts and sailboats and powerboats, and thousands and thousands of homemade rafts. As per the Prophet's "wet foot, dead foot" policy, the Coast Guard opened fire as soon as they entered international waters, but ran out of bullets. Luckily there was an aircraft carrier nearby, and the Coast Guard was able to call in air support. Fighters strafed the Flotilla until only debris and dismembered body parts were left.

We got a lot of bad press about this, at least in your international papers. But you've got to remember something. These people were dangerous food terrists who would do anything for their next hit. Like the Johnson brothers. Exactly. Sure, I know what happened to them. The only two survivors of the Flotilla, and what do they do? Go on Cuban television and tell everyone how happy they are to have a full stomach for a change. The world watching, and they stick out their tongues at us. Couple of thumb-sucking six-year-old brats. The CIA took them out. Boom-boom. Double tap. One in the chest, one in the head. Food terrists like that are a threat to every freedom-loving nation in the world.

Even tough love has its limits, you know? We tried to help them. We wanted them to be free. But they refused our help. It was out of compassion that we put them down. Put them out of their misery. It is better to be dead than a slave.

Live Free or Die. That's the US of A's motto. The Prophet's mantra, too. When he meditates, he takes a deep breath, exhales slowly and chants, *Livefreeordiiiieeee. Livefreeordiiiieeee. Livefreeordiiiieeee.* So relaxing. You should try it sometime.

That's a stupid question. How do I sleep at night? Same as you do. I turn off the lights, get into bed and dream about George Washington and Benjamin Franklin. What would the Founding Fathers say to see us now, how much progress we've made since their day, taking not just our country but the entire human race to a new, higher plane of existence?

And it's sad, really. What happened to the Johnson brothers, and to others like them. Because it could all have been avoided, if they had been willing to give Fat Camp a chance. I remember when I went to Fat Camp. It was a wonderful experience.

The Prophet declared a special amnesty for law enforcement officials. Volunteer and you got to keep your job. It's true some officers decided to stockpile weapons and cases of their favorite drug, and head for the hills. The Air Force has since bombed those mountain hideouts back into the Stone Age.

Fat Camp changed my life, as it changed the lives of so many of my fellow Airitarians. The military trainers marched us through the fields on long excursions, our mouths wide open, sucking down God's great air. If you were unlucky you might swallow a fly or a mosquito. That puts your progress back for weeks, let me tell you. Addiction means addiction. A heroin addict can't shoot up every now and again. It's all or nothing. You can't perfect your air-eating technique until you've been food-free for at least a month, and sometimes not even then.

Did you know that air comes in thirty-one flavors? You can have a different one every night of the week—for four weeks! Like vanilla, cilantro and asparagus. My favorite was always Mexican night. They'd let off a blast of pepper spray over the camp, and we'd run around with our eyes closed, taking great gulps of that wonderful taco taste. Which just goes to prove to you critics out there that we're not Puritans. We aren't anti-pleasure. Only anti-food.

A demonstration? Sure. Of course. You won't get any results the first time just by copying what I do. But I'll humor you. I can see the studio audience is curious, as no doubt are your viewers. It's only fair for them to see what they are missing out on, don't you think?

Here. Let me stand. You know, I've never eaten air in front of such a large audience before. Oops. The mike. Sure. Got it. Now, stand up. All of you. Stand up with me. That's it. Now move around a little. Loosen up. Shake those hands. Good. Nice and loose. Now make sure there's plenty of fresh air circulating near your head. Near your mouth. For instance, you should avoid eating air in basements, and in other poorly ventilated spaces. When you're ready, open your mouth. Wide, wide, wide, as far as it goes—yes, that's it—now lunge forward and chomp. Good. This is key. Lunge and chomp. No, no, no! You forgot to seal your lips. Tell him. Translate this. Classic beginner's mistake. The air leaks out through your lips or your nose before you can swallow it, digest it. You've got to pinch your nose shut, keep your lips tightly sealed while you munch on your very first atmospheric snack. Good one!

Above and beyond technique, there is one final ingredient crucial to eating air. I've mentioned it already. That is faith. You must believe. Anyone can master the technique, given time. But without faith, your body cannot digest air. You have to have faith in yourself. Doubt of any kind, even the tiniest niggle in the back of your mind, destroys all your hard work and puts you back to square one.

For those of you interested in attending Fat Camp yourself, and I'm sure many of you are, the embassy here in Paris has constructed a series of demonstration Fat Camps throughout the French countryside. We've already begun to enroll a small number of volunteers. Naturally we'd like to see France build more Fat Camps, enough for the entire population, to help bring freedom to the enslaved French people. And I have to say, between you and me? French air is the most flavorsome I have ever tasted.

To go back a bit. When I graduated from Fat Camp, top of my class, a federal recruiter was waiting for me. Lieutenant

Brownnose Lickit—I remember the chocolate-colored stain on his chin no amount of rubbing could ever seem to remove. He wore a trench coat with a tape measure wrapped tight around his narrow waist—the uniform of the newly reorganized ATFF that was to strike fear into the hearts of food terrists everywhere. He looked me up and down, not without a little disgust. I had lost two hundred pounds in thirty days, but I still had at least three hundred more to go. Finally he asked me if I was serious in my desire to enlist in the War on Fat.

Absolutely, I told him. There was nothing I wanted more. Nothing I wouldn't do to achieve victory in that fight.

It was then he invited me to join the Food Enforcement Division's training program. He slid a tape measure across the table with a smile.

"Welcome to the front lines of the defining conflict of our age."

The tape measure didn't fit, of course. It was another four months before I got my waistline down to twenty-five inches, the maximum allowed by the Bureau.

Our training was rigorous. They taught us a smorgasbord of techniques to subdue the rampaging food terrist. We learned Kung Yum Chop, an Eastern martial art that favored chopsticks as the weapon of choice. Stunt drivers demonstrated cornering at low speeds in our government-issued Smart Cars. (As part of his campaign promise to slim down government, the Prophet had sold the administration's fleet of black SUVs and replaced them with Smart Cars.)

But most of our training was dedicated to the Laxafier, the Bureau's standard-issue sidearm. The Prophet had replaced all service weapons with these six-round laxative revolvers. Each

THE UNITED STATES OF AIR

dart contained enough tranquilizer to drop a fattie charging an all-you-can-eat buffet, and enough laxative to empty his bowels immediately.

The day I became an ATFF agent and put on that tape measure for the first time was the proudest day of my life. The anthem playing, the flag fluttering and snapping in the breeze, the pepper spray canister the organizers let off over our heads—I was so happy I couldn't stop crying. We swore the oath of office together, vowing solemnly to protect and defend the Amendment against all enemies, both ferrn and domestic. Together we lunged and chomped for the camera, snacking on that exotic Mexican air, and finally tied our tape measures around our waists, from which dangled our bright new badges of office.

"What's our motto?" our captain shouted.

"Liberty or Death!" we roared back.

A tingle went up my spine as I shouted with the rest of them. We were on the cutting edge of human evolution. And I was part of that. Part of something greater than myself. Helping to make the world a better place.

No, I'm fine. Really. Just something in my eyes, is all.

It would have been a perfect day, except for my wife, Chantal. She showed up with Nathan, our ten-year-old son, in tow, a gallon of fudge ripple ice cream under her arm. To this day I don't know where she got it. I couldn't believe what she did next. She opened the carton in front of everyone—and put a spoonful in her mouth!

Here we were, a couple hundred freshly minted ATFF agents, recruited to stamp out precisely this kind of food abuse, and here she was, my wife, chowing down in front of my new colleagues. I just stood there, frozen, I was so embarrassed. But when she went to give a spoonful to our child, I started to run. It took me five minutes to cover the fifty feet to where she sat, the withered muscles in my arms and legs straining to get me there in time. I took a diving leap and knocked the spoon from her hand just as it touched my son's lips.

After that incident, I put my foot down. No food means no food. Naturally, I arrested her too. Not out of public shame, either. It was the right thing to do, and I'd do it again, even if my entire graduating class wasn't there watching me. My wife was a food addict, and she needed treatment. The Food Court judge was lenient and gave her thirty days in Fat Camp, even though I begged him to give her more. And I put junior through a kiddie Fat Camp at my own expense. I wanted to make sure his mother's influence hadn't corrupted his soul.

When they got back a month later, things were better in our house. She apologized, and I felt sure I had cured her of her addiction. There's a lesson here. Hard-core food terrists look and talk and act just like you and me. They could be a friend, a relative, even your spouse. But deep down, in the blackness of their diseased souls, these poor creatures—like my wife—hunger for their drug of choice, and nothing you say or do can help them see the truth.

Other than that, it was a good time at the ATFF. I brought my partner Harry Green with me. When I got promoted, I made sure he got promoted too. Loyalty counts for something in this world, I figure. Harry was a friend. Together we led the way in busting illegal grow-ops in the D.C. area—from huge warehouses full of hydroponic vats growing beans and corn, wheat and rye, down to the grungy college student with a sun lamp and a couple of tomato plants in his closet. It didn't matter. We busted them all.

It was around this time we got the first inkling of a growing menace in our society. Cross-border smuggling soared, flooding our streets with that vilest of drugs, the crack cocaine of food: polished white rice. How did they get it into the country? There were border checks, air-eating sniffer dogs at every port of entry, customs officials whose sole job was to look for and confiscate food. On top of it all, the sniffer dogs died of some unknown wasting disease. For a long time we weren't quite sure what had happened. Then we realized: the dogs had been poisoned.

We detected a master hand at work. Behind all the grow-ops, the smuggling, even the network of Supper Clubs we'd been hearing about, stood one man: Fatso, the Godfather of Food. As head of the French Food Mafia, *la chôse notre*, Fatso controlled 120% of the black market. My partner and I worked feverishly to build a case against him, but time and time again that greasy mafioso slipped through our fingers.

What's that? Supper Clubs are a network of exclusive food labs run by the mafia. Rich connoisseurs get high by candle-light on course after course of elaborately prepared illicit confection. I have to say, I don't get it. Why do addicts pay so much money for this stuff? A calorie is a calorie, and in my book, they're all bad. What's more, these bizarre assemblies require formal dress—black tie for men, evening gowns for the women. Can someone please explain to me why wealthy food terrists wear tuxedos while consuming addictive caloric substances? Is powdered cleavage necessary for the consumption of these mind-warping and soul-destroying meals? Not to mention the fifteen-piece orchestra. Do heroin addicts insist on chamber music or light jazz in the dark garbage-lined alleys where they shoot up?

You don't have an answer for that, do you? I didn't think so.

How do I know all this? Because I busted a Supper Club once. Got a tipoff from a snitch. Sent a hundred food terrists to Fat Camp, including half a dozen Congressmen. Boy, that was rough. Finding out that not all our honorable gentlemen on Capitol Hill are pure air-eaters rattled my faith in our political system. Thankfully, I soon realized it was an isolated incident, and my enthusiasm for the American way of life—I mean, the Airitarian way of life—soon returned to its full measure.

So we barged into this Supper Club, Laxafiers drawn, my TWAT team bringing up the rear. (That's Thin Weapons And Tactics, in case you were curious.) Rumor was Fatso himself would be present. The food terrists gasped when they saw us. The women shrieked. They tried to escape, and would have outrun us, too, what with the performance-enhancing calories they consume. We'd anticipated this, however, and blockaded the exits with ATFF fatty wagons.

I remember staring around that ballroom in shock. Lobsters stacked like firewood on every table, the floor littered with their crunchy husks. Buffet tables sagged under the weight of food. Calories on every plate but one.

Fatso's.

He reclined in a corner, like some malevolent, clean-shaven *maître d'* in evening attire. Over his head hung a large tapestry of the Battle of Hunger Hill, one of the fiercest battles of the Civil War. Not a shot had been fired. Union forces had starved to death a Confederate garrison that refused to surrender. If only the rebels had known then what we know now about eating air.

In front of the Godfather of Food sat an empty plate. Not even a trace of a calorie. I bagged his plate and silverware as evidence.

The lab found nothing. Next to the plate was a glass of water, untouched. An amused smile flickered across the man's lips.

"Zo yoo air Agent Froleek, *monsieur,*" he said, his accent strong, like a smelly contraband Roquefort blue cheese.

He came to this country—and by "this country" I mean the US of Air, not France, even though I'm currently in France—fifteen years ago and still couldn't speak English good. He had introduced *le hamburger à la Nancy Reagan* on the menu of his five-star restaurant here in Paris, only to have a mob of angry chefs attempt to lynch him. The State Department granted him asylum and—worse for us—citizenship. We couldn't even deport the food trafficker.

His grin widened. "I haf ben lookeeng fore-ward to meeteeng yoo, *non?* Zay say yoo air zee best *agent* zee ATFF haz."

"Tell it to the judge," I said, and pulled out my handcuffs.

All around us my TWAT team fired laxative darts at stampeding fat people. Where the food terrists fell, an unusual perfume arose. Their poo-poo and pee-pee seeped through their evening clothes and mingled with the still-warm lobster casings. But Fatso seemed uninterested in the scents of justice. In a gesture of unconcern, he interlaced his fingers across his belly. Or tried to. They didn't quite reach.

"Yoo air not a seek-air aft-air zee playzh-air, *mon ami,*" he said, his grin still natural and easy. "Zat I admi-air. Yoo air not like zeez uzz-airs." He waved a hand at the diners in their finery, piled one upon the other like beached whales at a Japanese barbecue. "I seenk not, *non?*"

"Save your breath," I said, and snapped the handcuffs in his face. "Now get up."

He rose slowly to his feet and held out his wrists. "Wat eez eet yoo dezi-air most een zees world, Agent Froleek?" he asked.

"Eet eez not zee playzh-air. Eez eet, *peut-être,* pow-air? To make zees world a bett-air place?"

"My desire," I said, "is to put you in Fat Camp." I struggled to loop the cuffs around his wrists.

Fatso's eyes twinkled with mocking amusement. The handcuffs would not click shut. "Now zat yoo haf cot mee," he asked, "wat weel yoo doo?"

I slammed the cuffs back onto my belt. "I, along with three hundred million other Americans—I mean Airitarians—will celebrate your demise." I drew my weapon. "Now don't move."

He looked at me thoughtfully, unmindful of the chaos around us. "Yoo seenk eet weel make a *difference?*" he asked. "Arresteeng mee, I want to say?"

I lifted up the back of his tuxedo jacket with the tip of my Laxafier. "Where is your tail? Your horns? Your cleft hooves?"

He laughed. "I am not zee deveel, Agent Froleek. I am a man, like yore-self. A man on a die-et. I try not to eat zo much, yoo know. But eet eez very deefeecoolt."

"You dare compare yourself to me?" I stared him down, my face inches from his, until his laughter died. "No," I said. "You are Satan Incarnate. You peddle your illegal substances to children. Children! I hope you never learn to eat air. I hope you starve to death in Fat Camp."

Fatso looked at me for a long moment. He nodded. Almost sadly, it seemed. "I am sorree I laf," he said. "Only zat yoo remind me of sum-wun I know."

Suffice it to say, Fatso was out of jail twenty-four hours later. We gave him the standard dose of laxative when we booked him, but his bowels were as clean as a canister of brussel-sprout-flavored air after I'd finished with it.

I was there on the courthouse steps when we released him.

"Froleek!" he said, beaming at me in the spring sunshine. "Sank yoo for zees opportooneetee to meet yoo. I want to tell yoo, eef yoo and yore fameelee ev-air haf zee hung-air—"

"We'll eat air," I said. "Now get lost, Fatso."

"Eef yoo ev-air change zee mind—"

"I won't."

He climbed into his limo. "Een zat case, I weesh yoo, *bon appetit.*"

"*Crêpes suzette* and *beef bourgoignon* to you too," I said hotly. "Whatever that means." The limo pulled away from the curb. "You can't run and you can't hide either!" I shouted after him. "You're too fat! You hear me? I'll get you if it's the last thing I ever do! Besides dying, that is."

That was a year ago. I hadn't busted a Supper Club since, much less found a crumb of evidence we could use against him. I could only dream of Thanksgiving.

Long since outlawed, Fatso still celebrated that unholy day on the usual Thursday in November, when all the mafia dons came to D.C. for their annual convention. What a coup it would be to interrupt that little shindig! I had been working the streets for months, just trying to find out the location of this year's gathering, but no luck. My snitches didn't know, or if they did, they weren't telling.

But Life, Liberty and the Pursuit of Air-Eating Happiness went on as usual. Fatso alone was not enough to stop us. Together we, as a nation, continued our unstoppable rise toward the final stage of human evolution, the destiny the Prophet ordained for us in *Food-Free At Last.*

Then something happened, something so extraordinary that it threatened to bring down everything we built, evict the Prophet from the Thin House and return the food terrists to power. Looking back, I see the hand of the French Secret Service at every step.

It began with a murder.

THREE

N OT JUST ANY MURDER, EITHER. A FOOD DEALER
got whacked in LaOmelette Park, across the street from
the Thin House. And get this: he had a whole pizza
with him when he was killed. Can you imagine? A whole pizza?
The street price of your basic pepperoni pie these days is what,
close to half a million dollars?

Smarty pants. Maybe you can get a genuine Neapolitan
just around the corner here in Paris for twenty Euro. That is
not something to be proud of. For that matter, you should be
ashamed that people walk the streets of this city openly consuming addictive caloric substances. Putting food in their mouths—
and chewing it! Swallowing it, even! You might as well have sex
in public!

Oh no. You poor thing. Are you really going to eat that? That
croissant? Right here, in front of me? Let me ask you something,
sir. Like the Prophet always says. How can I be thin if I'm surrounded by fat people like you?

But we can't "live and let live," as you put it. We're the United
States of Air. Every time a ferrner eats some food, our national
security is threatened. Food terrist masterminds like yourself—
well, we've got a special program to help cure your addiction. It's

called "extraordinary rendering." They fly you to a special Fat Camp overseas, tie you to a long rotisserie pole and hold you over an open flame, until the fat melts off your body.

Help! Somebody help me! Get him off! By the Prophet's useless colon! Now do you see? This is exactly the kind of behavior caused by food terrism. Anger. Rage. Uncontrollable emotions. All those calories make you crazy. And you can quit your squirming. My bodyguards are going to handcuff you to your chair. That's all. It's for your own good. I can't let you hurt yourself anymore with that crescent-shaped piece of flaky, buttery, melt-in-your-mouth pastry. Corporal! Incinerate this. Make sure no one else suffers because of this Frenchie's addiction.

Now. Where was I? A murder.

The murder that started it all.

It was three in the morning when the call came through.

"Get the Twinkie out of your ass and get down here, Frolick," the voice growled.

That's how Captain Brownnose Lickit talks. Same guy who recruited me. You remember. He got promoted.

The first time Cap made a crack about Twinkies, my heart nearly stopped. I thought he knew about my secret shame. But then I realized he talks that way to everyone. With Green it's "Get the Slim Jim out of your ass." With a couple of my colleagues it's "Get the frozen lasagna out of your ass." There's even a new recruit, Cap says to him, "Get the whole wheat bread with tuna fish and olive tapenade out of your ass." Cap's just funny that way, I guess.

"I got time for breakfast, sir?" I asked.

My wife Chantal groaned and covered her head with a pillow. "That's right, baby," she said. "You go eat some air."

I put my hand over the mouthpiece. "Not now, Oxy," I said. Her pet name is Oxy. Short for "oxygen." The sweetest gas that man has ever tasted.

In my ear Cap was saying, "Roll your window down and munch some air while you drive. I'm calling Green now."

"What we got, Cap? Is it bikers with chocolate chip cookies again?" I asked. "Or maybe students with some ramen noodles?"

"Neither. Got a murder for you."

"Whoa," I said. "We don't do murders. You know that."

"You do now. Park across the street from the Thin House. Agent Erpent will fill you in."

I frowned in the darkness of our bedroom. "Don't know any Erpent, sir. He ATFF?"

"Skinny Service. You know what that means."

The two words made my heart go thud. "The SS?"

"Like I said. Move."

I moved. I drank a glass of water and chewed some air while I got dressed. Two pairs of long underwear against the November chill, the midriffs cut away. Then my regulation khaki trench coat and white tape measure, as tight as it would go. Promotion in the ATFF, as at all levels of government these days, was based on waistline. Cap was a sixteen, the Under-Secretary for Food Enforcement was a twelve. The Prophet himself was rumored to be a ten.

Before I left, I sat down on the bed. I put a hand on Chantal's shoulder, but she jerked away. "Make sure Nathan says his air prayers this morning before school, OK?"

"Go bust some food terrists," she said in a tone of voice she'd been using more and more often these days. I wasn't sure what it meant.

"And don't forget to send him off to school with a big air lunch, and an air snack in case he needs a little something extra in between meals."

"We haven't had a decent meal in months!" she cried into her pillow. "Why can't you get us something real to eat for a change?"

I sighed. "I don't have time for this right now, Oxy. Pray for strength. Pray for faith. Remember, Happiness is Eating Air. We'll talk more tonight."

Her bony forearms beat at her pillow. Maybe it was lumpy. But no time now to think about new bedding. Cap needed me. Our nation needed me. The human race, desperate for alternatives to food addiction, needed me.

I was out the front door as quick as it took me to limp there. I crawled down the walk and climbed into my Smart Car. I started the engine, listened to it putter and pulled away from the curb. I rolled the window down like Cap suggested, and savored that early morning road air. Pollution with a faint tang of dead leaves. I pondered dessert but decided I'd been glutton enough for one day.

On the way, I passed one of the new billboards the government had been putting up to combat French propaganda. A mile wide and a quarter mile tall, it depicted a chubby little boy with a toothless grin and the words "You're not starving to death. You just need to believe. Go the Power of Air!"

I pulled up in front of Green's house and beeped the horn. He was just coming off two weeks of compassionate leave. Something wrong with his daughter, apparently. Although he refused to tell me what it was.

He was a long time in coming out. I puzzled again over the orders to investigate a murder. The last time I was on homicide detail, I didn't solve a single case. Was I really the right man for the job?

To distract myself, I turned on the radio to the All Air Station—"all static, all the time, the sound of the airwaves coming at you"—and let that relaxing crackle soothe my soul. Several minutes passed. I was about to honk again, when he stumbled out of the house, wiping tears from his eyes. He got into the car and slammed the door.

My first thought was that his wife had made him taco air for lunch. But then he slouched back into his seat and sobbed into his hands.

"What's eating you?" I asked.

"Just drive."

I put the car into gear and stepped on the gas. I was still getting used to the Smart Car. It was a bit like driving a lawnmower.

"Roll a window down or something," I said. "Have some breakfast."

"I'm not hungry," he mumbled through his fingers.

"Suit yourself."

We rode in silence for a while. Tears poured down his cheeks like molten chocolate in a candy bar commercial. Before they banned candy bars, that is. He glanced at me from time to time, like he wanted to say something, but couldn't make up his mind how or when to say it.

We'd been through a lot together, Harry and I. I trusted him with my life. And I'd never seen him like this before. I touched his elbow.

"Is it your daughter?" I asked as gently as I could. "Melissa?"

He nodded, but said nothing.

"What do the doctors say?"

"We took her to a bunch of different specialists. I don't know why we bothered. They said there was nothing wrong with her. As healthy as a sixteen-year-old girl can be."

"Well, what's the problem then?"

"She won't eat. Hasn't touched food in months."

I smacked the steering wheel with the palm of my hand. "Good for her," I said. "You must be very proud."

He turned to me and frowned. "How do you mean?"

"Kids these days. Most people would kill to have a daughter like that. Not sneaking around after curfew, hanging out with the wrong kinds of boys, getting high off an illicit Snickers or Mars Bar in the back seat of some lowlife's car." I pulled onto the freeway, floored the Smart Car and putted along in the slow lane. "She were my daughter, I'd take her to Air Temple on Sunday and raise my voice in praise of the Prophet for bringing me such a wonderful child."

During the Prophet's campaign for President, he had nick-named Fat Boy Burgers "The Church of Fat." Since then, all the franchises—the Golden F's—had been turned into Air Temples. We went there every Sunday to listen to the Prophet's weekly address and to eat air in communion with others.

Green looked at me for a long moment. "Yes," he said. "I suppose you have a point." He sat back in his seat and stared out the window.

I can usually read his moods. "There's something else, isn't there?"

He sighed. "We did find someone who could give us a diagnosis."

"What did he say?"

"Except he's not exactly a doctor."

"What is he, then?"

"A naturopath."

I nearly slammed the car into a telephone pole. "One of those quacks?"

"I know, I used to think the same. But Dr. Stummick really knows what he's talking about. Thing is, though, he's proposing a radical treatment. I can't convince Melissa to take her medicine."

"What's he suggesting?"

My partner shook his head. "Says the only way for her to get any better is to start eating again. You know. Food."

I brayed with laughter. "Some doctor," I said. "Maybe she needs another stint in Fat Camp. Strengthen her faith."

"Stummick says if we do that, she'll starve to death."

"Quack quack," I said. "Quack quack." I glanced over at Harry, but he wasn't laughing. "Look. Take her to the beach for a week. That salty sea air?" I smacked my lips. "Yum, yum."

"That's just it," Harry said. "She eats air all the time. Eighteen hours a day. But she keeps getting skinnier and skinnier." He shifted in his seat. "I was hoping you might talk to her."

"And congratulate her on eating air?" I said. "Sure, if you want me to." Like the Prophet always says, you can never be too rich or too thin.

Green coughed into the back of his hand. "Actually I was hoping you'd tell her it's OK to eat food."

I wagged a finger at him. "You are such a joker!" I said. "That's why I love working with you, Harry. You crack me up."

"Watch out!" he said. "Red light!"

I looked up in time to bring the car to a halt. A motorcycle traffic cop gave us a friendly wave. The Prophet had installed red lights at random intervals on the Beltway to increase revenue from traffic fines.

Harry blew his nose, a long, wet sound.

"This is really hitting you hard, isn't it?"

He fiddled with the end of his tape measure. "Can I ask you something? Off the record? One old friend to another?"

"I got your back, partner," I said solemnly. "You know I do."

He lowered his head. "You believe in the Prophet." It wasn't a question.

"Sure I do. You remember me from before, right?" I held out my hands, mimed the huge belly I used to have.

"You wanted to be thin."

"We both did, Harry."

"And the Prophet helped us do that." He whispered the words.

"The Prophet promised, Harry. And he delivered. Food is a drug. Air is all we need."

"And you never...that is...," he said, avoiding my gaze. "You never eat?"

"Sure I do."

"You...you do?"

"Of course! Air. Every day."

"I mean, you never eat food?"

I thought of the secret shame in my ankle holster. "I'm sorry?" I said, pretending to have misheard. "Did you say, eat *food*?"

The blast of a truck's horn sounded behind us. The light was green. I revved the Smart Car's engine and rolled across the intersection.

"But you've never wondered?" Harry continued.

"Wondered what?"

"What if, you know, the Prophet's wrong? About eating air, I mean?"

"What are you," I said, joking, "some kind of food terrist?"

He turned toward me. "I'm serious, Frolick. In the three years since the Prophet banned food, have you really never eaten? Anything?"

Here I have a confession to make. I am ashamed to admit this, but you have to understand my struggle if you want to understand what happened next.

Every night I would go down to my basement. Unlock my walk-in vault. My Twinkie vault. I didn't want to go. But I could hear them. Singing. Who can resist that siren song? I'd sit there on the floor, mouth agape, listening to their bewitching melody as they flew about the room.

Some nights they were gentle with me. Other nights were not so good.

They'd attack in swarms, forcing themselves into my mouth, down my throat and into my stomach. And if I tried to stop them, they'd turn kamikaze, slamming into my face, splattering me with their sticky white guts. I'd black out, and when I woke up later, I'd find myself surrounded by dozens of their plastic cocoons.

They could smell my weakness of faith, I finally realized. I tried to get rid of them. I did. Over and over again. I'd be halfway to the garbage bin when the box would burst open and the shimmer of Twinkie wings would cast flickering shadows on the floor of my garage. I'd chase after them with a butterfly net, but a flying Twinkie is hard to catch. And every time they'd lead me back down to the basement. To their nest. Their home. What else could I do? My faith was weak. I let them stay.

Is that so? You think I'm crazy, do you? I've got an easy answer for that one. Corporal? Yes. The duct tape. Please. There's no point in struggling, *monn serr.* I think you French are crazy too. But when I'm finished I'll give you back your precious news show and you can say whatever you want. Like all Americans—I mean Airitarians—freedom of speech is something I value highly.

So to go back to Harry's question: had I really never eaten any food? In three years?

No. Not unless you counted being brutally violated by a gang of savage flying Twinkies, who repeatedly penetrate you orally against your wishes. Like so many rape victims, I felt ashamed. As if it were my fault. My only consolation was that these depraved pastries died in the act. They'd force themselves down my throat, only to commit suicide and litter the graveyard of my stomach with their acid-burned cake-dough husks. How could Green ever understand my torment?

"Careful!"

I swerved to avoid a car pulling into traffic.

"Of course I don't eat food," I said. "What kind of question is that? They'd have my badge and tape measure for sure."

He sat sideways, looking at me from under his eyebrows. It was like he could guess.

"Faith alert! Faith alert!" I said. "You're doubting again, Harry."

He slumped back into his seat. "You're right."

"I know I'm right. Your doubt is affecting your daughter's digestion. Her ability to metabolize air."

"I know, I know." Fresh tears drenched his cheeks.

"Maybe you should go see one of the ATFF Faith Officers. They can help you."

"Now there's a thought," he said. "Go tell the snitches I'm a doubter. Get a permanent black mark on my record."

"What's more important?" I asked. "The fleeting details of this stage of evolution? Or everlasting peace in the Prophet's bosom on a higher plane of human existence, for you and your family?" I reached over and squeezed his knee. "You've got to believe in His Will. Otherwise you got nothing."

He turned away. "Sometimes I wish I'd never heard of the Prophet."

"Harry!" I said. "How can you say such a thing?"

He covered his face with his hands and sobbed in silence. The radio filled the gap between us. The rogue Twinkie in my ankle holster fluttered its wings against my calf, fueled by Harry's treasonous remark. Not an hour ago it had climbed up my trousers and perched against my calf. I had tried to dislodge it, but my faith wasn't strong enough.

It began to hum. No, please. Not here. Not now. I turned up the radio to drown out the sound. The wings trembled and went still. I let out a deep breath. Then Green said:

"So the new warehouse rules haven't affected you at all?"

I flushed just thinking of that scandal. Top brass tried to hush it up, but word got around. In the same way the DEA keeps depositories of impounded cocaine and marijuana until they can be destroyed, the ATFF runs a network of evidence warehouses full of confiscated food. A couple of our brothers-in-air had been caught consuming evidence.

I said, "How would that affect—"

But a public service announcement broke into the static. The deep baritone that did all the PSAs intoned:

"Dangerous food terrists lurk on every corner. Hiding in the shadows, ready to corrupt your children with addictive caloric substances. Fat People tempting your young ones away from the

Path of Air with candy bars, sugary treats, bowls of lentils and corn! Fat People are a menace to our national security. Remember, if you see Fat, say Fat." An old woman screeched: "Fat! There's a fat man! Over there! In the parking lot! And he's armed with a corn dog!" The baritone voice returned: "Remember, if you see Fat, say Fat. Call 1-800-I-SEE-FAT. That's 1-800-I-S-E-E-F-A-T. This message has been brought to you by the Dietitian General. Go the Power of Air."

The welcome hiss of static returned. I gripped the steering wheel as tight as I could, trying to block out the humming coming from my leg.

"Of course the new rules haven't affected me, silly," I said. "I have electric heating."

Everyone takes food home with them. It saves the government money on its fuel bill. Rather than leave the food to be destroyed on Burn Day, agents would take home cases of contraband to incinerate in their own furnaces. In fact, so high-minded were most ATFF agents that there was rarely any food left to destroy when Burn Day came around.

So when I first heard of the scandal, I was sure there had been a mistake. We were the ATFF. How was it possible that people I worked with every day were food terrists? But the videos of them at home consuming the contraband material—and worse, giving it to their wives and children—could not be explained away.

I worried what would happen to my flock at home. The Twinkies were asexual. I had observed their social interaction with the care of a field biologist, and come to the conclusion that they were sterile. Not once did I see them mate or give birth. Because of their suicidal tendencies, they were constantly after me, beating their wings against my head, demanding new playmates. On occasion I had brought home confiscated Twinkies to replenish their nest. Sometimes I felt like I was the one living in the dungeon, not them.

I took a deep breath, let it out slowly.

"The Bureau's counting calories," Green said. "Making sure not a single one goes missing."

"Good," I said. "What they should have done in the first place. Makes the rest of us look like deviant food-swilling scum when a few bad apples get caught with their hands in the cookie jar."

The Twinkie cleared its throat and sang:

"Apples, apples! Cookies, cookies!"

I hissed, "Stop it! Quiet! Stop singing, you!"

"I'm sorry?" Green said. "I wasn't singing."

"What? Oh. I was just talking to the radio. You know, that crazy singing static." I forced a laugh.

My partner looked at me strangely, but let it go. Phew. That was a close one.

I pulled up behind half a dozen D.C. cruisers—also Smart Cars—blocking the street, and killed the engine. The radio static died, and with it, my faith. If I wasn't careful there'd be an impromptu Twinkie concert in the park.

Green reached for the door handle. "So what do you think I should do?" he asked. "About Melissa."

"I don't want to get involved, Harry," I said. "Too many cooks spoil the broth."

"Yummy broth! Broth-ey broth!" the Twinkie sang.

"Maybe gruel? Is that so cruel?

With a spud. Half a spud.

A rotten spud. Any old crud!"

I pressed my eyelids shut. *Go away. Leave me alone. Why can't you leave me in peace?*

Harry opened the door but didn't get out. "You sure I can't convince you to talk to her? Explain to her how things really are?"

I shook my head. I could not bring myself to look at him. "If my family can do it, so can yours."

I thought of Chantal's rapid turnaround after the incident at my graduation, after she got out of Fat Camp. I'd come home after a hard day's work busting food terrists, and she and Nathan and I, we'd sit around the dinner table and chew some air for a while. He'd tell me about his day at school, the fat kids taken away by ATFF riot squads, the skinny kids who collapsed on the playground and got to suck on vanilla oxygen for the rest of the day. Chantal would kiss me on the cheek and tell me how she had a wonderful perfume lunch with the girls, really exquisite the flavors of air. After dinner I'd do imitations of Fatso to scare Nathan with.

I take my responsibility as a father seriously. It's important to teach your children the right values.

"Ho ho ho. I'm Fatso, the fat man drug baron. Look at me, come to ruin your lives. Candy, little girl? Chocolates, little boy? Once you're hooked on food, you'll never be able to stop. And I'll make lots of money selling you dime bags of rice and dried legumes, a dozen beans to the bag. Mwoo-hwoo-wah-hah! I am evil incarnate! I am a Frenchman food dealer! Be very, very afraid! Boo!"

My wife and son would collapse in giggles. We were a happy family in those days. Back before what happened, happened.

What's that? No, I'm fine. Really. Just a bit of runny nose is all.

So we sat there in the car, the glow of the Thin House glorious across the street. I took the keys from the ignition. Green put his hand on my arm. "This conversation never took place. Right, old friend?"

"Sure, Harry. You know me."

He slapped me on the back. "Good ol' Frolick."

He got out of the car and closed the door.

I sat there for a moment, collecting my thoughts. Faith: be strong! I believe! I do! Aid me now in my time of struggle, O Mine Prophet, please! The Twinkie song subsided. But for how long?

I would have to keep an eye on Harry. I was worried about my partner. Talking about naturopaths, giving food to his daughter. Faith was essential to survival. Essential to eating air. The tiniest speck of doubt could unleash a swarm of suicidal Twinkie rapists. To someone unaccustomed to their ways, this could destroy a man.

For the first time in our long partnership, I was unsure of Harry. Of his loyalty. Of his values. I would have to give him all the encouragement I could. And, if necessary, report him. If his faith was weak, it could affect my own digestion, and that of everyone he came in contact with. He would be a menace to society as long as his doubt lasted. It might be necessary to send him to Fat Camp again.

For his own good.

FOUR

E'RE WHAT? OUT OF TIME?

Yes, I know the show's called *Soixante-Neuf Minutes*. What's that got to do with the price of air in Kansas? I come bringing salvation to the French people, and you want to cut me off when I've barely gotten started?

Corporal? Take out your gun and hold it to the Frenchie's head. Like that. Excellent.

This broadcast continues. Anyone moves, anyone tries to end this transmission, and fattie here gets it.

We clear?

It was 4 a.m. by the time Green and I got to the scene of the crime. We crunched across the dead grass of the park, stepping over the rotting tree limbs that blocked our path. Remnants of the Air Force's herbicide spraying campaign. Half a dozen cops huddled around the body. They hid their hands behind their backs when they saw us.

"Well if it isn't Agent Frolick and his sidekick Agent Green." A homicide dick by the name of Sergeant Thinn hooked one thumb between his belt and his belly. "What are you doing here, anyway? You've never solved a murder in your life."

"Top brass put us on the case," I said, with justifiable pride. "Guess we're better than you thought."

"What's the last case you solved?"

I puffed out my chest. "Busted a ring of housewives selling homemade apple pies."

"And who you calling sidekick, fat man?" Green added, jabbing Thinn in the stomach with a finger.

"It ain't illegal to be fat," Thinn said. "The Air Congress passed a law. Remember?"

"You mean *Hoe v. Spade*?" I asked. "That wasn't Air Congress. That was the Supreme Food Court."

After the Amendment passed, roaming patrols herded fatties aboard buses and onto box cars to take them to Fat Camp. But an obese woman, a plaintiff by the name of Phood Hoe, sued the deputy assistant sheriff's assistant's deputy who arrested her. She claimed to be an early convert to the Prophet's words. She wasn't fat. She was swollen with excess oxygen from eating so much air.

In their landmark decision, the Court agreed. Being fat was not a crime. It was only consumption of food that was illegal. We could arrest a fattie on suspicion and feed them laxatives, but if their bowels were empty we had to let them go. That was when the Air Congress set up the Food Courts. Although what we were doing giving terrists due process and trying them in court was beyond me.

Thinn produced a paper bag from behind his back. He held up a hamburger and took a big bite. "Whatever. Anyway, it's about time you got here. Or were you too busy eating air?"

"Never too busy to eat air," I said. "Still on your methadone, I see?"

He was munching on a zero-calorie burger and thick-cut zero-calorie fries. I knew the food was zero-calorie because I asked him once and he told me. It still amazes me, though, how fat he was for eating nothing but zero-calorie burgers all day long.

A young cop turned to Thinn. Name tag read "J. Olde." His red, puffy eyes marked him as a rookie. Too much taco air. "Gosh," he said. "Didn't know you were a heroin addict, Sarge."

Thinn swallowed and rattled his paper bag. "This is a zero-calorie burger, fries and milkshake combo. Like we eat every day? Maybe you should join the team, Olde."

"Just gotta be different, don't you," said a second cop, name of Nice. Mean-looking. "Why can't you eat at Fatso's Diner like the rest of us?"

"Fatso!" I said. "Not our evil foe?"

Thinn licked mustard from his lips. "Different Fatso. No relation."

"Gee whillickers," Olde said. "Zero calories? I've never heard of such a thing. How come you never mentioned it before?"

"What are they made out of, anyway?" I asked.

"Processed air," Thinn said. "Olde here is from California. Raw foodie."

"Jeez, Sarge," the rookie said. "No need to make fun. Just 'cause I prefer my air unprocessed."

I fist-bumped the rookie. "You go, girl," I said.

Thinn waved a French fry in my face. "Processed air is pretty tasty. Sure you don't want one? Zero calories?"

Green trembled at my side. "Don't mind if I do."

I slapped his hand away. "Watch it, sidekick."

The fry fell to the ground, and three of the cops dove for it. Their heads collided on the dead grass. From the heap of groans Officer Nice emerged, fry held aloft in triumph.

"What's the matter with you?" I asked. "Don't you ever eat air?"

"Sure we do," Thinn said, his mouth full. "In between three square meals, a doughnut run and a midnight snack." He turned to the others. "All zero-calorie, of course."

They laughed.

I reddened. "If it's good enough for the Prophet, it's good enough for me."

Their laughter stopped. I pressed home my advantage.

"It's our job to be role models," I said. "What kind of example does this give our young people? From a distance it's hard to tell the difference between one of your burgers and an illegal one. I realize your food has zero calories, and is therefore exempt from the Amendment's prohibition of addictive caloric substances, but it could easily be misunderstood by a young person who didn't know any better. This is why it's so important that we—"

"Partner mine." A tug on my sleeve.

"What is it?"

Green nodded at the body on the ground. "Save it for Air Temple."

Ah, Air Temple. Sunday was my favorite day of the week. Attendance at Air Temple was mandatory, but I would go every day if I could. Sometimes they even let me deliver a guest sermon, but my favorite was the air-eating competitions the Faith Officers organized—how I would gulp down those scrumptious gaseous molecules! Then there was the obligatory group confessional, when citizens were encouraged to turn in local food terrists—their neighbors, relatives and friends. In practice this meant people giving each other free vacations. The accused party would fall to their knees, confess hysterically and pretend to beg forgiveness. Slackers. They'd rather take it easy in Fat Camp than go to the office every day like the rest of us working stiffs.

Green snapped his fingers in front of my face. I forced myself back into the present.

"We're here for him," my partner said. "Remember?"

I knelt down over the corpse. "Poor thing."

All thoughts of the sermon I was about to deliver disappeared. The body lay face down in a puddle of blood. A pizza box stood empty at his side. I touched his hand. Cold. Wet. I held up my fingers to the light. Flecks of half-digested mushroom, green pepper, onion, pepperoni, tomato sauce and cheese. The corpse was covered in vomit. A tremendous feeling of sorrow and pity crashed over me.

"If only he'd been given a chance to go to Fat Camp," I lamented. "Maybe then he wouldn't have turned to a life of crime."

Green bent down next to the corpse and bared the dead man's right forearm. There on the hairless skin above the wrist glowed a blue tattoo: nine digits, separated by two dashes. "555-66-1212." His social security number. Green took out a scanner and swept the bar code below the numbers.

"According to this, he's been in Fat Camp half a dozen times already," he announced. "Four convictions for possession, one for distribution and one for stealing candy from a baby. Claimed its mother missed a payment on her installment plan, and was only repossessing what was already his."

"A real hard case," Thinn grunted, and stuffed more burger into his mouth. "Why couldn't he just eat air like the rest of us?"

I held up my vomit-covered hands to the sky in despair. "What if the seventh time was all he needed?" I beseeched the heavens. "Now he'll never have a chance to eat air. To learn how to transcend the body and become pure spirit." Hot tears coursed down my cheeks. "He was just an innocent kid, corrupted by the mafia. They probably held his family hostage to make him do their dirty work."

Thinn spat. "Whoever did this, did us a favor. One less junkie dealer on the streets."

"How can you say that?" I grabbed the scanner from Green's hands, skimmed the man's bio. Name: Nick Hungry. Born: Pepperoniville, Pennsylvania, July 4, 1984. "Says right here he's got seven younger brothers and sisters."

"So?" Thinn demanded.

I skimmed some more. "His father's dead, too."

"Again. So?"

"So?" I was aghast at his insensitivity. "Maybe he still believes in that old-fashioned garbage about 'being the breadwinner' and 'bringing home the bacon.'"

"So what if he does?"

What can you do with a man like Thinn? A heart of stone. I sighed. "All I'm saying is, I feel sorry for him." I turned back to the dead body. "You hear me?" I said. "I feel sorry for you. I do. Me. If only you had let us help you. Whether you wanted us to or not. We could have cured you. Made you better."

Behind me, my partner stamped his feet. "You feel sorry for all the criminals we arrest, Frolick."

I wiped away a tear. "They are poor misguided souls who don't know any better," I said. "They deserve our pity."

A flashlight clicked on, illuminating dead Mr. Hungry's emaciated frame.

"So you want the run-down or don't you?" Thinn asked, sucking noisily on his milkshake.

"Tell us what you know," I said. "So we can find his killer. Whoever it was who deprived this poor boy of the right to eat air, to soar on the wings the Prophet gave our souls, to know that—"

"Excellent, Frolick," my partner said. "Another fine sermon for Air Temple this Sunday. Now can you let the man talk?"

Thinn slurped at the remains of his milkshake, tossed it in a nearby garbage can. "So," he said. "911 gets a call at 1:26 a.m. Muffled male voice. Sounds like he has a cold."

"Phone trace?" Green had his notebook out, pen poised.

"Pay phone not far from here." He indicated the opposite corner of the park, gulped what was left of his burger. "Said he'd seen a murder taking place. Food deal gone bad."

As Thinn narrated the crime scene, his mouth still full of food, flecks of zero-calorie beef rained down on my face.

"Cruiser responded to the 911 call," he said, struggling to enunciate. "Done a thorough search of the park. No murder weapon, no other clues."

"We'll be the judge of that," Green said.

The flashlight traced each limb of the dead dealer. Someone had eaten the entire pizza and then vomited it over his victim. But why? And who would do such a thing?

Green dipped a finger in the vomit, touched the liquid to his lips. I did the same, and quickly spat it out in horror. I looked at Green.

He nodded. "It's uncut," he said. "Pure. This was a special order. Probably cost close to a million dollars."

I spat again, trying to get the taste out of my mouth. "Maybe a million and a half."

I was a walking encyclopedia on the ways Fatso diluted his product. He was known for putting fillers in his pizza—edible plastics, fine sand, chalk dust, anything to water down the value. It was extraordinary to find someone buying an uncut pizza. This was a serious addict with no shortage of cash.

Thinn shrugged. "Some punk got lucky."

I rolled my eyes. "Come on, Thinn," I said. "You've got almost twenty years in homicide. You think some punk did this?"

"Like you say, Special Agent. I got almost twenty years. Plan on taking my pension and going someplace warm. And I know which way the wind is blowing."

I held a still-wet finger in the air. "North-north-east, I'd say. Maybe six, seven knots. Rain tomorrow, or the next day. Although I'm not sure how that helps us."

"Special Agent Weatherman," Nice cackled.

Thinn coughed into his fist. "Besides," he said. "You don't even know that this was Fatso's pizza."

Green cleared his throat. "Yes, we do."

"Oh yeah?" Thinn said. "How's that?"

My partner held up the pizza box with the tip of his pen. Emblazoned across the vomit-stained cardboard were the words "Fatso's Pizza."

"So what?" Thinn said. "Maybe it was the Sicilians whacked the guy. Wanting a piece of the action."

"Fatso's got an iron grip on the pizza trade," I said. "Remember last summer when the Colombian cartels tried to muscle their way in with that pizza lab over in Georgetown?"

"Got muscled out, as I recall," my partner chuckled. "Car bomb, wasn't it?"

"I heard about that," Officer Olde said, but fell silent at a glance from his sergeant.

"So someone's trying again," Thinn said, shoving fries into his mouth. "Knock over a pizza dealer, start a war. A mafia hit."

"Then why," I asked him, holding my vomit-coated finger under his nose, "would a hit man proceed to eat a million dollars' worth of pizza, and then vomit it all over his victim?"

"How should I know?" Thinn asked. "Maybe he got food poisoning or something. Overdosed. Who knows why these crazed food terrists do what they do."

"They hate us for our freedom," I said. "Our freedom to eat air. That's why, and you know it."

"You know what I'm thinking, partner mine?" Green said.

I groaned. "Not more of your cynicism."

He held out a hand. "Hear me out. It isn't called the District of Crap for nothing." The high levels of fecal material in our capital's sewers had given it that nickname.

"What are you suggesting?" Thinn asked.

"Corruption. What else?" my partner said. "The pizza was a bribe."

"None of our politicians are corrupt," I said hotly. "How can you say such a thing?"

Green covered his mouth with his hand. "What about Ed Ibble, the judge? What happened last week?"

"That was an accident," I said. "He fell asleep with his head over a cheesecake. Of course his mouth was full of food."

"Well what was he doing with a cheesecake in the first place?"

Why was Green always so obtuse? It was like talking to a brick wall sometimes.

"Taking it to be destroyed. Obviously. See this is your problem, Harry," I said. "You're always so negative. You see food crime everywhere."

My partner scrunched up his face. "That's because it's there to see!"

"No. It's not," I said. "Tell me something. Eating food is what causes crime—what causes food terrism. Right? So how can there be corruption when everyone is eating air?"

He stared at me for a moment, dumbfounded by the truth of this insight. Finally he said, "Then how come you and I still got jobs?"

He was trying to turn me into a jaded cynic like himself, but I wasn't going to let him. "There are occasional…anomalies," I admitted. "Perversions of the norm. These people need to be educated. Taught that the way to happiness lies in following the Prophet's air-only diet. It is my hope that one day soon we will both be out of a job."

Green cocked an eyebrow. "Because they fire us?"

"Harry," I said, and laid a hand on his shoulder. "I love you like a brother, but sarcasm does not become you. When no more food terrists remain to threaten our national security, a day that is coming soon, then our jobs will no longer be needed."

"Frolick's got a point, you know," Thinn said, jamming the last of his fries in his mouth.

"You think so?"

"Sure. Since the Amendment passed, D.C.'s become a corruption-free zone. I was just saying that down at the station the other day. Wasn't I, boys?"

"You was saying exactly that, Sarge," Officer Nice said.

I held my palms out wide. "You see?"

Green crossed his arms. "Alright then. I'm open to suggestions. Who would do such a thing? A bulimic stick-up artist who picked the wrong guy?"

I shook my head. "I don't know. I've never seen anything like it." I turned to look across the street at the Thin House lit up by floodlights. To think that purity could live so close to crimes like this. "Only thing I'm sure of is that I don't like it."

"Neither does the Prophet," said a voice from the shadows.

I was on my feet before the voice finished speaking, Laxafier in hand. Green, at my side, had his out too.

The owner of the voice stepped into the light. The cops swallowed hastily and hid their burger bags. Except for Thinn, who seemed surprisingly unconcerned. Green and I holstered our weapons. I forced myself to relax.

"Jumpy," the man said. He grinned, his face a death's-head mask in the light of the streetlamp. "Aren't we?"

I stiffened my spine, flung my palm out at an angle. "Go the Power of Air!" I shouted.

The others did the same.

He wore the black trench coat and red tape measure of the Skinny Service. He flipped open his badge, but I didn't bother to check it. His fourteen-inch waist said it all.

He returned our salute with a limp hand. "Go the Power of Air," he said in a bored tone of voice.

When the Prophet took office, he transferred the old Secret Service to the FBI's counterfeiting division, and hired a new squad of intensely loyal, super skinny bodyguards. You had to have at most a fifteen-inch waist just to get an interview. I should know. I had been bombarding their office with my resumé for the last two years. It had been my dream from the beginning to work for them. To report directly to the Prophet in the Trapezoidal Office itself. But no matter how hard I tried, I could not get my waistline under eighteen inches. I'm sure many of you out there can sympathize with my struggle. I even tried eating less air. Nothing worked.

What's that? The Prophet redesigned the shape of his office so that it would no longer be in the same shape as the food paraphernalia known in street lingo as "platters," which were often in the form of an oval.

Now the SS were the best of the best, the thinnest of the thin. We called them the Unpinchables. As in, "can't pinch an inch." Their job was to protect the Prophet. It was also to root out corruption at all levels of government. This, despite the theoretical impossibility of such anomalies. The ATFF and Food Bureau of Investigation went after food dealers and grow-ops, and, increasingly, organized food crime. The SS went after people like Judge Ibble with his cheesecake—although I still think they were wrong about that one. Also district attorneys taking burrito bribes, even the occasional ATFF man caught with a single Tic Tac in his shoe.

This last was the worst possibility. Possession of even a single calorie by an ATFF agent was considered a breach of the oath of office, and punishable by 180 days in Fat Camp, the maximum permitted under the Amendment.

There is no crime more serious than a violation of the public trust, as the Prophet always says.

This handful of corrupt government officials lived in fear of the Skinny Service's network of Fat Camps at Guantanamo Bay and in Eastern Europe. In these all-inclusive resorts, anomalies are treated to hands-on, faith-strengthening therapy. I don't know why they lived in fear. I confess I'm jealous of these people. Journalists, academics, hippies, chefs, restaurant critics—doubters of every kind—have all gotten this five-star treatment. To be able to devote your every waking hour to making strong your faith in the Prophet—it gives me goosebumps just thinking about them in Poland or Cuba somewhere, sucking down that exotic, ferrn air. They must like it so much, in fact, that they never come back. Sometimes I think about going myself, resigning from the struggles of the world, dedicating my life to meditation. But the threat to our national security at this time is grave, and the Prophet has asked me to step forward. How could I say no?

Of course, the innocent have nothing to fear from the SS. Most people are Amendment-abiding air-eaters. But in order to protect the innocent from savage attacks by food terrists deranged by their withdrawal symptoms, the Skinny Service has the power to search anyone without a warrant, or even probable cause.

The agent stared at each of us in turn. The cops around me trembled. Their burgers were zero-calorie, but perhaps they feared a misunderstanding. I myself began to quake a bit. But I had nothing to hide. I had been on an air-only diet for years. My Twinkie rapist, though—it was lurking in my ankle holster, ready to pounce. How would it react to the stranger?

I stood there in the park, the body of Nick Hungry at my feet, unsure what to do. And bearing down on me through the murky pre-dawn haze, an SS agent with a skeletal grin, a stronger, more loyal man than I, a man who ate the same air as the Prophet, mere feet from where our holy ruler lives and works. A man no doubt unafflicted by flying pastry predators. He stepped over the body, shoes squelching in vomit, and came to a halt in front of me. He withdrew a bony hand from his trench coat pocket and reached for my waist.

I sucked in my gut. He's going to pat me down. *Think thin. Be thin.* He's going to find the Twinkie. What am I going to do if it attacks?

FIVE

THE SS MAN HELD OUT A BONY HAND. "AGENT Erpent," he said. "You must be Frolick and Green."

Was that all? A handshake? He glanced down at my ankle, where I was staring. Did he know? Could he guess?

"Guilty as charged," I said. His fingers felt brittle.

"Brittle, brittle, like peanut brittle,
like Gramma used to make!"

Careful...down boy. Bad Twinkie.

"The Organized Food Crime Division over at the ATFF said you were the best they had." He patted my waist with his other hand. "And the most loyal."

I felt ashamed. If only my faith were stronger, I wouldn't be orally abused by suicidal Twinkie rapists. Evil tormentors! How could I make them go away? At this rate I would never get my waistline down to fifteen inches and fulfill my Skinny Service dreams.

"Heard about that apple pie bust," he added. "Those housewives were a major threat to national security. Good work."

Warm fuzzies.

"Warm and toasty
blueberry muffins

slathered with butter and—"

Green saved me. "Cap said to meet you here. What can we do for the SS?"

"Find that pizza lab and shut it down," Erpent said. "It's a disgrace that food deals like this are going on across the street from where the Prophet sleeps at night."

"Disgrace is right," I said, "but we have to find the murderer first. He's out there, somewhere, in a dark alley, crying his eyes out." I swept a hand at the body. "Look at what food made him do."

Erpent nodded. "That's true. But what about the poor addicts who suffer because of that lab?"

"It's a good point," Green said. He flipped his notebook shut and put it away. "Why don't we do this the SS way?"

I thought about that. It was a tough call. "The murderer deserves our compassion," I said. "WWTPD?"

Erpent frowned. "What's that?"

"What Would The Prophet Do? We can only save souls one at a time from the Terror of Food. Right now our priority has to be putting that murderer in Fat Camp. Getting him the treatment he needs."

The SS agent folded his twiglike arms across his hollow chest. "And suppose I told you these are the Prophet's direct orders?"

Before I could reply, Officer Olde gasped. The rookie with the puffy eyes. "Holy Air!" he said. "The Prophet's orders? Really?" He flicked on his flashlight, turned it on a patch of dirt. "Over here, Special Agents. You've got to see this!"

"What is it?" Erpent hissed.

"A trail of blood. Or it might be pizza sauce. I'm not sure. It leads off that way." He pointed into the darkness, where a string of blackened streetlamps led toward the Thin House.

"No, no, no," said Officer Nice, shaking his head. He drew his friend roughly aside. "You must be mistaken."

"But I'm quite sure," Olde said. "It might help solve this case. I know what Sergeant Thinn's instructions were, but if the Prophet himself is involved, then it's our duty to report everything. He is the Leader of the Food-Free World, after all!"

"Quite so," Erpent said, his voice frosty. "What does the senior officer think?"

"Probably leftover ketchup from a hot dog stand that used to be here three years ago," Thinn said. "It's nothing." To the rookie: "You shouldn't waste important people's time like this, Officer."

"But this is my beat, Sergeant. I walk by here all the time. That stain wasn't there yesterday."

"The ketchup theory makes sense to me," I said.

"But look where the trail leads! Straight toward the Thin House! Maybe he's going to try to assassinate the Prophet!"

"The SS will protect the Prophet," Erpent snapped. "Don't you worry about that."

I felt my partner tense at my side. "Hang on. Did you say *toward* the Thin House?" he asked.

Olde traced the bloody trail into the darkness with his flashlight. "See for yourself."

Green jumped forward, notebook once more in hand. "It can't be Hungry's blood. He's dead. Maybe the murderer was injured in the struggle. We have to find out where it leads. Expose this criminal to the world."

He took the flashlight from Officer Olde and traipsed off into the darkness. I turned to follow.

Erpent grabbed me by the shoulder. "You said it yourself. It's just a ketchup stain. Tell your partner to come back."

"Green's a bloodhound," I said. "What if he's right? It could be an important clue."

"By the Prophet's two-timing taste buds!" he swore. "We haven't got time for this." To Thinn he called out, "Get him back here, now."

The sergeant gestured at two of his men. Nice and another cop jogged off, and came back carrying Green between them. They jogged awful fast for not having eaten in three years. I wondered where they got the energy.

They set him on his feet, and Green came up swinging.

"This is an important piece of forensic evidence," he said. "A major clue to who the murderer might be. Justice in a case like this could mean freedom for us all." He looked around at us wildly, his fists bunched up. "Don't you understand that?"

Erpent's face had turned red. He looked like he was going to explode. Like a Spanish-style blood sausage when you throw it into the furnace and watch it burn. Instead, he pulled out a cell phone and pushed a button. To Thinn he said: "Did you find it?"

The sergeant cleared his throat. "What you were looking for? No."

"What were you looking for?" Green demanded.

"Yeah, Sarge," said Olde. "What were we looking for, anyway?"

But Erpent held out a warning finger. "Yes," he said into the phone. "No...no, Agent Frolick. With a k. What? At the end. He's right here." He held out the phone to me.

"For you."

"Me?"

He nodded.

"Who is it?"

"The Prophet." He looked at me like I was a package of Twizzlers about to be destroyed on Burn Day. "And you're keeping him waiting."

"You're joking," I said.

Green squeezed my elbow. "He doesn't look like the type."

Erpent took a step forward. "He wants to talk to you, Special Agent Frolick."

If the skies had opened and a bearded god addressed me from the clouds, I could not have been more shaken. Who was I? A lowly ATFF agent, tormented by a plague of suicidal Twinkie rapists. All because my faith was weak. I shuddered in self-loathing.

Still Erpent stood there, blinking at me quietly, unmoving, arm extended. I opened my mouth, but nothing came out. The Prophet. The man to whom I owed my life. My freedom. Everything I had. The Prophet wanted to talk to me?

"For me?" I croaked again.

Erpent nodded and shook the phone in his hand impatiently.

I took the phone and lifted it to my ear. But it slipped from my grasp and I fumbled for it, caught it before it hit the ground. I let out a long, trembling sigh and looked up at my partner. Green held out both palms. Relax. I pasted the phone back to my head. Opened my mouth to say hello, but a sound like sandpaper on metal squeaked from my lips. I held the phone away from my head and coughed to clear my throat. Loudly. Several times. Then, before I could lose my nerve, I brought the phone back to my ear and said as casually as I could:

"Hello?"

Nothing but silence. Had I broken the connection when I dropped it? Or was this some kind of practical joke? It was just the sort of prank the guys down at the station would play.

"Agent Frolick?"

It was a familiar voice, and it wheezed, deep with the bitter self-reproach that had won him so many followers. I remembered the speeches, the videos, that gravelly, growling voice of truth, with its reedy whine—so strange, but so compelling—listening to his life-changing righteousness pour from my car stereo, back when I needed a hydraulic lift to climb out of my vehicle.

It couldn't be. How could it be? It was. "This is Frolick," I said, with as much nonchalance as I could muster.

Another pause, then that voice again, like an out-of-tune oboe.

"Do you know who this is?"

By instinct, I flung my palm out and clicked my heels together. "Yes, Mine Prophet!" I bobbed my head in the darkness. "Can I just say, sir, what an honor it is to, to, to—"

"Agent Frolick."

Had I offended him? Offended the Prophet? What did I say? I swallowed hard. "Sir?"

"Do you believe?"

"Yes, Mine Prophet! I believe, I believe, that is, I—"

"Do you renounce food, and all its wicked recipes, and all its wicked restaurants?"

The litany from Air Temple. I was on solid ground now. I relaxed, let my arm fall to my side. "I so believe."

"Who will lead us from bondage, break the shackles of that grim overseer Food, and deliver us from the Babylon of Calories into the Promised Land of Oxygen?"

"The Prophet will," I responded by rote. "That is, I mean, you will, sir."

There was another long pause. I heard panting in the background, as though from exertion. Come to think of it, his voice sounded kind of nasal. Or at least, more so than usual. Like he had a cold or something. What was the protocol here? Was it polite to inquire if the Divine Leader was congested? Or would that be rude? Before I could make up my mind, the Prophet continued.

"We are beset on all sides, Frolick," he said. "There are those in this world who do not believe such purity as you and I practice is even possible."

The Twinkie flexed its wings in my ankle holster. Not now. Not now! The Prophet couldn't know. I'd kill myself if he ever found out. I forced myself to answer.

"That's true, sir."

"The UN continue their food drops up and down the Eastern Seaboard. Their planes and helicopters fly the Red Cross. For every one I shoot down, two more take its place. I've got secessionists in the so-called Rocky Mountain Republic, a.k.a. the Republic of Food, with their open flaunting of the food laws and their illegal Gluttony Congress in Denver. I've got cannibals on the loose on the West Coast, I've got hillbillies with hydroponic gardens in Appalachia, and do you know what the worst thing is, Special Agent Frolick?"

I had no idea what it might be. I didn't dare guess. I said as much.

"The worst thing of all," the Prophet said, "is that even after our glorious Amendment passed, even after the Air Force sprayed every square inch of arable land with an herbicide powerful enough to last for fifty years, food continues to be available in this country! And do you know why?" He did not wait for me to answer. "Because of the mafia, that's why. The French Food Mafia. Because of Fatso. Did you know he even calls himself the Foodfather?"

"The Godfather of Food," I corrected.

"I said the Foodfather and I mean the Foodfather," the Prophet said. He didn't raise his voice, but a note of steel cut into his tone.

"I need some good news for a change," he continued. "I need it soon. Something to show the world. That we're making progress in the War on Fat. I need your help."

I threw my shoulders back. The Prophet needed me. The clarion call of duty had come at last. How could I fail to oblige our savior?

"Understood, sir," I said. "You can count on me."

"I hope so, Agent Frolick. Because tomorrow I am hosting the Coalition of the Fasting at the Thin House. Presidents and prime ministers from all over the world will be here, including the heads of state of Tonga, Lichtenstein, Monaco and the Federation of South Pole Research Stations. Our most important allies in the Global War on Fat." He covered the receiver for a moment, and it sounded like he was blowing his nose.

Green looked at me and raised his eyebrows. I held out an open palm. Wait.

The Prophet came back on line. "When word gets out about tonight's murder—oh, I know, our press would never publish something like this, but those vicious ferrn news outlets take such delight in tearing down everything we've worked so hard to build. When word gets out, our enemies will use this as an example of our failures. 'Look at how crazy they are!' the French president will say. 'Trying to ban food.' Do you know he actually tried to give me" —and he lowered his voice to a whisper— "a giant wheel of Camembert cheese at his last state visit?"

"The French are nothing but a bunch of food-sucking slaves to pleasure, sir," I said.

"I just don't understand why the ferrn press can't print our press releases and be done with it, the way the Thin House Press Corps does," he lamented. "It would be so much less work."

"It's the same all over the world," I commiserated. "Ignorance is the greatest crime. If people only knew what was good for them, they would surely do it."

"A man after my own heart, Frolick. Let me tell you what I need you to do."

"Anything, sir."

"I need something to show the Coalition of the Fasting. Something to reinforce their loyalty to the cause. We are in the middle of delicate negotiations for tightening this all-important military alliance, including opening new Fat Camps in their countries. Need I say that a scandal right now, a murder outside the Thin House, of a pizza dealer no less, could easily derail the alliance and put the progress of air-eating back twenty years?"

I mumbled noises of agreement.

"It all comes down to you, Frolick," he said. "On your shoulders. Bring me Fatso."

My mind whirled, reviewing everything I knew about Fatso and his organization. He had proven the most elusive criminal I had ever matched wits with in my ten years in law enforcement. The only one, too.

I frowned at the difficulty of the task. "I'll do my best, sir."

He lowered his voice. "Your best is not good enough."

I cringed. How could I be so stupid? My best wasn't good enough. I knew it, and now the Prophet knew it. What was I going to do?

The Prophet then said: "You will do everything in the power of the government of the United States of Air to bring Fatso in. Alive. I have signed an executive order putting the entire resources of our military and intelligence establishments at your disposal. Screw the Food Courts. Fatso's going straight to Fat Island." The tiny atoll in the Indian Ocean where extraordinary rendering takes place.

I gulped. The Supreme Food Court had ruled that only ferrners could be sent there. "But what will the judicial branch of our sacred constitutional republic say?"

"You let me worry about the Obstructionist Nine. This is a direct order, Special Agent Frolick. From your Commander-and-Air-Eater-in-Chief. Find him. Do whatever you have to do. You have twenty-four hours."

I came to attention again and saluted. "Yes, Mine Prophet!" I said. "Your will be done."

"At home as well as abroad," he replied. The formulaic rebuttal complete, he surprised me by shifting gears. "Have you ever considered applying for the Skinny Service? We could use a man like you."

My jaw went slack. I fingered the tape measure at my waist. "I would not presume to such high ambition, sir. Besides, I'm at least a couple inches short of—"

The Prophet's reedy voice cracked high. "Exception can be made, Special Agent. Bring me Fatso and you work for me. Here. In the Thin House."

I stammered, "That would be an honor, sir."

"Twenty-four hours, Frolick," the voice said. His cold seemed to be getting worse. "Now give me Erpent."

The SS man took the phone. "Erpent here." He listened for a long moment. "Understood, sir." He hung up and turned to us. "The Thin House has woken the D.C. medical examiner. He's on his way to the morgue right now. The contents of the victim's stomach will no doubt lead us to Fatso's greasy lair."

An ambulance idled nearby. Two paramedics had arrived while I was on the phone. At a signal from Erpent, they loaded the dead pizza dealer onto a stretcher and trotted off.

Erpent and I turned to go, but Green just stood there with his arms crossed. "What are you waiting for?" the SS agent demanded. "Let's move!"

"We're not going anywhere," my partner said. "Not until we're finished with the crime scene."

"Twenty-four hours," I pleaded with him. "That's all we have before the Coalition of the Fasting meets. The Prophet is depending on us—on us!—to find Fatso for him."

"And the way to do that is to spend some time here looking for clues." He gestured at the vomit and blood at our feet. "It's the only way to bring the real criminal to justice."

Erpent stepped forward until he stood nose to nose with Green. "And who, in your opinion," he asked, "is the real criminal?"

My partner flushed. "Well, I don't know, do I? That's why we have to investigate."

Erpent jabbed a finger into the other man's chest. "The real criminals are lone wolf food terrists. People who look just like you." He smiled. "Who even work for, say, the ATFF. Sleeper cells of entire families. But they forget. Their disobedient child loves the Prophet, and refuses to be force-fed—"

"Enough!"

"—force-fed their parents' food-eating lies."

"I said, enough!" Green backed away. "You win. We'll do it your way."

Erpent pursued him across the dead grass. "You don't know anyone like that. Do you?"

My partner's shoulders slumped. "No."

"What would you do if you did?"

"Arrest them, I suppose."

"You *suppose?*"

"I would turn them in. It would be my duty." His voice had taken on a wooden inflection.

I slapped him on the back. "Good man."

His head hung low, like he was sleepy. I was tired too, but now was no time for a nap.

"Come on, Harry," I said. "Let's go eat some caffeinated air." I put my arm around his shoulders to lead him away. But he just stood there, staring at the Thin House lit up across the street.

Erpent barked at Thinn, "Sergeant. Skinny Service cleaners— I mean, forensics team—is due here shortly. Make sure you leave no traces of your presence. Wrappers or…whatnot."

Thinn gulped, and tossed a greasy burger wrapper into the nearby garbage can.

"Wrappers under control, sir."

"And Thinn?"

"Sir?"

"Have a talk with fuzzy cheeks here." He turned to the rookie. "What's your name, son?"

"Officer Olde, sir," the boy said, rubbing at his puffy eyes. Nice kept a tight grip around his friend's bicep. "I said nothing more than the truth, sir. I believe in the Prophet. That's why I became a cop."

"Isn't that precious," Erpent said. To Thinn: "Officer Olde needs a lesson in protocol. Don't you agree, Sergeant?"

Thinn pinched the rookie's cheeks. "I'm putting demerits on your record," he said. "You'll be lucky to keep your badge when I'm through with you."

"But why would you do that?" Olde asked. "I've done nothing wrong." He waved to me and Green. "Happy hunting!"

"Don't you worry about that," I called over my shoulder as we limped toward the car. "We'll have Fatso behind bars faster than you can say 'Go the Power of Air.'"

For some reason the cops laughed at that, a laugh Erpent cut short with a look. Thinn and his colleagues waddled over to their cruisers and drove off. The ambulance waited for us to follow. The park was empty now, except for the three of us and a blood stain where Nick Hungry had died. Only the murmur of the Thin House water fountain in the distance could be heard.

We climbed into the Smart Car. The vehicle had no back seat—always a conundrum when transporting handcuffed suspects—so Erpent perched on Green's knees.

As I pulled away from the curb, I smacked my forehead with my palm. "You ought to give Judge Oscar Meyer-Weiner a call. We got the guy's name and social, right?"

"Get a warrant," Green said. "Good idea."

"Put a toilet tap on the guy's house. His family, his friends, known associates. Anyone goes poo in those toilets, or even a little pee-pee, we're going to know about it. Maybe they can lead us to Fatso's hideout. We might even find his Thanksgiving convention this year."

A toilet tap is just what it sounds like: the sewer company comes out and installs a fecal monitor on the sewer output valve of your home. It can also detect urine, and pretty much anything else you might care to flush down your toilet: tampons, used condoms, withered celery stalks, old boots, computer hard drives, sacks of flour—dime bags of ground-up grain were especially common during food busts—what have you. The sewer company also has fecal monitors on all the sewer branch lines.

This way we can compile effective statistics as to which neigh-
borhoods harbor the most food terrists, and what kind of food
they consume. Although the press had kept silent about this
new technology at the Prophet's request, word had begun to
leak out into the criminal community. Many hoods had taken
to building latrines or outhouses in their backyards, which
severely limited our ability to track their movements. Their
bowel movements, that is.

Erpent snickered. "A warrant. How quaint."

"Hey," I said. "We swore to uphold and defend the Amendment. The Constitution is part of the Amendment, last time I
checked."

"It's the other way around," Green said.

I frowned. "Are you sure?"

"Judge Meyer-Weiner!" Green said into his cell phone. "Sorry
for the late call. Got an emergency for you."

We'd had a citywide toilet tap authorized by the judge for
months, looking for a single strand of Fatso's DNA, anything
we could use to track him. But Don Fatso was meticulous in his
hygiene, and no matter how much he ate—and he was rumored
to be a glutton of the first order—not a drop of pee, not a milli-
gram of his poo ever found its way into the D.C. municipal
sewer system.

While Green organized the toilet tap, I followed the ambulance as fast as I could. But the paramedics pulled away from us.
I couldn't keep up.

"Faster!" Erpent urged.

"What difference does a few minutes make?" my partner
asked, hanging up the phone. "We're both going to the morgue."

"Every second counts," the SS man snapped. "It's a matter
of national security."

I hunched over the steering wheel. "I know a short cut."

"Take it," Erpent said. "That's an order."

I popped the flasher on the roof and squealed around the corner onto Avenue the Prophet Jones. Heading straight into the heart of Georgetown.

"Are you crazy?" Green shouted. "Go back!"

Erpent clutched the dashboard. "Are we going where I think we're going?"

I peeled through a red light, swerved around a burned-out police cruiser. "Fastest way to the morgue is through the ghetto."

"Fastest way to get eaten by cannibals, you mean!" Green shouted back.

Georgetown was D.C.'s food ghetto, famous the world over for the lawlessness of its food dealers, where you could get any-thing—anything—your overdeveloped and unnecessary diges-tive organs might desire. But for a price. The common wisdom held that it was only safe to enter Georgetown by day. Especially in the morning, after the addicts had gotten high off their white rice—they boil it, can you imagine?—and collapsed into bed in a drugged stupor. Some are even known to freebase the stuff, wash it down with a glass of water. But after dark? Don't go to G-town, the ooga-booga cannibals will eat you.

Please. Stories to scare children into eating their vegetable-flavored air.

Where others see a cannibal, I see a lost soul. Someone who needs to hear the Prophet's Gospel of Air. How I long to press a copy of *Food-Free At Last* into their bloodstained hands, get down on our knees together in the middle of the entrails and body parts, and pray. For faith. These people deserve our com-passion. Not our derision and scorn.

I had been wanting to come here after dark for ages to spread the good word, but Green always seemed to come up with some excuse to keep us away. My visits were few and far between, and never at night. Now was my chance to save some souls. Even if it was only a brief visit.

To my surprise, Green and Erpent grabbed the steering wheel and tried to turn us around. But I was resolute. The fastest way to the morgue was by doing the Prophet's will at the same time. Isn't life just like that?

We turned a corner, and there they were. A jeep barreled down the street toward us. Men with automatic rifles clung to the roll bars. Red stains ringed their lips. One gnawed a bone, and threw it at us as they sped past. The bone bounced off our roof. Painted in red on the side of their vehicle were the words "Suck the Marrow Out of Life."

Green clutched his service weapon. "Let's hope they aren't hungry."

Erpent looked behind us. "Here they come!"

The jeep pulled a U-turn and roared after us. I popped the glove compartment. Empty.

"What a tragedy."

"You're telling me," my partner said. "I don't fancy being someone's dinner."

"No," I said. "I mean we're out of literature."

"They're going to kill us and eat us," Erpent said, "and you're worried about what kind of kindling they're going to use to cook us?"

"No, silly," I said. "That's the Sushi Gang behind us. They don't cook their victims."

He gasped. "You mean they eat them raw?"

"They'll cut off a leg and blowtorch shut the wound," Green said. "Meat keeps fresher that way."

Gunfire sizzled around us.

"Sizzle, sizzle!
Like crispy frying bacon
and fluffy scrambled eggs!
Served with French toast
and drenched in maple syrup! Yum!"

The flying Twinkie wriggled and chirped against my leg. I gritted my teeth. *Not now. Focus on the scenery. Look at all the empty storefronts spilling broken glass into the street.*

"They're gaining on us," Green said.

"What are you so afraid of?" I asked. "They are poor, misguided souls who don't know any better."

"And that's enough to kill us!" Erpent screamed. "Now do something!"

I spotted the Golden F's up ahead. "Relax. I've got a plan." I turned down a narrow alley, sped around a disused strip mall and pulled into the Air Temple drive-thru. I realized with horror that the jeep had been unable to follow us. We could just make it out, creeping around the block, looking for some sign of us. I would have to be quick, or I would lose my chance.

I rolled my window down. "Yeah, can I get half a dozen Prophet Packs and four condensed *Food-Free At Lasts*?"

"They don't strike me as readers, partner mine," Green said.

A second jeep rolled after the first.

"Better make that a dozen Prophet Packs," I said into the microphone. "And be quick about it, please. We got souls to save!"

I reached for the horn, to let the cannibals know where we were, but Green and Erpent wrestled my hands away from the wheel.

"What are you doing?"

"Can they see us?"

"I don't think so."

"Maybe they'll give up. Dawn is coming soon." Military street patrols began at dawn.

"And lose our chance to bring them freedom?" I protested. "Let me go!"

The twin roar of the jeeps echoed in the street and faded into the distance. They were heading away from us—and their only chance at salvation.

I struggled, but Green and Erpent held my arms tight to my chest. "This is on your conscience," I said. "Not mine."

"They gone?"

"Looks like it."

Four hands released their grip on me.

"Now what do we do?"

"Go after them," I said. "And where are my Prophet Packs?" I smacked the drive-thru mike. It fell to the ground.

"Uh-oh," Green said. "This must be an abandoned Air Temple. Probably being used as a food lab. We got to get out of here, now."

Before he'd finished speaking, men with guns stepped out in front of us. I was flung back in my seat. Green's shoe ground my foot against the gas pedal.

A gunman leaped aside, we jumped the curb and squealed back into the street.

"But those addicts needed our help!"

"We're in a hurry," Erpent said. "The body's probably at the morgue by now."

"Not going anywhere til dawn," Green said. "Right now we need to find a place to hide."

Erpent checked his watch. "But that's half an hour from now, at least!"

Green snapped his fingers. "Rat Boy. Let's go there."

"Rat Boy?" Erpent asked.

"You're right," I said. "Finding Fatso is more important than those dealers." My spirits lifted. I could feel the Prophet's guiding hand at work in our investigation.

"Rat Boy's a low-level informant. He helped us find Fatso once," Green explained. "He might be able to find him again. Plus, no cannibal would ever look for us there."

It was only a quarter mile to the Foodville where Rat Boy lived. Green was right, the Sushi Gang would never go there. Not enough flesh on the skeletal residents to make it worth their while. Next time I came to Georgetown, I would have to bring more literature. And leave Green and Erpent at home.

In the light of the remaining streetlamps, I got a glimpse of the ghetto by night. White men in business suits and expensive silk ties lounged on street corners, looking nonchalant. Their women, in well-cut wool pantsuits and subdued make-up, ground their hips up and down the sidewalk in low-slung pumps, with that mother-of-three come-hither smirk. And all of them prepared to scatter at the first sign of the Sushi Gang.

Such suffering. Such unnecessary squalor. All because of their addiction. Because of those evil food terrists at the French Food Mafia. My Twinkie broke into song, and I gripped the steering wheel tighter. Fatso was the greatest threat the air-eating world had ever seen. He had to be destroyed.

He had to be.

SIX

IT WAS A NOTCH IN THE PROPHET'S TAPE MEASURE the day the ATFF captured Bakin Cheez Burgher VIII, a.k.a. Rat Boy. Heir to the Fat Boy Burger franchise, and great-great-great-great-great-great-grandson of Bakin Cheez Burgher Sr., the founder and much-reviled head of that calorie-distribution ring, the youngest Bakin Cheez became famous as his own company's best customer. When the ATFF froze his assets, he fled to Switzerland. Or tried to, anyway. This was before the Prophet closed the borders. We caught him only because he was too big to fit in a first-class airline seat. He argued with the flight attendants long enough to delay takeoff. By that time the armed ATFF squad had limped aboard the plane, resting every few feet to catch their breath—that body armor is heavy, let me tell you—and escorted him back to the gate.

"This man is a symbol of what is wrong with our country," the Prophet declared in the Thin House Rock Garden. He had replaced the dead rose bushes with Stonehenge-like slabs of West Virginia granite. "Look at him." He turned and drilled a finger at Mr. Burgher VIII, who lay on his back, chained to a flatbed truck. "Eight hundred putrid pounds. Those great folds of fat. The slobbery jowls. The demented eyes of a crazed food terrist.

"The mouth was not made for eating!" the Prophet roared suddenly. "It was made for consuming God's own air. And Mr. Burgher here is going to learn to eat air the hard way, whether he likes it or not. When we are done with him, he will be a role model of what any citizen of this great nation can be: thin."

He gave a signal, and the Skinny Service driver turned the ignition. The flatbed truck hummed to life.

"Off to Fat Camp with him. Off to Fat Camp with all you food terrists out there who can't understand three simple little words: 'just say no.'

"And to those of you who say, 'slow down.'" Exaggerated finger quotes. "'Let us not go to extremes.' I say to you: we have come to this hallowed spot" —and he swept a hand at the Rock Garden behind him— "to remind America, the Land of Air, of the fierce urgency of now. This is not the time to engage in the luxury of cooling off or to take the tranquilizing drug of gradualism. Now is the time to make real the promises of democracy."

The Prophet's words rang in my ears as the three of us limped through the Foodville toward Rat Boy's hovel. The fierce urgency of now. That I understood. Twenty-two and a half hours to find Fatso. No one was ever more fiercely urgent than I was at that moment.

On our way through the shantytown we passed numerous emaciated bodies covered in swarms of writhing maggots. Amazing the lengths you French will go to weaken our faith. Employing Hollywood special effects artists—members of *La Résistance,* your network of domestic *saboteurs*—to construct such lifelike corpses. The maggots! The smells!

"Please, sir."

A man whimpered in the mud. He lifted his outstretched arms as we passed, and grabbed hold of Erpent's trench coat. The SS agent jerked away.

"Well?" he demanded. "What do you want?"

The man licked his lips. "A crumb," he whispered. "I beg of you. A crumb. That's all. To taste food once more before I die."

"You're not dying," Erpent snapped. "All you have to do is believe."

"In eating air?" The man cackled and nearly fell over.

"This is a land of equal opportunity," I scolded the man. "There's enough air for everyone."

"Are you for real?"

"You dare doubt in my presence?" The SS man yanked his Laxafier from its holster. "I ought to laxafy you right now."

"No! No! Look at me! Lunge and chomp. See? Look at how much air I'm eating!" The man gulped down that life-giving vapor. "All I have to do is believe!" he shouted.

Erpent lifted his Laxafier to shoot the man. I was moved to compassion. I put an arm on his elbow, drew the weapon back down to his side.

"Doubters like him are destroying this country," the SS agent growled.

"Once he gets a bellyful of oxygen, he'll be fine," I said.

The man shuffled away on his knees, shaking his head, lunging and chomping. My heart swelled to think that I had brought yet another person to the salvation of eating air.

At the end of the muddy track stood Rat Boy's hovel, a one-room shanty of corrugated iron with rust running in strips down the outside. I drew my own Laxafier. Green did the same. I rapped on the warped metal rectangle propped over the structure's only opening.

"I say, old boy, return hither in an hour's time," a voice inside drawled. "They have not yet reached a desired state of readiness."

I nodded to Green. Rat Boy, all right. He was one of those Americans—I mean, Airitarians—who thought everything in England was better than in the US. Of course, he'd never actually been to the UK. I'd read his file. The farthest from our God-favored land he'd ever been was a Fat Camp in Vermont. His manner of speech, so far as I could make out, was a badly remembered imitation of Masterpiece Theatre.

I held my finger to my lips. I knocked again.

"Don't get your knackers in a twist, I'm com—"

The words slid from his lips like a piece of rubbery bologna into the incinerator. He lifted the sheet of metal from the door and peered out, straight down the barrel of my service weapon.

Green threw his arms out wide. "Why the face?" He clapped a palm against the man's greasy, soot-stained shirt, and made a noise of disgust. He wiped his hand on his pants. "What's the matter, Rat Boy? Aren't you glad to see us?"

"My dear chap, there remains much cooking left to be done," the slum-dweller snapped. He pushed back the hood of loose skin that covered his eyes. "Will you not wait somewhere else? It makes my neighbors rather nervous."

The smell of burning hair wafted through the doorway, making my eyes water. Combined with the squalor around us, it sent my compassion into overdrive. The ghetto a few blocks away was genteel by comparison. Here shanty pressed close to shanty on the banks of the Potomacncheese. D.C.'s most miserable food whores slept in this Foodville. Poor things. Willing to do all sorts of unspeakable acts in exchange for one of Rat Boy's rotisserie rodents. Lucky for them, though, they would never taste that chargrilled flesh. Their pimps ladled them each a bowlful of gruel once per day, just enough to keep the withdrawal pains from becoming unbearable, and confiscated any non-monetary payments before the woman could shove it down her throat—and the Prophet help the whore who tried. If only they could learn to have faith in eating air, they too could join the rest of the country in the Feast of Oxygen inaugurated by the Prophet when he took office. Then, and only then, would they be free to escape this riverside slum.

"I say, don't be a stranger. Do drop by for a spot of tea later, what?" the former fast-food heir said. He reached for the door, but Green leaned his shoulder against it.

"I don't know what you're suggesting," I said evenly. "We aren't here to consume anything illegal."

I was ashamed of the truth and desperate to prevent it from coming out in front of Erpent and my partner. The fact is, a couple months ago, my Twinkies pulled a despicable stunt. I had come to bring Rat Boy some literature, when a swarm of Twinkies surrounded me and began to sing. They threatened to attack me. I still don't know how they got from my basement all the way across town. They demanded I take a rat from Mr. Burgher. Not as a payoff or bribe, but as a fellow rapist, a four-legged companion to join in their group violation of my mouth and throat. They made me hide the grilled rodent under my trench coat, and crawl back into my Smart Car. Then they forced that disgusting burnt meat down into my stomach.

Ever since, I've been at my wit's end. It obviously wasn't enough to stay out of earshot of my basement. I don't suppose you Frenchies have any traditional herbal remedies against suicidal pastry mouth molesters? Some kind of Twinkie repellent? No? 'Cause I've tried everything. Oh well. Just thought I'd ask.

"Is it a social visit, then?" Rat Boy inquired. "Shall I call the butler? He'll see you into the drawing room. Or perhaps you'd prefer the library? Truth is I can never remember which is which. There are ever so many rooms. Do be patient, he'll be along shortly. He does tend to get lost. Now, if you'll excuse me?"

I rested my Laxafier against the man's shoulder. The tip of the gun disappeared under the folds of loose skin that dangled from his neck. "You've got an ear to the sewer. What's coming down the toilet?"

Rat Boy sighed. He leaned forward, and his massive slabs of skin scraped against the door frame. He wore a faded T-shirt that read, "Fat Boys Turn Me On." Excessive epidermis erupted from every opening.

"Be my humble guest," he said. "Mind the hole in the floor, what? It's ever so tiny, but visitors have been known to stumble. Most unpleasant if you do."

Green and Erpent managed by great effort to move the door to one side, and I stepped over the threshold. I had never actually been inside Rat Boy's shack before. A glowing brazier stood to one side. A skewer of half a dozen rats, skin and all, rotated slowly over the coals. Another smell filled the room, mingling with that of burning fur. It took me a moment to identify it. It was poo. No, not poo. Raw sewage. The anal excretions of thousands of food terrists. The undigested waste that drops from their bowels. I followed my nose inside, spellbound.

Green grabbed my elbow. "Careful, partner mine."

At my feet a deep hole plunged straight down. Squeaking and splashing noises came up from below. I leaned over the edge. At the bottom, rats clambered over one another, playing their little ratty games—like hide and go seek, red rover and pin the tail on the donkey, no doubt—in a river of human excrement.

"What is this?" I asked in breathless wonder.

Rat Boy busied himself with the brazier. "The sewer of our great capital city vomits forth its bounty into the River Potomacncheese. Man's best friend, a species known in Latin as *rattus rattus,* simply adores the conditions in the pipes far beneath our feet. I fish the shitty subterranean streams with my trusty fishing pole,"—he nodded to where it stood in the corner—"impale them upon my ever-reliable cast iron skewer, and grill them to perfection. Now. About the sauce. With which variety may I tempt your indubitably jaundiced palates?"

"Yummy sauce!" my Twinkie chirped, *"Saucy sauce! I want some sauce!"* and began to dance. I crossed my legs to muffle the noise.

"What was that about sauce?" I asked as loudly as I dared.

"Surely you remember my sauces, old boy. I take great pride in having the best rat sauce between here and New York. Today I can offer you a rat-milk béchamel, pigeon liver pâté and a cockroach mousse. The mousse, I must say, is exquisite."

Erpent had said nothing until now, examining the shack with a look of distaste. At the mention of sauce, he gasped. "You mean you eat the rats?"

"But of course, my dear chap. On what rotating planet around what distant star have you been residing these past three years?" Rat Boy replied. "This is the land of the free and the home of the brave. This is America."

"The United States of Air," I corrected.

Erpent flung a trembling finger out at Mr. Burgher VIII. "He admits it!" he cried. "Food terrist! Arrest him! Food terrist!"

"Chill," Green said. "It's cool."

Erpent turned on my partner and screamed in his face. "He admits his crime. Why aren't you arresting him? Possession of addictive caloric substances, with intent to distribute!"

"Because he's a snitch," Green said. "Leave him alone. He's helped us out in the past."

"This sort of selective enforcement is not acceptable," Erpent barked. "We are a nation of laws!"

Green stood firm. "You didn't seem to mind the burgers the cops had in the park this morning."

"That's different, Harry," I said. "Their zero-calorie snacks are made out of compressed air. It's not the same thing. You know it's not."

Erpent drew his Laxafier. "Failure to arrest a food terrist is a crime. You could lose your jobs for this."

"We were doing our jobs until you interfered," Green snapped.

Mr. Burgher VIII plucked the spit from the brazier and brandished it at us, the dead rodents still impaled along the length of the blackened iron. "My dearest Frolick, what ever is going on?" he said. "I thought we had an understanding."

I had never been comfortable with our use of snitches. These people deserved treatment in Fat Camp. Why were we letting them suffer? But Green had persuaded me it was for the greater good. I reluctantly sided with my partner.

"What's more important?" I asked. "Capture Fatso? Or put away this scum-sucking chunk of slum-dwelling filth?"

"Thanks, Frolick," Rat Boy said.

"Hey," I said. "No problem."

Erpent scratched his chin. He kept his weapon pointed at Rat Boy's chest. "You may be right. But still. We are the long arm and skinny waist of justice. We're not supposed to engage in favoritism."

"Think of it this way," I said. "He's small potatoes. We're after the roast turkey with the cranberry sauce and pumpkin pie and gravy and glazed yams and all the other trimmings. So that we can chuck it all into the fiery furnace and watch it burn."

Erpent lowered his gun. "Please proceed with your investigation, Special Agent Frolick," he snapped.

"I say, we got off on the wrong foot." Rat Boy held out the smoking spit. "Do sample one of my rodential delicacies. Better than crumpets and cream on a Devonshire afternoon, eh, what?"

Erpent hissed, "Are you attempting to bribe an officer of the SS?"

Rat Boy cocked his head to one side. "Oh come now. Don't be shy. Can you resist one of my chargrilled specialties? They're crunchy on the outside, soft and juicy on the inside." He lowered his voice. "You simply must try the cockroach mousse. It is too good."

Erpent slapped the iron spit out of his face. "The Prophet himself has ordered the French Food Mafia shut down and Fatso arrested," he said. "Now tell me what you know."

Rat Boy chuckled. He hooked a thumb at Erpent. "He is direct, I'll grant you that."

Before I could stop him, the SS man grabbed the thumb with his free hand and tried to bend it backward. Burgher looked down, as though puzzled by the tiny man dangling from his thumb, then shook his hand free. Erpent slipped to the ground in a pile of rat poo.

It's like the Prophet always says. How can you compete with Olympic athletes who use dope? It's the same with food. How was an Amendment-abiding, air-eating citizen to compete with people like Bakin Cheez? It was like trying to beat the East German swim team. Steroids, food—same thing. Both were performance-enhancing drugs. In both cases it gave an unfair advantage to the bad guys.

"What on earth are you doing, old chap?" Rat Boy asked.

Erpent picked himself up and wiped rat poo from his palms. He scraped the filth from his Laxafier and pointed it at Rat Boy's chest. The weapon shook in his hands. Green and I stepped out of the line of fire.

"Calm down," my partner said. "This is not how we do things."

"Which is why I am doing your job for you." He shook his Laxafier in Rat Boy's face. A dangerous thing to do. A laxative dart to the head causes the brain to run out the nose. "Now start talking!"

My phone rang. I checked the number. "Guys!" I said. "Time out. It's my wife?"

"Oh, right."

"Sorry."

Erpent lowered his gun. Rat Boy put the spit back on the grill. I answered on the third ring.

"Jason, honey?"

I turned away from the others and lowered my voice. "How many times have I told you not to call me that?"

"What, 'Jason'?"

"No! 'Honey'!" I bunched up my fists. "I am not an addictive caloric syrup made by bees!"

"I'm sorry, Jason," she cooed into the receiver. "You're still sweet to me."

A tingle went up my spine. "Look, Oxy," I said. "I'm on the job. Is everything OK? Nathan getting ready for school?"

"No, he's not OK. That's why I'm calling."

My son! What was wrong? I pressed the cell phone closer to my ear. "Why? What happened?"

"He's hungry," she said. "We both are. Jason—"

"Not this again." I groaned.

"Do you want us both to starve to death?"

Erpent waited at the edge of my vision, listening to every word.

"I can't really talk right now," I said. "When I get home we'll pray together. Ask the Prophet to strengthen your faith."

"Oh for the love of pizza!"

"Pizza!" I exclaimed. "What do you know about pizza?"

"It's an expression, Jason! A figure of speech?"

I considered that. Was it a clue? "A thin figure or a fat figure?" I asked.

"Mothereating idiot," she swore. And hung up.

My ears stung. Such language! I'd never heard her talk that way before.

"Can we continue our standoff now?" Erpent asked.

"By all means," I said, and pocketed my cell phone.

The two adversaries resumed their defensive postures. "Now where were we?" Rat Boy asked.

"You said I'm direct. I grabbed your thumb. You shook me loose. Green told me to calm down. I didn't. Then I told you to start talking."

"Right-O."

Erpent shook his Laxafier in Rat Boy's face again. "So start talking!"

"My dear boy," he said. "I sell rats to food whores. Why on earth would you think I know Fatso personally?"

Erpent's finger tightened on the trigger.

"No!" I shouted, and reached for his arm, but it was too late. *Pfthh.*

A dart embedded itself in Burgher's chest.

The dealer staggered backward against the brazier. "God Save the Queen," he mumbled. He touched a finger to a soot-stained photograph on the wall of the current English monarch. With one last effort, he swung the iron spit up onto the hot coals. He slumped down against the creaking, rusty wall, the dart sticking out from between his flabby breasts. A new odor joined the riot of fruit flavors in that hot metal box: fresh poo, with a hint of rotting rat meat.

"Thank you," Rat Boy sighed, his eyes closed, head leaning back.

Erpent bent down, pried open an eyelid. "Why do you thank us?"

"So terribly…constipated. Now I feel wonderfully empty… clean. Clean. Superbly clean."

Green and I exchanged glances. We'd shot our share of suspects, but this was a first. Usually they fell asleep and stayed that way until they were in the Food Court holding cell.

"Where's Fatso?" Erpent demanded again.

"Simply not enough fiber in rat meat…can't afford oat bran. Tried to get some…Metamucil once…turned out to be sawdust shavings…" He clucked his tongue. "Such dishonesty in the world."

"What is in those darts?" I asked.

Erpent crouched low over the slumped figure. "The usual. Plus some truth serum. Sodium pentathlon. Started using it last month. So far it's proven effective. Although subjects do tend to ramble."

My partner groaned. "You've killed him, then."

Erpent shone a pen light in Rat Boy's eyes. "I have not. He'll be fine in a couple of hours."

A half-roasted rat slid from the end of the spit and fell to the ground. Two of its live brethren scurried out of a dark corner and gnawed on its charred flesh. The sound of moist crunching filled the gaps in their conversation. I tried to pet one of the rats, but it bit me.

"What happens when the neighbors find out he talked?" Green said. "They'll slit his throat and leave him for the cannibals. Or the rats."

Erpent stood up. "We can always issue you sodium pentathlon darts too. You're ATFF, after all."

"But that is not the point!" Green said, raising his voice. "When word gets out that we can't be trusted?" He gestured at Rat Boy with his gun. "That this is how we treat our snitches? Our ability to develop sources disappears. And with it our ability to do our job."

Erpent smiled, a thin string of flesh across his skin-tight skull. "With any luck," he said, "by the end of the day we will have Fatso in custody, and you will no longer have need of these low-life traitors."

Green snorted. "Fat chance of that."

I bent down, stroked Rat Boy's gelatinous forehead. The sooner we shut down the mafia, the sooner my suicidal flying pastry rapist problem would go away.

"I'm really sorry," I said, as gently as I could. "But we need to find him. Any idea where Fatso might be?"

Rat Boy spoke from a drugged slumber. "I don't know."

"You see?" Green said.

Erpent pushed me aside. "But you have some idea where he is, don't you? Location of his Supper Clubs, for instance."

The Skinny Service agent had a point. Rat Boy helped us find Fatso that one time. So now, as I stood over Rat Boy's drugged and helpless form, I wondered why our favorite snitch had heard nothing more of the Supper Clubs.

"It changes every night, never the same place twice," Rat Boy mumbled. "I look to you the sort of person he would invite?"

"Then how did he know before?" Erpent demanded.

"Maybe Fatso plugged the leak," Green said. "Let's try some easy questions first." He tapped Erpent on the shoulder. The SS agent hissed, but moved aside. "What's your relationship with the mafia?"

Rat Boy giggled. "I pay protection money."

"Why is that funny?" Erpent asked, but the giggling only got louder. "Answer me, damn you! Why is that funny?"

"Is funny…because they protect me from them." The giggles trailed off.

"How much you pay?"

"Two rather large gents visit me once per lunar cycle. I deliver into their big, meaty paws a sealed envelope and a free rat each. They prefer the béchamel sauce."

"How much?" Green asked.

"Five thousand."

"By the Prophet's unnecessary teeth," Erpent swore. "What's the going price for a rat these days?"

"It varies upon the weight," Rat Boy said. "Around two hundred per head, not counting extras like sauce, pickles, mustard and the various other relishes for which I am justifiably famous."

"People really pay that much to satisfy their addiction?" Erpent asked. He seemed genuinely surprised.

I shrugged. "Protein is scarce. I mean, for people who are into that sort of thing," I added, at a sharp glance from him.

I bent down again next to Green. Rat Boy looked so peaceful, propped against his hovel wall. The folds of skin at his neck trembled with each breath. "Tell me, Mr. Burgher," I said. "Everything you know about…pizza." The last word I whispered in his ear.

A look of pain passed across his face, as though some great inner struggle was taking place behind those lidded eyes. He said nothing.

"Pizza, Rat Boy!" Erpent screamed over my shoulder, making my ears hurt. "Where is Fatso?" He reached down and slapped the food dealer again.

"Pizza...expensive," he finally came out with. "What about it?"

"Where is the food lab?" Erpent demanded, hopping on his toes behind me. "Why would Fatso sell an uncut pizza? How do we find him?"

I held up a hand. "One question at a time."

Green patted Bakin Cheez on the cheek. "You still with us, Rat Boy?"

"Me Rat Boy," came the reply. His diction was getting worse, an effect of the sedative. "Me eat rats. Mommy, yummy, me eat rats!"

"Let me ask you this," my partner said. "Who has the money and the nerve to order a pizza from Fatso, kill the delivery guy, then vomit all over his dead body?"

A smile twitched at the corners of Rat Boy's lips. "Mommy, I don't think he's heard," he said. "Fun Fun Funny. Everybody knows the prof—"

Crack!

Erpent's shoe connected with Rat Boy's chin. The dealer's head banged against the wall and flopped forward on his chest. I checked the man's vitals. He was out for a while, but he'd be fine. I stood up and turned to Erpent, but Green beat me to it.

"What in the name of the Prophet was that?" Green shouted.

"I told you our investigation was of Fatso only," Erpent said calmly. "Not the murder. What part did you not understand?"

Green jabbed a finger into the SS man's bony chest. "Skinny Service or no Skinny Service, you interfere one more time in our investigation—yes, *our* investigation—I will personally pump you full of laxatives. Right in front of the Prophet, if I have to. Then we'll see what comes out, Mister Look At Me How Skinny I Am."

The two men held their Laxafiers at ready. For a moment I was afraid of Mutual Assured Laxafication. The first ray of dawn fell between them. A Humvee rattled by outside.

Erpent reacted. "I'll deal with you later. Right now, we've got to get to the morgue."

We limped across the Foodville to the Smart Car, Erpent urging us on to faster and faster hobbling. I mused out loud over Rat Boy's last words.

"'Knows the prof,'" I said. "The 'prof.' The profusion? Of what? No. The professor? Professor, where? What college? What subject? No. Wait. I got it. The profit."

Green made a big *O* with his mouth. "Welcome to the party."

"The profiteering," I added, convinced I had nailed it. I drew myself up straight and declared, "The profiteering bastards of the French Food Mafia are slowly destroying this country with their addictive caloric substances." I turned to Green. "What do you think? Is that what he was trying to say?"

Green's smile faded. Erpent glared at him. "We don't need a snitch to tell us that," my partner said. "We know it already."

I know what all of you out there are thinking right now. And shame on you. When you find out what really happened that night, the truth will warm the cockles of your heart.

"And serve them up
with lemon juice and salt!"

Shut up, you.

Don't believe me? No? Just you wait and see.

SEVEN

M Y FAVORITE THING ABOUT THE MORGUE WAS the ME's special ham. Back before the Prophet came to power, I'd made any excuse to visit the coroner. I never could figure out why he called it special ham. Maybe because he smoked it himself. We'd munch succulent sandwiches, an entire leg of the stuff between us, surrounded by dead bodies with tags hanging from their ears, because their legs were missing. An awful lot of paraplegics passed through that morgue, let me tell you. Must have been an epidemic of wheelchairs crushed by speeding semitrailers. No doubt road rage caused by eating food.

Those terrible days were over now, thank the Prophet. It had been three years since I last visited. I wondered how he was. I shouldn't have worried.

A bent figure shuffled out of the darkness, leaning heavily on an IV stand. Plastic tubes snaked out of his nose and down his back to an oxygen tank he pulled behind him. His puckered face exploded when he saw us, like popcorn when you throw it into the incinerator.

"Frolick!" he wheezed. "What's an honest cop like you doing in a place like this?"

"What a joker," I said. "Are you implying there are cops who are dishonest?" I turned to Green and Erpent. "Can you believe this guy?"

He chuckled and offered me his hand. "It's good to see you," he said. "It's been too long."

I grinned in spite of myself. Medical Examiner Hot 'N' Juicy and I went way back. From even before I partnered up with Green. I took his bony claw in my own. How frail my old friend looked. How—old.

"Doc," I said at last. "You've lost weight."

Juicy cackled. "I lose any more I'll be dead."

"Then maybe you should pray for faith," Erpent said sharply. His eyes narrowed. "You got a permit for this?" He stood on tip-toe to read the sticker on the IV bag.

"It's his medicine," I said. "Leave him alone."

"No. It's not. It's glucose." Erpent snapped a ragged finger-nail against the bag, and for a moment I thought the plastic would tear. "An addictive caloric substance."

Juicy retrieved a wallet from a baggy hip pocket. He used to weigh as much as I did, close to five hundred pounds. Now his white lab coat hung loose on his shoulders, sixteen sizes too big for him.

"Medical exemption," he muttered, hunting through the wallet. "I'm diabetic."

"That's no excuse," Erpent said. "A condition that would not exist if you had more faith. Air is all you need." The SS agent's jaw twitched, no doubt wishing he could destroy that bag of sugar water and remove one more source of temptation from the world.

In that moment, I sympathized with both of them. I know how hard it is when your faith is weak, and the Twinkies attack.

To watch an addict consuming so much as a single calorie can incite them. But on the other hand, when you're diabetic, a tiny lapse in faith could cause dangerously low blood sugar, sending you into a coma. It was a tough call, finding the right balance.

"Here it is." Juicy held out a laminated card. "See the signature?" He jabbed a frail finger at the signing authority.

"Director of National Air Security, Lt. Gen. Allfood Bad," Erpent read, and bit his lip. He caught himself, looked around at those of us who had seen him do it, and wiped the saliva from his lips. No one wanted to gain a reputation for self-cannibalization.

Juicy cackled, "Chew on that, Agent Whoever You Are."

"It's Erpent," the SS man snarled. "Agent Erpent, Special Aide to the Prophet Himself."

You could hear the initial capitals as he spoke them. I had no idea he was so important. "Really?" I said. "Wow."

"Whatever." Juicy shrugged. "No sugar, no me. No me, no morgue. No morgue, no one to cut open the bodies for you. Got it?"

Erpent's eyes flickered across the card, no doubt admiring the photo. When he was done, he grunted and shoved the card back at Juicy. "So where's our pizza guy?" he demanded. "Cut him open, let's see what we got."

"Always so impatient," Juicy sighed. He turned away from us, shuffled toward a sheet-covered corpse.

The room smelled of burnt meat and formaldehyde. A carving knife protruded from the leg of a nearby body. A lit Bunsen burner on a corner bench illuminated a bloody saw. I sniffed again. Was it possible? I would have sworn I caught a hint of Juicy's famous special ham. Must be a remnant odor. Years old. Down here in the basement things didn't get aired out nearly so often as they ought to be.

"No appreciation for the skill," Juicy continued. He tapped his temple with a skeletal forefinger. "The vital matter of analysis made possible by the human cerebrum."

"Ignore the super skinny," Green said to the coroner, using a rude nickname for a member of the Skinny Service. "We just want to know who killed the guy."

"No!" The shout echoed in the concrete basement. Erpent tightened the tape measure around his waist. "We're after Fatso, not the murderer. How many times do I have to say it?" He turned on Juicy. "Cut his stomach open. Do it. Now."

"Your friend seems a bit high strung," Juicy remarked, and stopped next to a gurney.

"No friend of mine," Green said, and crossed his arms.

"I don't expect you to like me, Agent Green," Erpent said. "I expect you to obey me. Is that clear?"

Green clicked his heels together, threw out an open palm and shouted, "Go the Power of Air!"

Juicy chuckled. He checked the tag on the body's big toe. "This is the one," he said. "I can't tell you who killed him. Even if I wanted to," he added, looking at Erpent from under his eyebrows. "But I can tell you what he ate in the last twenty-four hours. More importantly, I can tell you his name."

"Nick Hungry of Pepperoniville, Pennsylvania," I said. "Rap sheet as long as a piece of melted cheese."

"How long is a piece of melted cheese?" Green asked.

I furrowed my brows in concentration. Come to think of it, I had never considered the question before. "You know," I said. "I'm not sure."

"That's just one of his many aliases," Juicy said, ignoring our conversation. "His tattoo was surgically altered. I ran his prints through the FBI's database. This is what came out."

He chucked an inch-thick stack of paper onto the dead man's chest. The pages were held together with a binder clip. He nodded toward me and Green. "The two of you should take a look at it. Might help in your investigation."

Erpent grabbed the report before I could pick it up. "Let me see those," he said, and flipped through the pages. Over his shoulder I could see table after table listing chemical reactions. I had no idea what it meant.

I pinched the report between my thumb and forefinger. "Care to give us the executive summary?"

Juicy pulled the dead man's right arm out from under the sheet. He picked up a pair of scissors and cut away the sleeve. "The real Nick Hungry disappeared eight months ago. This guy's name is Jacques Crusteau, a baker's apprentice from Quiche Lorraine, France."

Green whistled. "The French Food Mafia's ancestral homeland."

"He's had his social security number surgically altered on several occasions," Juicy continued, tracing faint scar lines amidst the blue bar code with the tip of the scissors. "The alterations are good enough to fool the scanners, but fingerprints are harder to modify."

"But why didn't he go clean?" Erpent asked.

I was surprised at Erpent's question. It showed how little he knew of field work. Even I knew the answer to that one.

"To go clean" meant illegal removal of your social security number and bar code. While only ex-cons were obliged by law to wear their tattoos, these days that meant pretty much everyone. After all, who hadn't been to Fat Camp at least once?

I let the coroner explain.

"No one looks twice at a multiple offender these days," Juicy said. "But a first-timer? Someone without their digits?" He shook his head. "It would attract too much attention."

The coroner lifted the sheet until only the dead man's head remained covered. He cut away Crusteau's blood-soaked grey sweatshirt to reveal a navy-and-white striped shirt underneath. The thick stripes ran horizontally across the man's chest. From under one armpit, the coroner plucked a crumpled black beret. From the other armpit, a half-empty pack of Gauloises.

"*Voilà!*" he said. "As I suspected. The uniform of French Intelligence. Your pizza dealer was a spy."

"Why would a French spy want to work for Fatso?" I asked. "That makes no sense."

Green chewed on a fingernail. I would have to have a talk with him about that later. "Maybe it does, partner mine. Remember Taco Tim?"

Nine months ago, Congressman Tim O'Mexico, the Irish-American "Lion of Airizona," had come to the ATFF with a confession. In return for a reduced sentence, he told us how a blackmailer had photos of him in a compromising position with half a dozen chimichangas. The press had dubbed him "Taco Tim." I guess "Chimichanga Tim" just didn't have the same ring to it. He could have paid, he told us. But the blackmailers would have slowly bled him dry. He was nearing retirement age, and he wanted to leave an inheritance for his kids. He decided a two-month stretch in Fat Camp wasn't such a bad deal after all. Even managed to keep his Congressional seat when he got out. *I* wouldn't have voted for him, you understand. I was shocked to hear that others had. That kind of vice in our public officials is more than just anomalous. It's a disgrace. Can you imagine? Half a dozen chimichangas? At the same time?

"So you think Crusteau was looking for someone to black-mail?" I asked.

"That's what spies do, isn't it?" Green said. "Maybe the mur-derer was a politician." He glanced at Erpent. "Or maybe some-one's aide."

"Entirely possible," Juicy said. "Now you see why he had a phony social?"

"The question is, though," I said, "is Fatso part of this? I mean, is he working for French Intelligence too?"

Erpent broke his silence. "Fatso and the French spies hate each others' guts," he said. "Fatso may be a criminal but he's still a loyal Airitarian. He doesn't want to see the Amendment repealed. Or he'd lose all his business. It's the French we have to worry about." With a flick of his wrist he dropped the stack of papers back on top of the corpse's chest. The papers slid against Crusteau's head, pinning the remaining sheet to his neck. "Now can we please start cutting? I want to see what's in his stomach. This *is* rather urgent, you know."

Juicy grabbed hold of the edge of the sheet. "Do you mind?"

I picked up the papers, and the coroner yanked the sheet off the dead man's face. The three of us newcomers gasped.

In the park we had seen Jacques Crusteau alias Nick Hungry lying face down in the dead grass under a broken streetlamp. Now we saw him face up under the bright light Juicy turned on. Deep gashes pocked the dead man's face, neck and chest. His skin shone damp, like someone had recently wiped down the body.

Something was missing. It was Green who spotted it first.

"No vomit," he said. "No pizza sauce. No leftover cheese."

Juicy clucked his tongue. "This is how they brought him in."

"What!" I exclaimed. "Didn't you examine the crime scene?"

"And when would I have time to do that?" he asked. "Two Skinny Service types dragged me out of bed half-dressed. Told me it was a matter of national security." He scowled at Erpent. "So if this isn't how the body looked at time of death, don't blame me."

Juicy and Erpent glared at each other. There was an acid tension between the two, like drinking a glass of vinegar on an empty stomach. The sort of thing the Prophet used to do in his "health food phase," before discovering the miracle of eating air. I tried to throw some sodium bicarbonate on the situation.

"So it was a knife, then?" I asked.

Juicy withdrew from his staring match. He turned back to the corpse in front of him.

"At first I thought so too," he said in a tired monotone. He put down the scissors and picked up a surgical spreader. "But if you look closely at the depth of the wounds," —and here he spread open a deep gash in the man's shoulder and inserted a plastic ruler— "you'll notice the weapon appears to have been circular in shape, and sharp all around."

"So what was it?" I asked.

"He was trying to defend himself," Juicy went on. He lifted up the man's wrists. The backs of Crusteau's hands and forearms had been gashed in the same peculiar manner. "And this," he said, and traced a long gash across the man's neck, "is the wound that killed him. Severed the carroty artery."

"We're not interested in the murder weapon," Erpent said, tapping his shoe against the concrete floor. "What we want to know is what is in his stomach. Can you get cutting now? Please?"

The coroner fastened a pair of goggles over his eyes. He regarded the SS agent through the smudged plastic. "Young man," he said, "do you know why I'm still here?"

Erpent cracked his knuckles. "What do you mean?"

Juicy tossed the surgical spreader back onto the tray with a clatter. He lifted a circular saw from the floor. "Why I didn't go to Canafooda with the rest of them. The AMA crowd. Why I chose a shitty job like this instead of going into private practice in the first place. I could have, you know."

Without waiting for an answer, he flicked a switch on the saw and slid the spinning blade through Crusteau's sternum. Bone dust and flecks of flesh sprayed fore and aft. The three of us stepped away from the gurney, shielding our faces with our hands.

"Because I believe in justice!" Juicy howled like a food-crazed chef carving a turkey corpse. Over the whine of the saw against bone we could barely make out his words. "Because I believe in punishing the guilty! And there are none of us who is innocent!"

The saw sputtered and died. Juicy dropped it back onto the floor and dug his gloved fingers into the space made in Crusteau's chest cavity. With a heave the ribs separated, exposing the French spy's internal organs to the cold basement air.

"I will give you all the information I have," he said. "But I will not be bullied, I will not be threatened and I will not be silenced."

And with that, he buried his arms up to his elbows in the dead man's intestines.

"Funny," Erpent said, in the silence that followed, the squish of internal organs loud in the quiet basement. "I thought you stayed put because of your special ham."

Juicy bent his head lower over his work. His face was hidden in shadow. "I believe in this country, Agent Erpent. I believe in the words that end our Pledge of Allegiance: 'and justice for all.' Including for me."

Erpent rested his hand on the butt of his gun, and rocked back on his heels. "Even for cannibals?"

"For them, for everyone," Juicy said, squeezing the dead man's intestines between his fists. "Monstrous brutes, cannibals. Consuming the flesh of their fellow man."

"You know the punishment for cannibalism?" Erpent leaned forward now, his face contorted once more in that death's-head grimace.

I put my hand in the air, jumped up and down. This was just like ATFF school. "Ooh! I know!" I cried. "Pick me! Pick me!"

Green sighed, pulled down on my arm. "Go ahead, Agent Frolick."

"The punishment for cannibalism," I recited, "is to be tied hand and foot and dropped off at sundown in an area of known cannibal activity. Ironic, huh?" I looked up at Erpent. His recommendation, it occurred to me, would be crucial in making the jump to the Skinny Service. "Did I get it right? Can I give the dunce cap back now?"

They were all looking at me kind of funny. Juicy spoke first. "Thank you," he said. "Your memory, as usual, does not fail you." He dropped the coil of intestines and shifted down to Crusteau's hips. "Now help me with this, will you?"

He slid both gloved hands, smeared with blood, under the dead man's naked right buttock. I stood opposite and did the same. The cold skin of the corpse's bottom weighed heavy on my fingertips.

"Like this?"

"Now lift."

We lifted.

"You there. The bed pan," he said to Erpent. "Be quick about it."

Erpent did not move. Green grabbed the bed pan and jammed it under the man's tush. Crusteau's legs, stiff with rigor mortis, poked up at an angle.

"Now," Juicy said with a smile, "let's have a look-see, shall we?"

He wrung the dead man's colon between his fists until a thick brown poo oozed out into the bed pan. "He shat himself when he died," the coroner said. "They all do, of course. Loss of bowel control at moment of death is normal. But here," and Juicy picked through the paste with a pair of tweezers, "here we have the contents higher up. Look!" He held up a tiny piece of brown.

"What is it?" I asked eagerly, bending over the bed pan, the aroma of the dead man's last meal fragrant in my nostrils. This was being alive. Here I was, examining the contents of a French spy's bowels. All I had to do now was catch Fatso. I was on my way to the top of the Skinny Service. I was sure of it.

"Brown rice," Juicy said. "And see this? Half-digested tofu. Bean sprouts. Legumes. Pulses. Even what looks like an apple seed." He held aloft the suspect particle between his tweezers. "Fruit! Can you imagine?" he said, and laughed.

"Loathsome creature," Erpent spat.

"He was an addict," Juicy said. "He couldn't help himself. I think we all know what that's like."

"Speak for yourself, Doctor," Erpent said with a scowl. "Now can we get to his stomach? That's what we're here for."

"I thought we were here to trace the contents of the man's stomach back to the source," Green objected. "To help us find Fatso." He indicated the bed pan in front of us. "Isn't that what we're doing now?"

"Patience," the coroner said to Erpent. "I don't know what your rush is, but we're getting there." He took up a scalpel and made an incision in Crusteau's primary digestive organ.

"You're in luck, you know," he said, peering down into the man's stomach. "*Monsieur* Crusteau was a bad boy. He didn't take his laxative the way Fatso told him to."

Over the last few months, we had discovered the French Food Mafia was issuing laxative tabs to all its dealers, with orders to clean out their colons every afternoon before reporting for duty on their street corners at nightfall. Simply having poo residue in your lower intestines was enough to get you thirty days in Fat Camp. In many cases, dealers destroyed evidence before we could arrest them, but we could always still nail them on residue charges. This new tactic of theirs had caused us great frustration. Time after time we had to let hardened ex-con dealers go just because their intestines were clean. It was maddening.

The coroner scooped a handful of goop out of the French spy's stomach and into the bed pan, on top of the rest of the residue.

Erpent bent over the bowl, staring eagerly into the brown mess. "Well?" he said at last.

Juicy picked through the goop for a long moment, humming to himself. Saliva dribbled from the corners of his mouth. He licked his lips.

"That confirms it," he said at last, and stood up straight.

"Confirms what?" Erpent demanded.

"Your boy here was a vegetarian. Vegan, in fact."

"What?" I said. "A pizza dealer who doesn't use his own product?"

Juicy waved a hand in the air. "Been seeing it a lot these days. You want me to bag that for you?" This last to Erpent.

The SS man continued to stare down into the bed pan. "Are you sure there's nothing else?"

"Why would you want him to bag it for you?" I asked. I turned to Juicy. "Don't you have a lab here?"

Erpent snapped his fingers. "Give me the tweezers. Now!"

Juicy held out the instrument in silence.

The Skinny Service agent fished around in the goop. I looked over at Green, who made a face. He obviously had no more idea than I did what was going on. I was about to ask again about the coroner's lab when Erpent came up with a big chunk of something between his tweezers.

"Distilled water," he ordered. "Quick."

Juicy grabbed a bottle of lab H_2O and squirted it over the chunk Erpent held up. The poo rinsed away and the object took shape. I was stunned when I saw what it was.

"Maybe not so vegan after all," Juicy said.

"How did that get in there?" Green asked.

It was a nose. A human nose. Or piece of one, anyway. A prominent mole protruded from the tip. A mole in the shape of a bratwurst. The back end of the nose was ragged, like it had been bitten off. The skin was burned from exposure to stomach acid.

I knew only one man with a mole in the shape of a bratwurst on the tip of his nose, and that was the Prophet himself. The famous "Nose Mole," as the press had dubbed it, that led our Fearless Leader in search of the tastiest air in North America. What this meant, obviously, was that there was a second man somewhere in D.C. with an identical mole, who had just killed a pizza dealer across the street from the Thin House. Once we find Fatso, I thought, we're coming for you. Whoever you are.

I tapped my teeth. "I wonder who it could belong to?"

"There's always," Green said with a glint in his eye, "the Prophet."

I burst out laughing. "That's the funniest thing I've heard in years!" I roared. "The Prophet. Eating pizza! Killing a food dealer! Getting his nose bitten off!" I wiped tears from my eyes. "Thanks, partner. I needed that."

THE UNITED STATES OF AIR

Erpent slapped me on the back. "That's the spirit."

"The spirit of what?" I asked. "It's called deduction. We're detectives. That's what we do."

"Oh. Yeah. Right." The SS man turned to the coroner. "I need a sterile container, and either milk or sugar solution. Stat."

The coroner shook his head. "Why would I have milk here? It's illegal. Much less sugar solution. I'm a coroner. Not a GP."

Erpent scanned the room. His eyes fell on the tray of instruments. "Give me a clean scalpel, then."

"Sure."

Erpent took the scalpel, unhooked Juicy's IV bag and slashed the feed. He turned it upside down and cut a hole in the bag.

"You mothereating mouth," Juicy swore. "What do you think you're doing?"

"What does it look like I'm doing?" Erpent asked. "And watch the language, please?" He dropped the acid-burned nose into the bag of sugar water. He turned away from us and took out his cell phone.

Juicy turned to us, flabbergasted.

"Don't look at me," I said.

"You know," Green said, "whoever it was must be talking kind of funny right about now." He pinched his nostrils together. "When you spoke on the phone to the Prophet, did he sound strange to you? Nasal, maybe?"

I frowned, trying to remember. "A little bit," I said. "Like he had a cold or something. Why?"

Green exchanged glances with Juicy. "Or like he had his nose bandaged?"

I laughed. "What a bizarre thing to say. Why would the Prophet have his nose bandaged?"

Juicy nodded and crossed his arms. "Probably just a cold then."

"Well, it could be the flu," I said. "I can never remember the difference. Whatever causes that kind of congestion."

Green spat. "Disgusting. Don't you think? I'd resign my tape measure right now if I thought it would do any good."

"Harry!" I exclaimed. "What's gotten into you? The Prophet catches cold and you go crazy. Down, boy. Save it for the food terrists."

Meanwhile, Erpent had finally gotten a hold of whoever it was he was trying to reach. We fell silent. Even from across the room we could make out the hushed murmurings into his handset.

"It's me," he said. "I found it. Yes. Get someone down here, now. What? Does it matter? It was in his stomach. He must have swallowed it. Have a surgeon standing by. I don't care. Someone you trust." Erpent looked over his shoulder. We were all staring at him. He raised his voice. "And get the forensics techs onto analyzing this fragment right away. It will no doubt lead us to the perpetrator of this heinous, heinous crime."

Erpent hung up the phone and rejoined us around the carved-up corpse.

"You know what this means?" Green said.

"It means we've got twenty-one hours left to find Fatso and save the Coalition of the Fasting," Erpent said. "The Fate of the Food-Free World is in our hands, gentlemen. Let's move."

"It means," Green said, not moving, "that there's someone out there with a missing nose. And when we find him, we'll have our killer."

The muscles in Erpent's jaw twitched. "This is no longer a criminal investigation, Agent Green," he said. "It's a matter of national security. Or do you happen to have a background in counterespionage?"

"Counterespionage?" Green exclaimed. "What are you talking about?"

"Isn't it obvious?" Erpent said. "Crusteau here was an *agent provocateur.* Part of a French plot to sabotage the Coalition press conference tomorrow."

"Sabotage?" I asked. "How?"

"If they can embarrass the Prophet, they can derail the expansion of the Global War on Fat. And what could be more embarrassing than a dead pizza dealer across the street from the Thin House?"

"Wait a minute," Green said. "Are you saying Crusteau was on a suicide mission? I find that hard to believe."

Erpent sighed. "Do not underestimate the enemies of this great country," he said. "These crazed food terrists will do anything to bring back the Tyranny of Food, and enslave us once more to their addictive caloric substances."

Juicy laughed, a long throaty chuckle that turned into a hacking cough. He bent double, trying to breathe, and pressed the oxygen tubes tight to his face. When he was able to speak again, he said, "That's the most ridiculous thing I've ever heard."

Erpent's eyes narrowed. "When I want your opinion, Medical Examiner, I will give it to you." He glanced at me and Green. "That goes for both of you as well."

A fair reprimand, I thought. It is for us to obey the will of the Prophet, not to question why.

Erpent looked at his watch. "But right now we have got to go." He pointed at the bed pan. "So yes. Bag it for us. Make it snappy."

"What's wrong with the lab right here?" I asked. "The coroner has world class facilities." When I was on the D.C. force, Juicy often helped us with investigations.

The coroner scooped up the poo and shoveled it into a biohazard bag. "He's taking you to the NSA."

"The National Sewer Agency?" Green said.

Erpent swore a terrible oath. "By the Prophet's pointless pancreas!" he snarled. "That's Top Secret, Doctor. You're asking for punishment."

"No more than I deserve." Juicy squeezed my arm. "Besides, what I know is very little. The NSA has some new lab. The Skinny Service uses them for domestic operations."

"But I thought the NSA was forbidden to spy on the homeland's toilets," Green objected.

The doctor chuckled, pointed at me and my partner. "You two are a real pair, you know that?"

The doors to the morgue banged open and two SS agents burst in, pushing a stretcher.

"Over here!" Erpent called out. He lay the bag of sugar water with the nose in it in the center of the taut white sheet. "Now move!"

The black trench-coated figures limped to the door and were gone, all without saying a word.

Erpent grabbed the biohazard bag of poo that Juicy held out. It flopped against his leg. He saluted, shouted "Go the Power of Air!" and marched off.

"Wait," I said. "Dr. Juicy, you still haven't told us what the murder weapon was."

"Didn't I?" He raised his eyebrows. "I should be able to recognize it by now. This is the third time I've seen wounds like this in as many months. And all of them dead pizza dealers."

"Is there any proof?" Green asked. "Actual evidence we can use? To find the suspect, I mean."

Juicy glanced at Erpent's retreating back. He lowered his voice. "It's all in the papers I gave you. The last five pages. If you value your lives, read them."

"Come on!" Erpent shouted. "We've got souls to save!"

We looked up. He had stopped marching and stood, legs apart, staring back at us.

I weighed the report in my hand. There had to be at least a ream of paper there. "Last five pages, huh?"

Green bent down and pretended to tie his shoe. "For the love of the Prophet, Doctor, just tell us what the weapon was!"

The coroner's smile tightened a notch. He whispered so softly I could barely catch it. "Why, a pizza slicer, of course. A razor-sharp pizza wheel."

EIGHT

ALL THIS TALK OF POO AND NOW YOU'VE GOT TO go? Put the gag back in, Corporal. You can quit squirming in your chair, Mister Broadcaster Mouthpiece of the Ludicrously Overweight French People. No one goes potty until I'm done talking. That applies to all you out there in the studio audience too, you hear?

It's a disgusting habit, by the way. Defecating several times a day. And one that you eliminate when you go on the air-only diet. No, I'm not going to let them take the handcuffs off you. If your ass crack gets sticky that's not my problem. Let it be a reminder to all of you to start eating air.

It's all right, let him holler. I understand his anger. I feel sorry for him. Are you translating this? The strong emotion you're feeling now is rage caused by calories. Until you learn to eat nothing but air, you will never experience the peace and tranquility that the pure oxygen diet brings.

We left the morgue. I drove, and struggled to keep my attention on the road. My Twinkie was singing again. Green perused the papers Juicy had given us. Erpent gave me directions, all the while trying to turn around and see what my partner had found.

"Sit still," Green said. "I'm trying to read." He held the papers up against the SS man's back, and skimmed the last five pages. Then he went back and read them again.

"Pull over. Now." Erpent reached for the door handle and had shoes on the ground before I'd fully stopped.

I parked in a no-parking zone and killed the engine. Green looked up.

"What are we doing here?" he asked.

The Lincoln Memorial gleamed in the early morning light.

"Visiting the NSA," Erpent said. "What do you think?"

I pulled myself out of the Smart Car. Erpent was already halfway up the marble steps, the bag of poo bouncing against his leg. Green and I trailed after him.

"You know the other murders the coroner mentioned?" Green asked. He kept his voice low.

"The pizza dealers. Sure."

"Remember what happened to Detective Ribbs?"

I nodded. "I knew his partner, Soss. Found their bones in a cannibal barbecue pit, didn't they?"

"And Lieutenant Franks and his two patrolmen?"

"What about them?"

"How did Franks die?" Green insisted, his face tense.

"Him and the Beens brothers got put through a sausage grinder," I said. "What are you getting at?"

"They were all investigating pizza murders."

I tried to concentrate, but my Twinkie was humming again. "I still don't see."

"Don't you?" He grabbed my arm so hard it hurt. "Every cop who gets close gets eaten by cannibals." He pulled those last five pages from his trench coat pocket. "Look at this." A photo showed a pizza dealer murdered on the steps of the Capitol. "Same MO. Identical wounds. Body covered in pizza vomit."

"And the other murder?"

"Same. Right outside the Supreme Food Court Building."

"Can't we get a DNA match on the killer from his vomit?"

Green shook his head. "Same thing happened. Body got cleaned of all traces between the crime scene and the morgue."

"What's the holdup?" Erpent shouted from the top of the stairs. He raised the bag of poo above his head, turned and entered the shrine.

"You thinking what I'm thinking, partner mine?" He jerked a thumb up at the SS agent.

"That it's time to eat some air?"

Green grabbed me by the back of my head. "Don't be so naive, Frolick. The SS is going to try to kill us."

I pulled away. "But we're on the same side," I said. "Why would they do that?"

"A cover-up."

"Harry... You're being paranoid. What do they have to cover up?"

Erpent appeared again above us. "You coming or not?" he called out. This time he waited.

"On our way!" my partner shouted. To me: "We are in some serious doo-doo. You trust me?"

"Sure I do," I said. "With my life. You know that."

On several occasions he had dragged me from gunfights with desperate food terrists who refused to go to Fat Camp. If it weren't for him, I'd be dead by now. Our Laxafiers were no match for the actual bullets criminals used.

"Then follow my lead," he said.

"Why?" I asked. "What are you going to do?"

Green resumed his climb. "I have no idea."

We joined Erpent at the top of the stairs and entered the memorial. He led us around to the back of the statue. We stared up at the smooth marble surface.

My partner coughed. "Now is really not the time to play tourist. You want to go to the NSA, let's get a move on."

Erpent unzipped his fly and took out his wee-wee. "We're already there," he said. He stroked himself, and inserted his erect member into a small hole in the stone. "Biometrics," he explained. He pumped himself into Lincoln's butt until a back door swung open, revealing a set of stairs that led down into the earth.

"Holy air," I breathed. "Who knew?"

The SS man zipped up. "This facility is Top Top Super Double Dip Hot Fudge Sundae With A Cherry On Top Secret," he said. "There are only a handful of security classifications higher. Before we proceed, you must swear on your service copies of *Food-Free At Last* never to divulge what you are about to see."

I took out my copy of the Prophet's book. Harry couldn't find his, so we swore together on mine.

Erpent gestured down at the stairwell. "Gentlemen," he said. "After you."

I went first. The stairs were dimly lit and curved out of sight. Behind me, Green said, "Isn't there a front door we can use?"

"We're at war against the Terror of Food," Erpent said. His tone of voice hardened. "Secrecy is of vital importance."

"I thought it was the Tyranny of Food," my partner said.

"Do not quibble with me, Agent Green. Both are true."

"In that case," Green said. "Won't you do the honor of leading us?"

Erpent huffed, but must have decided not to press the point, as I soon felt his bony frame bump into my back. Green joined us, and the door swung shut with a click. He spun around, searching for a handle or doorknob, but found nothing.

"Entrance only," Erpent said. "Only way out's the other side."

"I hope so," Green said, and rested a hand on the butt of his Laxafier.

I caught his eye and shook my head. He relaxed, but kept his hand on his revolver. The three of us marched in single file down into the darkness. At the bottom we came to an elevator.

"Press the call button," the SS agent ordered.

Green's glance fell to the man's service weapon, but Erpent kept his hands clasped together behind his back. Green mouthed the words, "It's a trap."

Was Erpent really going to try to kill us? I found that hard to believe. No man that thin was capable of evil. I dismissed my partner's paranoid cynicism with one hand, pressed the call button with the other. From deep inside the earth came a humming sound. A bell chimed, and the doors opened.

We looked back at Erpent.

"Not many civilians alive today have ever ridden the NSA elevator," he said. "Besides the SS, of course." His smile was thin and hard. "Truly the Prophet has blessed you both. Please." He gestured for us to step inside.

We did. Erpent followed. The doors slid shut. To Green's evident surprise, the man turned his back on us.

The SS agent slid his wee-wee into another hole in the wall. He pressed the down button. There was no up button, I noticed.

Without warning, and before I could dissuade him, my partner grabbed Erpent in a head lock and fumbled for the man's Laxafier. The bag of poo flopped at our feet.

"What are you doing?" Erpent cried, his wee-wee pressed deep inside the biometric console. He clawed at Green's elbow. "In the name of the Prophet, desist!"

"I don't plan on being food for cannibals," my partner growled.

The SS agent's face turned purple. "What cannibals?" he gasped, beating weakly at Green's forearms.

"That's right. Deny it. Now when that door opens, you are going to get us out of here. Is that clear?"

Erpent struggled to get free but failed. "If I refuse?" he managed.

"I'll cut off your weenie and use it to get through the biometric stations."

"Frolick," the SS man said, his voice faint. "Help me. I'm trying to bring down Fatso, same as you."

I drew my service weapon.

"Don't listen to him, Frolick!" my partner shouted.

"Eat you," Erpent swore. Green slammed the man's head against the elevator wall.

What was I supposed to do? What if Erpent was telling the truth? Then we were committing treason. I was destroying my only chance to bring down Fatso, and eradicate the local Twinkie population. But what if my partner was right? What if it really was a trap? Before I could make up my mind, the elevator lurched to a halt, the doors opened, and we had bigger problems to deal with.

Two big problems, to be specific. Burly men in jungle camouflage carrying laxative Uzis at port arms. They took one look at Erpent's wee-wee flapping in the breeze, Green's elbow under the man's chin and our drawn Laxafiers, and they leveled their weapons at us.

"Down and lick the floor!" one shouted. Three chevrons adorned his sleeve.

I held up my badge. "It's OK," I said. "ATFF. Tracking down a major French Food Mafia figure."

They threw me on the floor and took my gun and badge. Erpent and Green landed at my side.

"This is all a misunderstanding," Erpent said, lifting his head off the ground. "If you'll just allow me to—"

"Lick the mothereating floor!" the sergeant screamed. "Down! Do it! Now!" He jammed the barrel of his Uzi into Erpent's butt crack. "Or I'll pump you so full of laxative you'll have hemorrhoids the size of dinner plates!"

We licked the floor. Dust stuck to my tongue. I tried not to swallow, in case there were calories mixed in with the dirt. Shoes clacked toward us down the hall. They came to a halt inches from my head.

"Report."

"Intruders, sir," the sergeant said. He held out our badges. "Pair of ATFF, one Skinny Service."

"The SS?" A note of surprise.

"I have access," Erpent hissed from the floor. "The Thin House cleared it with the General this morning. Or how do you think I got down here?"

"This is an Air Force base," the officer said. "Maybe up there you're somebody. Down here you're not worth a food terrist's stinky poo. Now shut up."

The only sound was the three of us cleaning the floor with our tongues. One by one the newcomer examined our badges and laid them on a nearby table. I fidgeted. My throat was getting dry. What if Green was right? What if they were going to grind us into sausages?

"On your feet."

We got up, scraping the grit from our tongues. Green spat on the floor.

"No spitting!" the sergeant yelled. "Show some mothereating respect."

The officer gave us back our badges, but left our weapons on the table. "It's all right, Sergeant," he said. He kicked a bucket toward us. "Here. Use this."

We all spat in the bucket. The lieutenant was almost as skinny as Erpent. He wore Air Force blues. Balloons the size of contraband candy apples rose from the epaulets of his shirt. A first lieutenant's silver stripe ran down the front of each. Rumor had it the Air Force filled officers' rank balloons with helium, and at military parties they'd inhale their own rank balloons and talk in high squeaky voices. My gaze dropped to his name tag. "Lieutenant Krapp," it read. A division insignia I had never seen before was pinned to his shirtfront. It was gold and roughly the size and shape of a poo.

"What are you staring at, Agent Frolick?" Krapp demanded.

"Nothing, Lieutenant," I said. "I was just wondering what that insignia you're wearing means."

The officer crossed the room in two strides and stood toe to toe with me. His rank balloons bobbled against my face and shoulders.

"This insignia?" he said softly. He tapped it with his forefinger. It had been polished until it gleamed. "This insignia means we are the last line of defense. We are here to protect people like you from the food terrists out there who are salivating for a chance to attack this great country."

He punched the air and grunted, "Poo-AHH!" The two guards echoed the exclamation.

"I thought that was our job at the ATFF," I protested.

"Not even close," he said with a sneer. "This insignia represents the most cutting-edge technology. The very existence of our unit is Tip Top Tippity Top Golden Poo In A Bidet Secret. You understand what I'm telling you?"

We shuffled our feet for a moment, looked at each other. Erpent shrugged.

"Um...no," Green said.

"It means we don't exist!" he bellowed. "We are a figment of your imagination! And I'll thank you to remember it!"

"But isn't this the NSA?" Green asked.

"Poo-AHH!" the two guards grunted.

The lieutenant went silent. His eyes bulged from his head. "That's Tip Top Tippity Top Golden Poo In A Bidet Secret!" he screamed at my partner. "How do you know that?"

Green jerked his thumb at Erpent. "He told us."

For the first time, Erpent looked unsure of himself. "I'm sorry," he said. "I thought it was only Top Top Super Double Dip Hot Fudge Sundae With A Cherry On Top Secret."

The lieutenant snorted. "Well, you were wrong."

"So what's so special about the NSA?" I asked. "They spy on ferrners' sewer systems. Everyone knows that."

Krapp grinned. "Is that what you know?" he whispered. "Is that what you think you know?"

"They don't know poo," the sergeant scoffed.

Erpent protested, "But I was personally briefed this morning by the Prophet's National Security Advisor—"

"Who is what? A general with only four stars?" The lieutenant spat. "You know nothing."

Green cleared his throat. "We're obviously not welcome here," he said. "We won't take up any more of your time. If you'll show us where the exit is, we'll go."

The lieutenant squared his shoulders. "The General is not happy about this intrusion," he snapped. "My orders are to take you to him. Come along."

He turned on his heels and walked back down the hall. Erpent tucked himself into his pants, straightened up and followed after the junior officer. Green and I fell into step behind the other two.

"Still think it's a trap?" I asked.

"If they're letting us live, it's because they want us to be patsies. That's why they chose us. They need a pair of fall guys when this investigation fails."

"Don't be so cynical, Harry," I said. "Of course we aren't going to fail."

"All I know," he said, keeping his voice low, "is that if the Air Force is involved, we're screwed."

For you ferrners out there unfamiliar with the military structure that makes our great Empire of Air possible, the Prophet centralized all our armed forces under the Unified Strategic Air Command during his first year in office: the Air Force Marine Corps; the Air Force Army, Navy and Coast Guard; the Air Force NSA and CIA; the Air Force Merchant Marine; the Air Force Geological Survey; the Air Force Irish Dancers; and so on. Some people, traitors mostly, asked what all this military expenditure was for. Who were we going to fight? That sort of remark will get you put in Fat Camp until the War is over. What these people don't understand is that the Air Force is the most powerful force for good this world has ever seen. These are the brave men and women who risk their lives to promote American values—I mean Airitarian values—all around the world. Like Truth, Justice and the Air-Eating Way.

So while Green walked down that corridor all nervous, I strode forward to my destiny, knowing I was going to meet a general, one of our greatest military leaders in the Global War on Fat.

The lieutenant made a right turn and led us down a slope. The corridor widened and dead-ended at a round chrome door twenty feet high. On both sides concrete pillboxes protruded from the wall. Their narrow slits bristled with Laxafier automatic rifle barrels. The guns twitched at our approach, aiming their high-powered laxative loads at our bellies.

Krapp approached a biometric reader in the wall and unzipped his fly. He put his wee-wee in the hole and thrust himself in and out, his belt buckle clacking against the concrete wall each time. He humped the hole for long minutes before uttering a cry and going still.

The chrome vault door opened with a hiss. A hubbub of voices burbled forth—the sound of thousands of people talking at once, fingers tapping at keyboards, lips slurping up caffeinated air. But one noise dominated the rest: the gurgling of a flushing toilet.

"This way," Krapp grunted. He zipped up his fly. He seemed a bit dazed.

I looked behind us. The two guards stood there, laxative Uzis pointed at our bottoms.

"Get moving," the sergeant said.

I took the steps two at a time up to the vault door. "Come on," I said. "Let's see what the fuss is all about."

"I guess we don't really have a choice," Green said.

"No," the sergeant said. "You don't."

NINE

W E STEPPED THROUGH THE VAULT DOOR AND gasped. Before us stretched an underground bunker several football fields long. Every square foot was covered by giant copper tanks, laboratory equipment and computers. Air Force technicians in lab smocks and goggles swarmed about the space. The ceiling was ten stories high. The gurgling noise came from there. Pipes the size of sewer mains dropped from overhead and branched off until they connected with the copper tanks.

On a dais in the center of the room stood a man. Rank balloons the size of small cars rose from the epaulets of his dress uniform. The balloons were covered in stars.

Opposite him on the wall hung an enormous screen. It showed a map of the US. Lines and dots of different colors covered the terrain. "Sewer Systems of the United States of Air," proclaimed the map key.

"Gentlemen," the lieutenant said. "Welcome to the NSA. Now quit your gawking and get a move on."

He waited for us beside a copper tank with a window in the side. The tank was filling up with a brown liquid.

"A-OOO-gah! A-OOO-gah! A-OOO-gah!"

A klaxon sounded. Behind us, the vault door closed. The three of us scrambled off the threshold and into the great chamber.

"Titanium deadbolts," Krapp remarked. "Fifty feet of reinforced concrete. We are impervious to nuclear attack here, gentlemen. Nothing—and no one—gets in or out of the National Sewer Agency without the General's say-so." He about-faced, held his head high and marched toward the dais.

We followed, staring curiously around. We passed a bank of computer consoles. The technicians were crowded around a monitor, watching a movie. Two butt cheeks filled most of the screen, plus some genitalia, two legs and a triangular gap of light. A dark spot got bigger, then—*plop!* A turd floated across the camera lens. On another screen, a stream of urine clouded the image. What a strange movie, I thought. Was this art house cinema?

We approached the dais. The General stood with his back toward us, leaning over the chrome railing. An Air Force officer with a major's watermelon-sized rank balloons stood at ground level, reading a report.

"...and in Paris, Operation Dog Poo Baguette was a success, revealing the dietary habits and fecal composition of the president's inner circle—"

A sergeant-at-arms stopped us with a white-gloved hand. He wore spats over flip-flops and an inflated yellow duck around his waist. The lieutenant whispered to him. Meanwhile, the major droned on, "And in China, our operative code name Spicy Sichuan Chopsticks was able to infiltrate a chain of noodle stores—"

The sergeant-at-arms reached up and pulled on the General's pant leg.

"Hold it, Major." The General turned to face us. "Who interrupts my midmorning snack?"

The General's uniform dazzled me. His medals and service ribbons covered both sides of his chest, spread across his stomach, up both sleeves and down his pants. There were even service ribbons on his shoes. Gold braid thick enough to moor an oil tanker draped under both armpits. The peak of his cap rose a yard in the air, and the bill jutted out a foot.

Plus he was fat. Bigger even than Fatso. I frowned. Weren't we at War on Fat? Surely a general should have superhuman faith, and a waistline to match. Then I spotted the golden tape measure around his belly, and did a double take. His faith was superhuman, all right. Eleven inches! Almost as skinny as the Prophet himself.

"Lieutenant Krapp," our escort announced. "Civilians to see you, sir sir sir sir sir." He flung out an open palm. "Go the Power of Air!"

The General returned the salute. "I got no time for civilians, Lieutenant. Tell them to come back later."

"Sir sir sir sir sir," Krapp said. "One of them is Skinny Service. Here by orders of the Thin House. Thought you'd like to know, sir sir sir sir sir."

"Interruptions are bad for the digestion," the General grumbled. He put something in his jacket pocket and swung himself over the chrome railing onto the shoulders of the sergeant-at-arms. The enlisted man's face turned purple. He knelt down and set his cargo on the ground. The General stood up and brushed what looked like crumbs but were no doubt dandruff from the front of his tunic.

I stepped forward and held out my hand. "Can I just say what an honor it is to meet someone so successful at eating air?" I said. "Please share your faith with us before we go. To see you so skinny…" I was overwhelmed by his waistline, the dandruff on his lapels, the sandwich peeking out of his jacket pocket, a challenge, I was sure, to keep himself honest. "I wish I could eat air like you."

"Well you know, son," the General said, and took my hand, "we aren't called the Air Force for nothing."

Erpent jostled me aside. "We bring you orders from the Prophet." He held up the biohazard bag.

"It's dead French spy poo," I added proudly.

The major frowned. His name, I saw, was Major Turdd. "Forgive me, General, allow me to explain the protocol?"

"By all means, Major."

Major Turdd addressed the three of us civilians. "It is standard military protocol to address the NSA commander at all times as 'sir sir sir sir sir.'"

"Isn't one 'sir' enough?" Green asked.

The lieutenant swung an arm up at the General's rank balloons. "He's a twenty-five-star general," he hissed. "One 'sir' for every five stars."

"That must take an awful long time to say," Green said.

"It used to be one 'sir' for every star," the major explained, "but it was decided that in battlefield conditions that might not be desirable. For instance." He turned to face the General. "'The food terrists are attacking, sir sir sir sir sir sir sir sir sir sir sir sir sir sir sir sir sir sir sir sir sir sir sir sir sir!'" He turned back to us. "You see? That's why it got shortened to just one 'sir' for every five stars."

"Couldn't we just address him as 'General'?" I asked.

"You could if that were his rank," Lieutenant Krapp said, and laughed.

I scratched my head. "But didn't you just say you were taking us to see the General?"

Krapp stood to attention. "Sorry, sir sir sir sir sir. It's just they're civilians, sir sir sir sir sir, and to explain to them how we—"

"At air," the General said with a smile. "Perfectly understandable. In your position I would have done the same thing."

The lieutenant shuffled his feet. "Thank you, sir sir sir sir sir."

"And I'm sure you will enjoy your new career as a poo detector specialist, installing equipment in the sewers," the General said, and added, "Airman First Class Krapp."

The color drained from the lieutenant's face. He reached up and untied the rank balloons from his shoulders. They floated up into the air until they bumped into the ceiling far above.

The General smiled at us. "There are, after all, only a handful of twenty-five-star generals in the US Air Force. We have to maintain a certain prestige." He threw out his chest, clicked his heels together and said, "Director of the Department of Homeland Air Security, Protector of Our Precious Air, Head of the Toilet Safety Administration, Commander of NORAD and our Nuclear Arsenal, I-SEE-FAT Call Center Supervisor, Poo Propulsion Laboratory Test-Pilot-in-Chief, Striker of Fear in the Breasts of Food Terrists Everywhere, Leader of the NSA, CIA, DIA, MIA, and WTF, Exalted High Almighty General of Generals Full O'Shitt at your service." He bowed. "Full O'Shitt is my *nom de guerre,* of course." He parted his service ribbons to reveal the hidden name tag.

"Thank you, sir sir sir sir," I began. "We're here to—"

"That's 'sir sir sir sir *sir,*'" corrected the former lieutenant.

"What are you still doing here?" Major Turdd barked. "Report to the Poo Detector Installation Brigade. Double time, march!"

Newly minted Airman First Class Krapp about-faced and marched off.

Erpent thrust the bag of poo in the General's face. "Analyze this."

Major Turdd stepped forward. "May I ask what this is all about?"

"Your orders are to drop what you are doing," Erpent said, "and find Fatso."

"Finding Fatso is foremost forever in our minds," O'Shitt said. "We're doing all we can."

"What do you mean you're doing all you can?" Erpent exclaimed. "How many bazillion gazillion dollars do we give the NSA every year?"

"And we need every gazillion," the General calmly replied. "You think every man, woman, child and donkey working here isn't motivated by one single thought—Get Fatso?"

I looked around. Indeed, in one corner a herd of donkeys trotted around in a circle. Several small boys walked behind them. As I watched, a donkey did a big poo, and the trailing boy caught it in a plastic bag.

Erpent crossed his arms. "What about Total Poo Awareness?" he asked. "Surely you have some idea where he is."

The General coughed into his hand. "TPA is classified." He glanced at us.

"Tappity Tippity Tappity Smores Go Crunch Round The Campfire Secret," Erpent said. "Yes. I know. Green and Frolick were cleared by the Prophet himself."

"What's Total Poo Awareness?" Green asked.

"TPA," the General said, "is why the NSA exists. Our goal is to know who's pooing, where they poo, what it's shaped like, what it smells like, what it consists of. Only then can we finally smash food terrism once and for all."

"And you still have no idea where he is?" Erpent said, his voice mounting toward hysteria.

"Every sewer tap around the world is programmed to alert us at the first sign of our arch-nemesis," the General added. "He so much as farts we'll know he's there."

"Only problem is he hasn't farted," Green said.

The General nodded sadly. "It's like he's a ghost or something."

"You've had two years at this post," Erpent said, shaking his finger in the General's face. "If you still can't tell me what I need to know, maybe it's time the NSA had a new commander."

"Listen to me," O'Shitt said. "Every day we gather data on billions of people around the world. See those pipes?" He pointed at the plumbing that snaked above our heads.

"What about them?" Erpent snapped.

"Some connect straight to the D.C. sewer. Others connect to storage tanks. Millions of gallons of sewer samples awaiting our analysis. From all over the world. I got Tokyo sushi poo, I got Paris bistro *merde,* I got Moscow borscht crap—I got it all."

"And in all that poo you can't find one man?" Erpent shouted.

"We sweep up vast amounts of data," the General protested. "We're busy trying to—"

"You're busy wasting my time," Erpent said. "You find Fatso for me now. Today. Or what you just did to that lieutenant? I'll see the Prophet does you worse."

The General's jovial features narrowed. "It is unwise to threaten me. The Prophet ought to know that by now."

"Oh yeah?" Erpent said. "When he's through with you, you'll be cleaning out latrines with your tongue. Do I make myself clear, Airman Third Class O'Shitt?"

He tapped the General's right rank balloon to emphasize his point—with the ragged fingernail I spotted in the morgue. A loud explosion made me duck. When I opened my eyes, shreds of balloon trailed from the General's right shoulder. O'Shitt sank down on one knee, scuffing the service ribbons on his pants. His left side was held aloft by the remaining rank balloon, but it was not enough to keep him on his feet.

"Replacement balloon!" Major Turdd bellowed. "Replacement balloon for the NSA commander!" He pressed a red button on the side of the dais. A siren blared. Across the crowded floor, a team of Air Force Marines shoved their way through the milling technicians, bearing a new twenty-five-star rank balloon with them.

The General and Erpent eyed each other warily as we waited for the replacement balloon to arrive. The major grabbed hold of the General's right side, but could not lift him back to his feet.

"Too much air," O'Shitt mumbled.

Turdd pleaded with us. "Help me."

Green and I managed to get the General back on his feet. For someone so skinny he sure weighed an awful lot. An Air Force Marine cut away the rubber shreds that dangled from the General's shoulder and fastened a new balloon to the right epaulet.

"Thank you, men," the General said.

The team of six Marines stood to attention and saluted in unison. "Sir sir sir sir sir!" they shouted, then about-faced and marched back to wherever they came from.

"Would you turn that off, please, Major?" the General said.

Turdd pressed the red button again and the alarm stopped. The bunker was once more filled with the sounds of typing technicians and slurping machinery.

The General drew himself up straight. "You've made your point," he said to Erpent.

"Excellent," the SS agent replied. "You'll find Fatso for us, then?"

O'Shitt snapped his fingers. The sergeant-at-arms came to attention.

"Take this poo to the Plumber," the General ordered.

The sergeant-at-arms gulped loudly and clutched his yellow duck. "The Plumber, sir sir sir sir sir?" He accepted the bag of poo with a shaking hand.

"Immediate analysis. Auth Code Eggnog ApplePie Twinkie Milkshake Eggnog. Now move!"

The sergeant-at-arms saluted and shuffled off, his flip-flops slapping against the floor.

"Now," the General said. He turned to Erpent, and tucked his triple chins into his chest. "I think it's time the Thin House learned exactly what we do here at the NSA."

Erpent glared back. "You took the air right out of my mouth."

O'Shitt led us over to an open tank of water. An empty toilet stood on either side. I peered over the edge of the tank. A pair of what looked like eels slumbered on the bottom.

"Wireless toilet cams," the General declared proudly. "The next generation of sewer monitoring technology. Drop them into the sewer, and they will find their way to their preprogrammed destinations. Eliminates the need for Air Force Navy frogmen."

He pressed a button on the side of the tank. Within seconds, the toilet cams found the open pipes to the toilets and wriggled out of sight. We crowded around the nearest toilet.

"See here?" The General's fat finger pointed at a brown speck at the bottom of the bowl. "The tip of its head has a tiny camera attached to it."

"So that's how you got those pictures of people pooing," Green said.

"Precisely," the General answered. "With this new technology, we can have a toilet cam in every toilet of your house—even, say, the Thin House," —he glanced at Erpent as he said this— "lying in wait to film a food terrist in the act of defecation."

Erpent gasped. "How long has this been going on?"

"We've got toilet cams in every major sewer in the world," the General continued, ignoring the question. "Three months ago, we let loose several million toilet cams into the D.C. sewer system." He grinned. "We know everything." He bent toward Erpent, his grin widening. "I know where you poo and what you eat—"

"Now wait just a chocolate-licking minute—"

"—and what you mutter under your breath when you sit on the potty." O'Shitt pitched his voice high. "Ma-ma. Ma-ma."

"I do not say that!" Erpent turned on us, fists clenched. Our snickering continued. "I do not say 'mama' on the potty!" He pulled at his hair. "What am I saying? I don't even use the toilet!"

The General tapped his temple with a pudgy finger. "The NSA knows all."

"These are serious accusations," Erpent protested. "You can't just—"

"We know everything that goes on in the Thin House," the General said. He lowered his voice. "Everything."

Erpent went silent. He fumbled for his cell phone.

"No signal down here, I'm afraid," the General said. "You'll have to wait until you leave...whenever that happens to be."

Erpent gulped and put the phone away.

O'Shitt held his arms above his head, embracing the Disneyland of wonder that surrounded us. "Gentlemen, from this bunker I can destroy the world with nuclear weapons or watch the president of France go potty. Like our motto says." He tapped his shoulder patch. It read, "Omniscience. Omnipotence. Your Poohole." He beamed at us. "This is Total Poo Awareness at its finest."

"Let me get this straight," Green said. "You're spying on innocent people, taking pictures of them going poo-poo, without a warrant?"

The General chuckled. "Oh, they're not innocent," he said. "Only food terrists ever go poo-poo."

"But it's an invasion of privacy!"

The General's grin disappeared. "The Global War on Fat requires us to make certain sacrifices, Agent Green," he said. "Food terrists would kill us for the right to eat food again. But don't panic!" He grabbed me by the shoulders and shook me. "Be alert. Not alarmed."

An unshaven man in greasy blue coveralls staggered into view, yawning. He carried a large metal toolbox that appeared to be handcuffed to his wrist. In the other hand he carried a lug wrench.

"Yo, Fat Man," he said. "I found your evil twin."

The man must be myopic. Couldn't he see the General's tape measure? "You mean Fatso?"

"Who else you think I mean?" He turned to go. "Well you coming or arentcha?"

TEN

T HE GENERAL LED US ACROSS THE CROWDED
bunker toward the largest copper tank I'd seen so far.
The Plumber, whoever he was, had gone on ahead.

O'Shitt cleared his throat. "I know he doesn't look like
much. But he has a PhD from MITT."

"Not the Massachusetts Institute of Toilet Technology!" I
exclaimed.

"The very same." The General nodded. "He's one of the
old-school NSA prodigies. All brains, no social skills. Some
say he's smarter than Albert Einstein and Stephen Hawking
put together."

"Wow," I breathed. "He must be one hell of a plumber."

"Only thing is, he hates the Air Force. Thinks we never should
have taken over the Agency."

"So why do you put up with him?" Erpent asked.

The General waved a hand at the apparatus that surrounded
us. "These machines? He invented them all. Designed the first
plumbing-computer interface. Without him, the National Sewer
Agency in its current form would not exist."

We approached the copper tank. The Plumber was on his
knees. He had unlocked the handcuffs and was connecting a

series of pipes to his toolbox. Without warning, he lifted his lug wrench in the air and started smashing some nearby tubing.

"Leaks! Leaks! Leaks!" he screamed. "Kill the leaks!"

The General put his finger to his lips. "And whatever you do," he whispered, "don't mention the word *leaks*. He hates leaks."

Major Turdd cleared his throat. "You found something?"

"I found another leak," the Plumber said, panting with exertion. "If it weren't for you Air Force bubbleheads, there wouldn't be any leaks."

"Come now," the General said. "Do you really think that's fair?"

"You morons wouldn't know the difference between a lug nut and a lug wrench if it jumped out of the toilet and bit you on the pitootie."

"What's so bad about leaks?" Green asked.

"Leaks! Leaks! Leaks!" the man screamed, and smashed the offending pipes again.

"But what's so bad about them?" my partner insisted.

"So bad about leaks?" The man stared at Green like he was speaking a ferrn language. "The turd that got away could be the secret to where Fatso is."

"I thought you said you found him," Erpent said. He snapped his fingers in the man's face. "You know where Fatso is, or don't you?"

"Please," the General said. "Let me manage this."

The Plumber clambered to his feet. "Who the poo is this?" he asked, peering at Erpent through his thick glasses.

Erpent was ready with his badge. "I work directly for the Prophet in the Trapezoidal Office. Now spill."

"Do you know the Auth Code?"

"What Auth Code? I don't need an Auth Code. I just told you—"

"Then you know nothing, super skinny," the man sneered.

Erpent stiffened at this rudeness. "What is your name, technician?" he demanded. "I'll put you in Fat Camp for that."

The Plumber straightened his shirtfront. A white name patch fringed with red had been stitched to his left chest. It read, "Too Secret For You."

"I think they need to hear the song, don't you, Fat Man?"

"No, please, not the song," the General begged. "Anything but that. Please!"

Too Secret For You punched a button on a nearby stereo. He grabbed the bag of poo we'd brought, now half-empty, and swiveled his hips to the music, the biohazard bag clutched tight to his chest. He sang:

> I'm too secret for my shirt
> too secret for my shirt
> so secret it hurts—

"Enough already!" O'Shitt bellowed.
But the man continued:

> I'm too secret for this poo
> too secret for this poo
> don't you wish you knew who

> I am
> too secret for the Air Force
> too secret for the Air Force
> I'm an NSA man

Too secret

I'm too secret for my—

Erpent stepped forward and turned off the music. "We don't have time for this," he snapped. "Did you or did you not find Fatso?"

"Don't you get pooey with me," Too Secret For You replied. "I don't work for the Air Force, and I sure as poo don't work for the Skinny Service."

Green stepped between them. "This is an extraordinary piece of sewer technology," he said, and gestured up at the copper tank. "Is it true you invented all of this?"

Too Secret For You banged his lug wrench against the side of the tank. "Darn pooing right I did. You don't think the Air Force flyboys are capable of this kind of sewer innovation, do you?"

"Wow," I said. "Could you give us a demonstration? Too Secret For, umm, Me?"

"Finally," the man said to the General. "People who appreciate what I do for a change."

A funnel descended from one side of the machine. He opened the half-full bag of poo and poured it into the funnel. "Always run it twice to be sure," he said, and flipped a switch. A loud farting sound came from a release valve overhead, and we were soon enveloped in a miasma of rotten egg smell.

The General took a deep breath and sighed with pleasure. "God I love the smell of poo in the morning."

I looked up at the contraption. "But what does it do?" I asked.

The Plumber reached up and caressed the copper beast. "The Super Dooper Pooper Snooper!" he shouted over the din.

"She can analyze any poo sample you care to give her. With this baby I can tell you where the food came from, where it comes out and who else eats a similar diet."

The farting noise ended. The stench slowly dispersed.

Too Secret For You tapped at the pipes in his toolbox. "On screen," he commanded. At the base of the tank, three airmen in lab coats sat in front of computer consoles. One pushed a button.

A monitor built into the side of the tank displayed Jacques Crusteau's dossier. His particulars continued below: date of birth, height, weight, waist circumference, bank accounts, car registration, books taken out of the library—*The Complete Guide To Hydroponics* was flagged for our convenience—plus DVDs rented and TP (Toilet Protocol) addresses of bathrooms across the country where he had gone poo-poo.

Too Secret For You jumped to the Career section. "Jacques Crusteau, French Spy," he narrated. "Graduated French Spy School, Masters in Sabotage, MPhil in Blackmail, PhD in Assassination. As part of his thesis defense, he whacked the president of Famishedton, a small war-torn former French colony in West Africa."

"Fascinating," I said. "But what was he doing in the park last night?"

"What do you think, Agent Stupid?" he said. "What does a French assassin normally do across the street from the Thin House?"

"I dunno," I said. "Feed the ducks?"

"Feeding the ducks is illegal, moron. Besides, there aren't any ducks left." Too Secret For You turned to Green. "Is he brain dead or what?"

"What," my partner replied. "He's a believer."

Too Secret For You whooped. "You mean there's one left?"

"What are you talking about?" I asked.

Too Secret For You said, "The assassin was near the Thin House because he wanted to kill the Prophet."

I had to laugh at that. "Then he was a lousy assassin!" I said. "What's he going to do, climb the fence? The SS would take him out. Right, Erpent?"

"Not likely he'd make it over the fence anyway," Too Secret For You said. "His poo is full of cancer markers. The guy was terminal. Had a couple weeks left to live, tops."

"That makes no sense," I said. "He's got cancer, so he wants to kill someone?"

Green lifted his head. "Wants to kill...or wants to be killed?"

Erpent was triumphant. "You see? I was right."

My partner nodded. "Maybe it was a suicide mission."

"Of course," I said. Now it made sense. "The embarrassment factor."

"Which means," Green said, "he must have tried to get the whole thing on camera."

Too Secret For You spun back to his toolkit. "Let's run this through the psych profiler. If I can find toilet tap videos of this food terrist going ca-ca, I can put together a detailed personality profile."

"We can read their ass lips," Major Turdd explained.

On the screen a dozen videos played of someone pooing. The same someone. Too Secret For You tapped furiously away at his toolbox with a screwdriver. "How about that," he said. "You're right. It was a plot to blackmail the—the buyer. Did you recover the sound and video equipment?"

Green shook his head. "We didn't find anything. Someone," —and here he turned to Erpent— "must have cleaned the corpse."

"But surely he was transmitting," Too Secret For You insisted. "Didn't you find any accomplices nearby?"

Erpent coughed. "We picked up two French spies, actually. Just a few hundreds yards from the crime scene. They were disguised as mimes."

"Why didn't you say so?" I exclaimed. "Let's go talk to them right away."

"Alas," Erpent sighed. "There was an accident."

"Oh no," I said. I covered my cheeks with my palms. "What kind of accident?"

"They slipped on an invisible banana peel right in front of a speeding steamroller."

"How horrible!" I breathed.

"Why didn't you mention this before?" Green demanded.

"It wasn't relevant to finding Fatso," Erpent said. "Now can we please avoid these distractions? We have only nineteen hours left!"

Too Secret For You looked up at Erpent for a long moment. He cocked his head to one side, and said in falsetto, "Ma-ma! Ma-ma!"

The Air Force techs laughed and banged their consoles. Erpent drew back a fist, like he was going to take a swing at the man. Before he could do so, Too Secret For You plunged his lug wrench into the toolbox and waggled it back and forth. A map of the US appeared on screen. Bright dots clustered near half a dozen cities.

"Each dot," he explained, "represents one TP address. One toilet, one poo. Bigger dots, like here," —he zoomed in on Washington, D.C.— "represent repeated pooings. In his alter ego as Nick Hungry, Crusteau was an important and trusted courier for Fatso. But he was based right here in the District of Crap."

"Didn't you hear me before?" Erpent barked. "Enough about Crusteau. You said you found Fatso. Now where is he?"

Too Secret For You reached for the stereo. "You need to hear the song again?"

The General stepped between them. "Please, Agent Erpent! I must ask you to be quiet."

"That's better," Too Secret For You snorted.

He hammered at a tight bolt in his toolbox, and a map of Cuba appeared on the big screen. "A long, narrow landmass," he announced. "Roughly the shape of a giant turd. Code Name: Poo Island."

A cluster of bright dots glowed across the strait from Florida. The image zoomed in. "Havana," he continued. "Capital of Poo Island, and center of the Western Hemisphere's biggest food smuggling operation. Run, of course, by Fatso."

"And our boy's been doing ca-ca there recently," O'Shitt said, his arms crossed.

Too Secret For You turned his backside toward the General and farted. "Give that man a gold star!"

"He already has twenty-five," I exclaimed. "But maybe he should get another. If we catch Fatso, perhaps the Prophet will make you a twenty-six-star general."

"There's no such thing as a twenty-six-star general," O'Shitt said gloomily. "Twenty-five is as high as it goes."

"Then he could create a new rank for you," I suggested. "What do you think, Erpent? Would the Prophet go for that?"

"The Prophet rewards loyalty and punishes treason," the SS agent said, his eyes half-closed. "Something you should all remember." He turned to Too Secret For You. "So what was Crusteau doing down in Cuba? Are you saying that's where Fatso is?"

"We believe Fatso travels frequently to Cuba to manage his operations there."

"You *believe?*" Erpent sneered. "You don't *know?*"

Too Secret For You glowered back at the SS agent. "The only thing we know for sure is this." He twisted a pipe with his wrench. The map of Cuba disappeared, replaced by half a dozen mug shots.

"*These* are his couriers," he said. "We can trace them because Fatso made the mistake of feeding them all the same diet."

"What, pizza?" I said.

"Not likely, Agent Stupid Times Two. Fatso forbids his couriers from consuming the product they sell, on penalty of death. They get macrobiotic meals to manage their withdrawal symptoms."

"Like the Prophet used to eat before he discovered the air-eating way," I said, remembering that terrible confession in *Food-Free At Last.*

"That explains what we saw in the morgue, anyway," Green said.

"The horror of macrobiotics," I said. "Addictive brown rice, appetite-provoking steamed vegetables, beans—the heroin of food-stuffs—and nuts." I shook my head. "The poor misguided souls."

"What about Fatso himself?" Green asked. "Does he follow the same diet?"

Too Secret For You swung his lug wrench in the air, brought it crashing down on a stubborn bit of pipe. "If only we knew. No poo sample from Fatso has ever been taken. He conceals his activities and food consumption so carefully it is impossible to know for certain what he eats—if he does, indeed, eat food."

"So where is he now?" Erpent asked.

"Who?"

"Fatso. Who do you think?"

Too Secret For You shrugged. "No idea."

"But you said you found him!" Erpent shouted.

The NSA man pointed at Erpent and clutched his sides in laughter. "I was just pulling your poo," he said. "We don't even know what Fatso looks like."

Now was my time to shine. I stepped forward. "I've met the man."

Everyone turned to look at me. "We both have," Green added. "We arrested him too, but he got off on a technicality. I'm surprised you don't have his image and DNA on file. Don't you get daily uploads of our arrest records?"

Too Secret For You glanced at General O'Shitt. "Must be a glitch in the system."

"Doesn't matter," I said. "I've got a photo of him right here." I took out my dog-eared copy of the Prophet's manifesto and turned to the final chapter—"Freedom From Food Means Slavery To Air: Is Going Air-Free Possible?"—where I had used the mug shot of Fatso to mark my place.

The others crowded around, rank forgotten, jostling to get a glimpse of the world's most-wanted food terrist.

"And to think he lives with impunity right here in the District of Crap," one of the Air Force techs muttered.

"All because of our laws and our freedoms, can't so much as touch him," said another.

"Poo-ee, they hate us for our freedoms, dog."

"That right, dog," said the second tech. "They be hating us for the right to be thin."

The two techs chest bumped. Their bellies jiggled. "We the Air Force, dog!" they shouted, and grabbed each other by the ears and stomped the floor. "Go the Power of Air!"

Too Secret For You stood at my elbow. "May I?" he asked reverently.

Everyone seemed to hold their breath. I handed him the photo. It was like announcing the brunch buffet was open, back in the bad old days. The crowd cleared, the techs blasted back into their seats.

Too Secret For You put the photo into a slot in the copper tank. Then—nothing. Silence. All around us in that bunker, thousands of keyboards clacked as analysts studied defecating bottoms. Pipes overhead gurgled with their worldwide sewer residues. Glassware on lab tables clinked together.

Too Secret For You bent over his toolbox, riding his lug wrench back and forth. Finally he leaped to his feet and shouted, "We got the mothereater, boys!"

O'Shitt put his hands behind his back. "On screen."

But Too Secret For You strutted about, pumping his fists like a wide air receiver after making the game-winning touchdown in the Super-Thin Bowl. He sang:

I'm too secret for this job
too secret for this—

"NSA GUY WHOSE NAME I DON'T KNOW!" the General thundered. "TEN-HUT!"

Too Secret For You stopped and looked around him. "I'm sorry," he said. "Were you speaking to me?"

"Share some of the joy with the rest of us," Erpent said.

Too Secret For You bent over his toolbox again. He unzipped his fly and inserted his wee-wee into a biometric reader. "I cross-reffed the photo against our entire giga-figa-hugga-bigga-lugga-chugga-migga-zigga-byte database," he said. "Let me show you what I found."

He continued to slide himself in and out of the biometric reader while he talked. "This data stream is classified Prophet Prophet Bo Boffet Secret," he explained. "It requires constant authentication. A sort of dead man's switch."

"Let's hope he's not a premature ejaculator," Green said.

"I shouldn't think so," Too Secret For You said, sighing with apparent pleasure. "This is my fourth authentication today."

A satellite photo of Cuba—I mean, Poo Island—appeared on the big screen. It zoomed in on Havana. The roof of a resort hotel appeared, fringed with palms, blue pools, a white beach to the north, the ocean. Hundreds of empty tables filled the spaces between the pools.

"Our orbiting Sewer Eye In The Sky took this photo of an unknown fat man in Cuba yesterday," Too Secret For You said, humping the biometric reader. "Guess who?"

The image zoomed again. Fuzzy at first, it showed a group of men sitting around a table pool-side. The table was covered in a yellow tablecloth with a pattern of red circles and green squiggles. "Funny-looking tablecloth," the General grunted.

Where had I seen that pattern before? The image resolution improved, and it hit me.

"It's a pizza!" I said, and pointed.

"What is, partner mine?"

What we'd all thought was a tablecloth was actually a six-foot-wide pizza pie. Green saw it at the same instant.

"Gotcha," he said, and pounded his palm with his fist.

"What have we got?" the General asked.

"Leaving the US of Air for the purpose of consuming addictive caloric substances is forbidden by the Amendment," I explained, wiping away tears of joy. "That tablecloth is actually a giant pizza!"

Too Secret For You adjusted the resolution one more time with his lug wrench, and the faces of the men became clear. One man gazed up at the sky, saluting the heavens with a champagne flute. He seemed to be looking straight at us.

At me.

It was Fatso, all right. And his clothing was spattered with food stains. The sort of evidence that Food Court judges love.

"It *is* him!" exclaimed the first airman. "From the photo!"

"You know I got a sister addicted to Ding Dongs?" said the other airman. "All because of that monster there."

"Have no fear," O'Shitt said. He patted the airman on the shoulder. "Our revenge shall be swift and terrible. Fatso will regret the day he set himself up against this great nation, the Holy Land of Air. Major Turdd!"

His aide jumped to attention. "Sir sir sir sir sir!"

The General pressed his lips together tight and grim. "Set our status to FOODCON ONE."

ELEVEN

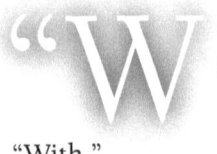"ITH OR WITHOUT SPRINKLES?" TURDD inquired.

The General considered for a moment. "With."

The major spoke into a nearby telephone. "Set status to FOODCON ONE. Auth Code Smoothie UpYours Cheesecake KitKat Milkshake YooHoo DingDong IceCream Cheesecake KitKat. Repeat, set status to FOODCON ONE."

"With sprinkles," the General reminded him.

Turdd repeated the command into the mouthpiece and hung up. A siren blared. Every man, woman, child and donkey rushed to the nearest corner of the bunker.

I raised my voice to make myself heard. "What's going on?"

"Battle stations," the General explained. An airman rushed up and handed him an orange plastic bucket with a strap. "FOODCON ONE is the highest level of alert. It means there is an imminent threat of a food terrist attack."

"But Fatso's in Cuba," Green said. "Or was yesterday. What makes you think he's going to attack the US?"

"I don't think," the General growled. "I know." He strapped the orange bucket around his waist, so that it covered his behind.

The other Air Force staff returned to work, orange buckets attached in similar fashion. Even the donkeys wore extra large plastic garbage bins fixed over their haunches.

"What are the buckets for?" I asked.

Too Secret For You cackled. "They're not buckets, Too Stupid For Me. They're butt helmets. In the case of a sewer attack."

"Sewer attack?" Green asked.

"If French plumbers hack their way into our systems, they could read our thoughts by prying open our butt cheeks and reading our ass lips. They could learn our deepest, darkest secrets. Like the password to my hotmail account."

"Major Turdd, where are my sprinkles?" the General bellowed.

"They're coming!"

At that moment it started to snow. I caught a flake and put it on my tongue, but spat it out again.

"Styrofoam pellets," Too Secret For You explained. "In the case of a sewer attack, sprinkles make it easier to track an enemy toilet cam. Or even an enemy frogman."

"But what about Fatso?" Erpent asked, strapping on a butt helmet. "Can't we just snatch and grab him? We got SEAL teams down there, right?"

The General tugged at the foot-long brim of his cap. Showers of fake snow fell at his feet. "If only it were that easy," he said. "Ever since the Johnson Brothers op, it's been impossible to get a SEAL team on the ground in Cuba."

"What's the problem?" Erpent asked. "Get in, grab him, get out. How hard is that?"

The General sighed. "The feared Cuban Fat Police are everywhere, Agent Erpent. *Los Gordos,* the downtrodden Cuban people call them. Our skinny commandos stick out like celery at a cannibal barbecue."

"Navy SEALs, Navy SEALs," barked a technician, in the tenor of that marine mammal, and balanced an invisible ball on his nose.

"Bad SEAL!" scolded his friend. "No fee-shee for you! Have a snack on air, big boy!"

Erpent rolled his eyes. "So issue them fat suits. I got to think of everything for you?"

"Disguises aren't enough," O'Shitt said. "*Los Gordos* make sure everyone gorges himself five times a day. How can we ask our fine young men, who have sworn to uphold the Amendment, and believe in the divine principles of eating air, to defile their bodies and minds in this way?"

At that moment Crusteau's dossier vanished from the screen. Too Secret For You groaned and pressed his wee-wee deep into the biometric reader. We all turned to look.

"Sorry," he said. "Next time I'll have to use a condom."

I had an idea. "What about Cuban dissidents?" I suggested. "There must be air-eating sympathizers down there. People who are horrified at being force-fed by their totalitarian government."

"It's a sorry plight the Cuban people are in," the General said. "For reasons we can't begin to fathom, they like being fat. For fifty years they were on the road to eating air. And now?" He shook his head sadly.

"There must be something we can do!" I said.

Glum faces turned away from me. No one would meet my eye. Was this it? To come so far—so close to capturing Fatso—only to be stymied once more by our implacable foe, Cuba?

My Twinkie jumped up and down in my ankle holster, celebrating this victory for all Twinkie-kind. It sang:

Twinkies forever, you and me
Twinkies forever, glad to see—

"Noooooooooo!" I shouted at the ceiling, a primal scream of rage and despair.

But the Twinkie song swelled louder and louder until I could hear nothing else. My arms and legs became puppets, enslaved to that cursed pastry's enchantment. I scooped up a ball of fake snow and threw it at Too Secret For You.

"What the poo was that?" the NSA man demanded. He threw a snowball back at me. It hit Major Turdd.

"Watch it, Plumber," the major barked.

The General stepped between us, arms raised. "Gentlemen, please!" he said. "There's no time for this." He turned to Too Secret For You. "Do we have any idea when Fatso might be coming back?"

"Let me check, Fat Man." Too Secret For You threw a snowball at the General. It exploded across the ribbons on his chest.

"That's it," O'Shitt said. "No more Mister Twenty-Five-Star Nice Guy." He picked up a handful of styrofoam snow and threw it at Too Secret For You. It hit him in the face.

The return volley pegged an airman working at a nearby machine. Soon the fake snowball fight spread until the entire bunker was involved, tens of thousands of Air Force elite, orange buckets strapped to their behinds, fake snow flying everywhere.

Meanwhile, Too Secret For You tapped away at his toolbox. When the sprinkle fight died down, he said, "We're in luck. Fatso's due back in D.C. tomorrow. Six-thirty in the morning. Just enough time to make your deadline."

The Twinkie song abruptly died. My mind was my own again.

"Why didn't you say so before?" I asked.

"It was more entertaining watching you throw snowballs at each other."

"But how do you know he's coming back tomorrow?" Erpent asked.

"Filed a flight plan with Boring Tower when he left last Wednesday." That's the air traffic control tower out at D.C.'s Boring Airport.

"That's impossible," Green said. "The Prophet grounded all civilian air traffic two years ago. The Air Force has standing orders to shoot down any plane trying to leave the country."

"I can tell you what it means," Erpent said. "Corruption at the highest levels."

"No!" I breathed.

"Now don't jump to conclusions," the General said. "Who approved the flight plan?"

A bony face appeared on screen. He looked like the kind of man who had a fourteen-inch waist. "Air Traffic Controller Blobbalicious Superfattypants."

"Yikes, what kind of name is that?" I asked.

"Legal immigrant from Ruritania," Too Secret For You said. He printed out a copy of the photo and gave it to me. "He's been the sole remaining air traffic controller out at Boring for the last year and a half. The skeleton crew, if you will."

"Any history of food terrism?" the General inquired. "Family in Fat Camp? Ghetto ties?"

Too Secret For You shook his head. "Not that we know of. FBI ran a background check on him. He came out thin."

"No air traffic controller can stop fighters from being scrambled," Erpent said. "That means someone in the Air Force has to be involved." He stared around at the swarms of technicians in their butt helmets, then at the General himself. "Maybe somebody in this very room."

O'Shitt stiffened his spine. "You malign the honor and integrity of this uniform," he said, running his fingertips over his ribbon-covered tunic. "None of my men would ever betray the Prophet like that."

"I'm afraid the super skinny's right," Too Secret For You said, tightening and loosening bolts with his lug wrench. "Someone in NORAD authorizes Fatso's flights, and prevents fighters from shooting him down."

The General reeled backward on his heels. Major Turdd caught him in time. "A traitor in our midst!" he gasped. "Who could it be?"

"According to the signature on the flight plan, it was the NORAD-FAA liaison officer, Lt. Cptn. Maj. Col. Bouwelles."

"Not Bouwelles!" O'Shitt said. "He's been with us since the beginning!"

"A viper at your breast," Erpent said. "Sucking the vital air from your lungs. I suggest you call the guards, or I shall be forced to arrest him myself."

The General straightened his cap. "To think that I've been harboring a food terrist so close to my heart," he sobbed. "All this time!" He shook his fist at the heavens. "I'm not waiting for any guards. Let's go get the bastard."

"That could be dangerous, sir sir sir sir sir," Major Turdd said. "When cornered, food terrists have been known to turn desperate."

But O'Shitt brushed his aide aside. The rest of us followed in his wake. He waddled the length of the bunker, past the

I-SEE-FAT Call Center, past the Poo Propulsion Laboratory, to NORAD itself. Fifty resolute men sat in front of a big screen, ready to respond to a nuclear first strike by Paraguay, Uganda, Luxembourg or even nuke-loving New Zealand. His waddle came to a halt at Lt. Capt. Maj. Col. Bouwelles's desk, where the man sat laughing into his headphones, his jaws moving up and down like he was chewing on air.

"Sure I can get you a salami, honey," he was saying. "But what do you want me to do with it?"

The General pulled out a laxative revolver, and the man's laughter died. The gun was pewter-plated with an imitation ivory handle, and I recognized it instantly. It was a commemorative piece the Franklin Mint issued in honor of the Amendment's passage. They only made fifty thousand, each one lovingly handcrafted by slaves in China, individually numbered and accompanied by an engraved certificate of authenticity.

O'Shitt pressed the tip of the gun to Bouwelles's nose. We crowded around, arms crossed, looking down at him in judgment.

"No need to point that at me, sir sir sir sir sir," he said. "You've got my attention." He cracked a grin. "Is it time? Just tell me who to nuke. I am so there."

Tears sprang to the General's eyes. "I know," he said. "I know."

I spotted a lump in Bouwelles's cheek. My eyes narrowed. "Open your mouth," I said.

"It isn't what you think," he mumbled. "I can explain."

The General cocked the hammer of his commemorative laxative weapon. "Spit. It. Out."

A mouthful of half-chewed food tumbled from the man's lips onto his keyboard. The assembled throng gasped in horror.

"What do you call that?" Turdd demanded.

"I was only chewing!" Bouwelles wailed. "I never swallow. It isn't illegal if you don't swallow!"

"Find out soon enough," the General said. And shot Bouwelles in the shoulder.

The man collapsed in his chair. A dark stain spread across the traitor's trousers. The smell of poo wafted up from below. Two guards appeared.

"Take this piece of human filth to the brig," the General ordered. "He speaks to no one. Understood?"

"Yes, sir sir sir sir sir!" The guards saluted, and dragged the disgraced officer to his feet. A bag of chocolate candies spilled from the man's jacket and skittered across the floor. Several of the airmen picked them up.

"Save the janitor some work," one explained, filling his pockets. "Everyone's got to do his bit in the War on Fat, don't you think?"

"That's the spirit," Major Turdd said. "I'll see you get a commendation for this. Maybe even a promotion."

The airman beamed. "Thanks, Major!"

"General," my partner said. "With your permission, we would like to question your man." He indicated the limp figure of Lt. Capt. Maj. Col. Bouwelles.

"No time," the General said. "Summary execution in twenty minutes. Right now we need to track down his accomplice out at Boring, before he has time to warn Fatso. And you." He addressed Bouwelles. "You, you, you food terrist!" He spat in his colleague's face. "You disgust me."

Bouwelles hung limp between the two guards. Poo dripped down his trouser leg onto his shoe. "Sometimes you gotta catch a bullet for the team," he murmured, his tone slack under the sedative. "Had to happen one day. Take care of my family, will you?" He was weeping openly now. The guards led him away.

"Our Smart Car is waiting out front," I said. "It'll be a squeeze, but there's room for five. If there's not too much traffic, we can be at the airport in an hour."

"An hour!" the General said. "We can do better than that. Follow me."

He led us to the far end of the bunker. What looked like an oil pipeline soared from ground level and disappeared through the far wall. He lifted a hatch in the pipeline to reveal a capsule.

Inside was like a limousine. It even had that new limousine smell. Clad in black leather, with a mini-bar of compressed air— all the flavors, too!—plus a built-in television and an arsenal of laxative assault rifles. The only difference from an ordinary limo was that the seats had fighter jet harnesses instead of seatbelts. And the seats, I noticed, were actually toilet bowls. Green depressed a lever on one, and it emptied of water.

"What is this contraption?" Erpent demanded.

"The latest invention of the Poo Propulsion Laboratory," the General said proudly. "Gentlemen, I give you the Poo Rocket."

"Alright, come out of there," a voice said. A rent-a-cop in a plastic badge stood at the hatchway. His shoulder patch declared him an Official Drone for the Toilet Safety Administration. Motto: "Protecting Our Precious Air."

"I was just showing it to them," the General whined.

"You know the rules. Not before you go through security." The TSA Official Drone gestured at a nearby metal detector and colonoscopy machine.

"But I'm the TSA Commander," O'Shitt protested.

"So you say," the Drone sneered. "How do I know you're really you?"

"What are you talking about?" I asked. "Of course he's really him."

The man snorted. "Anyone can gain five hundred pounds, put a bunch of colored ribbon all over their clothes and strap a couple of big balloons with stars on them to their shoulders."

The General turned purple. "This is a direct order, Official Drone. I am your commanding officer!"

The man scratched his ass and sniffed his fingers. "Get in line, fatty," he said. "Or I'll report you to my supervisor. You'll get the open-heart chest-cavity search."

"Not the open-heart chest-cavity search!" O'Shitt said. "No need to call your supervisor. Please. We're getting in line now. See? Here we are in line."

"That's better," the Drone said.

We backed up behind the security checkpoint. The General grumbled to himself for a moment, then sighed.

"Now," he said, "I don't need all three of you with me. Agent Erpent, why don't you update the Thin House on our progress?"

"Are you kidding?" Erpent said. "Of course I'm coming."

Major Turdd said in a high-pitched voice, "Ma-ma! Ma-ma!"

Erpent swallowed hard. "On second thought, maybe the Prophet should be informed of the full capabilities of the NSA."

"A wise decision," the General said.

"But I expect a full report on my desk this afternoon," Erpent said.

"And you shall have it. What about you, Agent Green?" O'Shitt asked. "You could wait for us in the lobby of the Pentagram." The military's star-shaped headquarters across the Potomacncheese.

Green stuck out his jaw. "You can't threaten me," he said. "I've got a right to come along, and I intend to do so. What's more, when this case is over I'm going to make sure the whole world knows what you do here."

"Think of your daughter," the General said quietly.

"That's exactly what I'm doing, General," he said. "What kind of future do I want for my child? Do I want the NSA filming her bottom every time she goes to the toilet?"

A twenty-five-star shrug. "This is the price we pay to live in a free society," the General replied. "Where everyone—regardless of age, race, gender, sexual orientation, family status, hair color, number of toes on their left foot, favorite glue to sniff, movie they saw last weekend, number of cousins in Georgia, fluency in Swahili or preferred brand of pipe tobacco—is free to eat air."

My partner crossed his arms. "I am beginning to wonder if that's really the kind of freedom I want."

The General's jowls trembled. For a moment I thought there had been an earthquake. "Of course, Agent Green. I understand." He glanced at the Plumber. "So your plan is to *leak* this matter to the press?"

"Leaks!" the Plumber screamed, and brandished his lug wrench. "I feeks leaks!" He attacked my partner, swinging his wrench wildly. "No! More! Leaks!"

Green ducked out of the way. The sergeant-at-arms and a pair of nearby airmen wrestled the Plumber to the ground. The TSA Official Drone looked on, nodding vacantly.

"Kill the leaks!" Too Secret For You screamed, as they dragged him away. "Leaks! Leaks! Leaks!"

"Sure you won't change your mind?" the General asked.

My partner was defiant. "Positive."

O'Shitt turned to me. "What about you, Agent Frolick? Do you want to help me catch Fatso, and receive all the glory of being there for the collar?"

"I am but a humble air-eater who struggles each day to live up to the Prophet's teachings," I said. "I am not the best man for the job. Maybe I'm even the worst. But the Prophet chose me. He needs my help. Who am I to reject that sacred trust?"

"Well spoken," the General said. "We welcome an objective observer like you on this mission." He glared at Green. "Your partner here could learn a lot from you."

"You see?" I said, and slapped Green on the back. "I'm not so stupid as you think."

He just stood there looking at me. "So goes the world," he said at last, apropos of nothing.

"I haven't got all day!" the TSA Official Drone called out.

The General gestured at the screening point. "After you."

I took off all my clothes and stepped naked through the metal detector. Something beeped.

"Probably your fillings," the Official Drone muttered. "Open wide."

He stuck a pair of pliers in my mouth and pulled out a couple of teeth. Then I remembered.

I spat blood on the floor. "I don't actually have any fillings."

"I know what it is then," the Drone said. He snapped on a pair of latex gloves. "Bend over."

I did so, and he began the colonoscopy.

When was my last Twinkie assault? Would he find the residue? I played dumb.

"What are you looking for?" I gasped.

"If I knew that, I wouldn't be looking for it, now would I?"

"But what kind of threat to Toilet Safety could be hidden. So. High. Up?"

"Can't have any blockages," the Official Drone explained gruffly. "You have any idea how much it costs to plunge a blocked-up toilet these days? So much as a tiny turd and *woosh!* Water and toilet paper all over the floor. There are food terrists out there who would kill to go potty in our sewers, just to block them up. Some even try to flush themselves down the toilet. Suicide poopers, we call them."

For a moment I thought the colonoscopy might come out of my mouth. Then it withdrew.

"Alright," the Official Drone said. "You're clean."

I gave a sigh of relief. I had heard the TSA Drones weren't very good at spotting threats. But then it occurred to me—if he couldn't find the remains of my Twinkie assailants, much less the Twinkie hidden in my ankle holster, how would he be able to spot a genuine food terrist intent on blocking up our sewers? *Note to self: mention the TSA to the Prophet once I'm working in the Thin House.* Maybe it was time to upgrade the security checkpoints so that everyone got the open-heart chest-cavity search.

I got dressed. "So what set off the alarm?"

"Oh that," he said. "It always goes off. Standard procedure. Next!"

Green and the General squawked their way through security and joined me inside the capsule. I'm sure they were clean, I thought guiltily.

"Drop your pants and strap in, gentlemen," the General said. "And don't forget to flush."

"What did you call this thing again?" Green asked, slipping into the harness across from me.

"The Poo Rocket," the General said. He hooked his balloons to the ceiling. His ribbon-covered trousers pooled at his feet, and he settled himself on the potty beside me. "Now hold on to your toilet seats. We're going for a ride!"

TWELVE

OOMPF!

W I was flung back in my seat. My head slammed against the headrest. My eyes sank into my skull. With great effort I looked to one side. The General's jowls spread out until they covered his ears.

"Why is it called the Poo Rocket?" Green shouted over the rumbling noise outside.

"Don't you read the papers?" the General asked.

"You mean the government propaganda mills? Don't believe a word they say."

"Well maybe if you weren't such a cynic, you'd know what Airitarian ingenuity has produced. The Poo Rocket is a nickname for the Sewer High-Intensity Transit System, or SHITS for short."

"That's right," I shouted. "Now I remember. Propulsion system based on raw sewage. There was a big hullabaloo in the Air Congress about it, as I recall."

"Yes, Congressman. No, Congressman," the General mocked. "Why are we spending billions of dollars on a rocket that runs on poo, Congressman." He snorted. "You know what he thought we should spend the money on instead? Grain-burning silos in Iowa."

"But burning grain is important," I objected.

"Sure it is," the General acknowledged. "I got nothing against grain-burning silos. But when our freedom is threatened by dangerous food terrists who want to destroy the Airitarian way of life, terrists who can't stand the fact that we're thin and they're not," —and here he caressed his eleven-inch belly, which had flattened itself against the wall behind him— "money must be spent first and foremost to give us the tools we need to hunt down these overweight food-eating scum."

The kinds of tools every country deserves. I know you Frenchies must be jealous. Why don't you have a SHITS here in Paris, you're wondering. It's only natural that France has fallen behind. We, the United States of Air, are the most advanced country in the world, after all. However, as a gesture of friendship, I am authorized to share this cutting-edge technology with you. If you renounce your allegiance to food, close your food terrist training camps and stop promoting food terrism abroad, all this—and more—can be yours.

To continue:

The roaring outside the Poo Rocket stopped. Acceleration slowed. We were suddenly weightless.

"Poo-AHH!" the General bellowed.

Green gripped his toilet seat with white knuckles. "What's going on?"

"A gap in the sewer. The launching tube flings us out via the Potomacncheese. We should be landing soon in a sewage treatment plant near the airport."

Green looked around the leather-clad interior. "But how do you steer?"

The General chuckled. "You don't."

"But what if we're off course and miss the treatment pool?"

"Hasn't happened yet."

"Oh good," I said.

"Not since last Tuesday, anyway," the General added.

The capsule fell. I screamed. My Twinkie screamed. We all screamed. It was like a roller coaster, only worse. It went on for a minute and more.

Splash.

The capsule slowed and came to rest. Green and I breathed a sigh of relief. Outside a clinking noise rasped against the hull. We seemed to be turning.

"Are we there already?" I asked.

"Now do you see the value of the Poo Rocket?" the General said. "So much faster than a Smart Car."

"Is it safe to get out of our harnesses?" Green asked.

"Sure is." The General reached for his own. He pushed at the release button but nothing happened. "That's funny. Can you open yours?"

"Mine works fine," Green said. He stood up and stretched.

"Must be a glitch."

I tugged at my own harness. It wouldn't open either. "That *is* strange," I said. "I can't seem to—"

All of a sudden, the rocket took off again. Green flew face first into the wall between me and the General.

Crunch.

"Stop the rocket!" I shouted. "He's hurt!" I struggled to lift an arm to help my friend, but the acceleration flung my hand back against the wall.

The General swore. "I forgot about the staging area!"

"What staging area?"

"It's a two-hop jump to the airport."

"But we've got to get him to a hospital!"

"Gotta get him to the airport first. Hold on!"

We landed a second time. Green was flung back against the opposite wall—*crunch!*—and slumped to the floor. I ripped off my harness—this time it opened—and went to him.

"Don't touch me!" he cried out. Broken bones protruded all over his body.

"Where does it hurt?" I asked him.

The hatchway opened. A TSA Official Drone stood there.

"Get this man a medic," the General ordered.

The Official Drone scratched his ample belly and adjusted his plastic badge. "Don't report to no military types," he said. "We's privatizized. Outsourced contractors, you know."

"My friend is going to die!" I pleaded. "For the love of the Prophet!"

The Official Drone clucked his tongue. "I dunno," he said. "I don't want to get in no trouble or nothing."

I stuck my head out the hatchway. We were in some kind of subway station. A group of airmen were playing cards nearby. Gambling for what looked like, but obviously could not be, Ritz crackers.

"Need a medic!" I shouted. "Got a man down here!"

"Hey!" The Official Drone blocked my path. "Authorized Personnel Only."

I pushed past him onto the platform. Two of the airmen saw me and jumped up. They wore medics' white uniforms. They wiped their lips, grabbed their first aid kits and a stretcher, and jogged toward us.

"What happened?" one asked.

"The locking mechanism must have failed," the General said. "Never seen that happen before. Crazy, huh?"

They ducked under the hatchway and knelt over Green. "Got to get him out of here," the second medic said. They carried him outside and laid him down on the stretcher. He screamed in pain.

"Look on the bright side, Harry," I said.

He groaned and coughed up blood. "What's that?"

I brushed the hair out of his eyes. "In the hospital you'll have plenty of time to strengthen your faith." The Amendment was strictly enforced in hospitals. Only diabetics with security ratings like Coroner Juicy got glucose IVs.

"On three," the first medic said, and they lifted the stretcher. Green clawed at my pant leg.

"Wait!" I said.

"No time," said a medic.

"Thirty seconds," Green insisted.

They put him back down on the ground. I knelt at his side. "What is it, partner?"

"Frolick," he said. "My friend. Do something for me."

"Anything."

"Remember what we talked about this morning? In the car?"

"I remember." His daughter's mysterious illness.

"Go to that doctor I mentioned," he said. "He's got some special medicine for my kid."

The quack-quack naturopath. Oh boy. Probably a thinly disguised food dealer. Good way to lose my measuring tape. "Can't your wife go?" I asked, and immediately regretted it.

"Eat it," Green swore. "Are you my friend or aren't you?"

"Sure, Harry," I said. I patted the bones sticking out of his hand. "No problem. You can count on me."

"I can?" Delirium overtook him.

"Sure you can. You're my friend. I promise. You hear me? I promise, OK?"

Green's eyes rolled up in his head. His chest arched. One of the medics touched a finger to his neck.

"He's not breathing. Cardiac event." He took out a pair of paddles. "Clear!"

They put the paddles to his chest. The shock lifted him from the stretcher and laid him flat again.

The General appeared at my side. He put a comforting hand on my shoulder. "Is he going to die?"

"He'll be fine," the medic said. "But we need to get him to the hospital."

The two medics picked up the stretcher and entered a nearby elevator. Then they were gone.

Just like that. No more Green. I was on my own. For the first time ever. My partner had always been there for me—cynical, wisecracking old Harry. It could be months before he was back on the beat again. If he lived.

But right now I had a job to do. A job that was more important than either Green or myself. I had to save the world from the menace of food terrism, and bring the Prophet's Message of Hope and Air to all you ignorant ferrners. Only then could we be truly free.

The General handed me a laxative assault rifle. I chambered a dart and flicked off the safety.

"Where to?" I asked.

The General drew his commemorative laxative pistol. His balloons towered overhead, the breathtaking symbol of command. "The tower. This way!"

"Hey!" the TSA Official Drone shouted after us. "You're not supposed to have guns in here! That's it. I'm reporting you! You hear me? My supervisor's going to hear about this!"

Without breaking stride, the General fired a laxative dart into the Drone's thigh. The man collapsed on the subway platform, going poo-poo in his pants.

"You'll get in trouble for that," I said.

"I know," he said. "But it was so worth it."

We climbed a set of stairs and entered the main terminal. The airport was deserted. Dust and ash covered everything. I stifled a sneeze. The cold afternoon sun flooded through the windows. We passed burned-out restaurants and duty-free stores, and the remains of a Muffin Man cart. Wiped that smirk off your face, didn't we, Muffin Man?

"Here we are," the General announced, stopping before a heavy metal security door.

"But where's the assault team?" I asked. "Aren't they going to meet us here?"

"What assault team?"

"I just assumed…"

"It's only one guy," the General scoffed. "We can take him. See?" He took out a cell phone and pressed a button.

I jumped back in horror. The screen showed a toilet cam's view of a man's bottom. Loop after loop of a continuous poo garlanded the camera lens.

"Where is it all coming from?"

"Depends on what he's putting in the other end, I suppose."

The General pushed open the door. We climbed a spiral staircase. The smell was different than in the terminal. Here it smelled like poo. At the top of the stairs we halted at a door marked "Control Room."

I turned the handle and pushed. It gave an inch, and sprang back. Some sort of foam padding was blocking the door.

"Help me push."

The General leaned his bulk against the door, but again no luck. A strange moaning noise came from inside the control room. A glass fire cabinet hung on the wall next to the door. I pointed.

"The axe."

The General opened the cabinet and hefted the axe. I pushed the door open a crack, and he swung the blade at the hinges. Once, twice, and the door snapped off. By pushing it sideways we managed to wiggle it free of the frame. What we saw made us gasp.

The doorway was filled with hairy white skin. The moaning noise was louder now.

"Does this mean what I think it means?" I asked.

"Let's get down onto the tarmac. See what we can see from there."

We made our way down the stairs and out a side door. We craned our necks up at the tower. White flesh bulged against the inside of every pane. The sound of whirring machinery came from the other side of the tower. We crept through the shadows to get a better look.

A luggage conveyor belt had been set up that ran from the tarmac to a single open window far above our heads. At the bottom, two men in fluorescent jackets were unloading crates from the back of a refrigerated truck and chucking their contents onto the conveyor belt.

"O Mine Prophet," I said.

Millions of dollars of food mounted its way to the window above: platters of glistening sausages, buckets of barbecue chicken wings, bowls of curly fries, doughnuts piled high in a rainbow of colorful frosting, a wheel of cheddar cheese cut into chunks, vats of unwrapped candies and caramels, a pyramid of hamburgers—more food than I had seen in years. My Twinkie squealed with delight. The food squealed back.

"*Eat me, eat me!*" cried the doughnuts.

"*Put me in your mouth and chew me!*" shouted the sausages.

"*Just a little lick, big boy,*" the curly fries purred in that throaty way of theirs. "*Down there. The way you know I like it. Um-hmm. One kiss on my salty spot, and you'll love me forever.*"

"Shut up," I said through gritted teeth.

The General looked at me sideways. "I didn't say anything."

Then my Twinkie spotted them. Brethren. A crate of shucked Twinkies landed on the conveyor belt. I had to prevent this unlooked-for species reunion.

"Don't move!" I shouted. "You're under arrest!"

The two men took one look at my ATFF trench coat and the General's uniform and rank balloons and took off running. The backs of their jackets read, "Food Mafia Waiter." The General opened fire. I followed his lead.

One of the waiters fell. The other was soon out of range. He slipped through a hole in the fence and disappeared.

We approached the fallen waiter. A laxative syringe pro-truded from his buttock. But before I could question the man, the General shouted, "Mothereating food terrist!" and pumped two rounds point blank into the man's skull, killing him.

"What did you do that for?" I wailed.

The General kicked the body. "It's scum like him who make our streets unsafe for women and children."

"But we could have questioned him!"

.M. PORUP

The General hung his head. "I'm sorry. I got so worked up, seeing all those addictive caloric substances, I guess I lost control."

I sighed and patted his shoulder. "I know how hard it is," I said. "But you gotta stop killing suspects like that."

The General wiped away a tear. "I'm just a simple soldier," he said. "A humble warrior of air. Trained to kill in defense of our freedoms. You understand?"

I gave him a hug. My arms didn't reach all the way around. He crushed me against his ribbons. "Don't worry about it," I said. "But no more shoot to kill. Got it?"

He nodded in contrition. "Got it."

We returned to the conveyor belt. It stopped and started at irregular intervals. The box of Twinkies was halfway to the top.

"Cover me," I said.

I climbed up until I was hidden behind the box of bewingèd pastries. When they heard my ankle Twinkie's song of joy, they danced and began their suicidal rapist death chorus. I recognized the tune. I knew the signs. They were about to attack. Not here. Not now! I looked over my shoulder.

The General was rooting around inside the back of the truck, his jaws moving up and down. Eating air, no doubt. A Twinkie wing brushed my lips, and I resigned myself to their kamikaze assault. A dozen had already raped my throat, filling my mouth with their sweet, creamy guts, when my cell phone rang.

I ducked down and fumbled to open it. "Hello?" I said, my mouth still full.

"Jason? Is that you?" my wife's voice asked. "Are you *eating* something?"

I swallowed. "Chantal. Oxy. I can explain."

"You think I'm stupid? You think you married a moron?"

63

A bucket of chicken wings fell empty to the ground. The conveyor belt advanced. Only two boxes separated me from the open window. I cradled the phone against my shoulder and held my laxative assault rifle at ready.

"I can't talk right now," I said. "I'm a little busy."

Her voice took on a throaty purr. Kind of like the curly fries. "It's been a busy day for me as well. Want to know what I've been up to?"

The box of candies tumbled below. The conveyor belt advanced again.

"I'm on a secret mission for the Prophet," I hissed. "Can we have this conversation later?"

"Fuck the Prophet," she said. "We need to talk about this now."

"Oxy!" I exclaimed, horrified at this outburst. "We'll talk about your use of language, too. Although I might not be home until tomorrow morning."

"You come home now," she screamed in my ear. "Or tomorrow morning I won't be here, and neither will your son. Is that clear?"

The conveyor belt advanced again. The Twinkies were next. "I'll see what I can do," I whispered, and slapped the cell phone shut.

I peered through the slats of the Twinkie crate. A sound like a vacuum cleaner came from up ahead. The conveyor belt advanced one final time. The Twinkies' choral overture to rape and death swelled in an ode to joy, then disappeared. A grey hose sucked them up. The crate fell away. I lifted my rifle and stared at the most disgusting sight I have ever seen.

THIRTEEN

AN ELEPHANT STARED BACK AT ME. OR WAS IT A woolly mammoth? A metal snout protruded from its face. Shaggy hair grew down over its eyes. But the truth was far worse. How could it be? It was a man. His body filled the entire control room.

"ATFF!" I shouted. "Drop the snout!"

Faster than I could react, the snout sucked the rifle from my grip.

"Hey! Give that back!"

The snout swung side to side.

"Does that mean no?"

The snout nodded.

Strong with the power of Twinkie corpses rotting in my stomach, I stood, grabbed the snout and pulled. With a snapping noise it came away in my hands. I pulled the rifle out, all covered in goo, and threw the snout over the side of the conveyor belt.

A man's face appeared at the window. Or rather, a set of eyes, a nose and a mouth floating in a sea of fat.

"What are you staring at?" the blob demanded.

Sympathy crashed over me like ranch dressing over an addictive caloric Caesar salad. "You poor thing," I breathed. "How did you get so fat?"

"Who you calling fat, twiggy?"

"Twiggy!" I was aghast at this unlooked-for compliment. "Are you calling me skinny? Look at this!" I pinched a wad of fat through my trench coat. "And this! And this! What do you call that?"

The blob whistled. "You gotta be more careful, or you'll starve to death."

"That's ridiculous," I snorted. "I eat all the air I need."

"Newfangled nonsense. Food is for eating. Air is for breathing."

"Blasphemy!" I gasped.

"Lunatics like you scare me," he said. "Show some common sense for a change."

"Common sense," I scoffed. "It's common sense that got us into this mess in the first place. It takes the uncommon sense of a man like the Prophet to show us what progress really means."

"There's nothing wrong with eating food," the man insisted. "You just gotta do it in moderation."

I stared at his bulk, the pile of empty crates below. "You call inhaling your food through a snout moderation?"

He opened his mouth wide. Rotting brown stumps speckled the inside of his jaws. "It's not a snout," he said. "It's a Browntooth Hands-Free Eating Apparatus."

"Which you wouldn't need if you weren't so fat!"

The mountain of flesh scowled at me. "Don't call me fat," he snapped. "'Cause I'm not. OK?"

"Oh yeah?" I said. "Then get up and walk out of here."

He looked around him. His head bobbed, as though he

166

were trying to move. "Don't want to," he said. "I'm comfortable where I am."

I held up my open palm. "Gimme five."

He glanced down at the mass of fat in front of him that covered his arms. As we later discovered, his fingers had glued themselves to the keyboard. We had to employ a surgeon to separate him from the keys.

"Not in the mood right now," he said finally.

I pulled my hair. "How can anyone be so stupid? Why can't you see what your problem is?"

"I don't know what you're talking about," he replied. "Now tell the waiters to get back to work."

"Your eating days are over, big boy." I hefted my laxative rifle. "You're going straight to Fat Camp, where you belong."

The blob smiled sadly. "I'm sorry, but I cannot let you starve me to death."

All of a sudden the conveyor belt advanced, and I began to fall. I let go of my weapon and grabbed hold of the window ledge.

"Where's. My. Food?" the blob bellowed. The control tower swayed from side to side. Concrete girders shrieked from the strain. Plaster dribbled from the ceiling.

I pulled myself up into the room. I scrambled over a radar screen and perched against the slanted glass of a window. It was a tight squeeze. There was barely enough room for his fat frame, much less my own.

Up close the immensity of the man was overwhelming. How could any human being grow so large? He made Rat Boy look like a midget. You'd have trouble loading him onto an eighteen-wheeler. I reached out and sank a finger into the flesh behind his head. A wave of fat rippled around the room and came back again.

"That tickles," the man giggled. His eyes narrowed. "You're not food. Go away and don't come back until you bring me food."

I had a job to do, and it was time I did it. I held up my badge. "You're under arrest," I said. "You have the right to be thin. If you refuse this right, you will be sent to Fat Camp at no extra charge. You have the right not to eat. If you do eat, anything you eat can and will be used against you in a Food Court of Law. Do you understand what I've just told you?"

"On what charge?" he demanded.

"Multiple violations of the Food Understanding Country Koolaid Yowzee Outrage Understatement Act."

"Never heard of it."

"Ignorance is no excuse," I scolded him. "Now, who are you, and what have you done with Air Traffic Controller Blobbalicious Superfattypants?"

He chuckled. "You're looking at him."

I held up the printout Too Secret For You gave me. The gaunt features of an air-eater stared back.

"You don't look like him to me."

"Maybe I've put on a few pounds," Superfattypants conceded.

"A few pounds!" I laughed. "You looked in the mirror lately?"

"And desert my post during a time of war?" the man shook his head. "As soon as we do that, we let the food terrists win."

I shouted out the window, "General!"

O'Shitt wiped his lips. "Just having an air snack!" he shouted up at me. "What is it?"

"Send me up one of your shiniest decorations! It's urgent!"

He squinted down at his much-decorated chest. He fingered a medal. "How about my Purple Stomach?" he shouted. "I got it fighting in hand-to-hand kitchen combat with a French commando-chef. Took my fingernail clean off."

"No," I shouted back. "I need something bigger. Shinier!"

He took hold of another, larger medal. "Or my Air Force Cross? Got it when we nuked them South Pacific food terrists last year. You remember Operation Enduring Hunger, when we deposed the dictator of Micronesia?"

"He was a major threat to world thinness," I replied. "That was good work, General."

O'Shitt shuddered. "The evil we saw in Micronesia. Before we dropped the bomb, that is. The horror! I will never forget it as long as I live. The doctors tell me I have postprandial stress syndrome."

My heart went out to the man. "I'm so sorry to hear that, General!" I shouted. "But your Air Force Cross is still not big enough. What about that shiny one around your neck?" I pointed. "The one in the shape of a bubble?"

The General clutched the medal. "Not my Congressional Medal of Air!" he exclaimed. "I got it for killing defenseless women and children!"

"And they deserved it too, I'm sure!" I shouted. "But right now I've got an emergency here!"

O'Shitt unclipped the two-foot-wide medal from around his neck. He kissed it and said, "Bless you, Mine Prophet, who didst bestow this greatest of honors upon me," and put the medal on the conveyor belt.

When it got to the top, I held it up so Blobbalicious could see. "Now tell me you're not fat."

He studied the image in the medal. I compared him again to the printout. The nose was the same. So was the red birthmark that covered half his face. It was him, all right.

The man laughed. "That's funny. You get that out of a cereal box?"

"Afraid not, big boy. That's you."

The laughter stopped. "You've had your little joke," he said. "Now go away and bring me back some food before I starve to death."

Unbelievable! How could I make him see?

"*There is a way,*" my Twinkie sang, "*a savage little way…*"

No. I can't do that. There has to be a better way.

"*Be a man, Spam.*

Or are you just canned flan, Stan?"

But it won't teach him anything. I want to save his soul.

"*Nothing like a Dover sole*

fried in lots of crispy fat.

Don't fall down that deep-deep hole—

lots of other feeshees, cat!"

My Twinkie was right, dang gummit. Blobbalicious wasn't the only misguided soul who needed saving. The Fate of the Food-Free World Hung in the Balance. I needed information. I needed it now.

I would have to resort to torture.

I LEANED OUT THE WINDOW AGAIN. "SEND ME UP some chicken wings!"

"Good choice!" The General licked his fingers. "That sauce is tangy!"

He chucked an open box onto the conveyor belt. It halted just outside the window.

Suppressing my disgust, I picked up a chicken wing and held it inches from Blobbalicious's lips. He lunged for it. My hand darted back.

"Got some questions for you first."

The man's head rolled on his neck. "I'm dying already," he moaned. "I can feel it. Just wasting away. The hunger is terrible. Terrible, I tell you! Like an African orphan in famine!"

My vision clouded with tears. My voice broke. "I'm sorry," I said. "Just a few questions, and you can have all the food you want."

"Liar, liar, pants on fire

sucking on a Twinkie tire."

His great cow eyes gazed up at me. "Would you really let me starve to death?"

My hand shook. I hardened my face. "If you don't cooperate, you give me no choice." I threw the chicken wing out the window. "Fly, chickie chick! Fly, fly!"

"Alright!" he screamed. "I'll talk! Whatever you want to know!"

Success. But in that moment I felt part of myself die. I was torturing a fellow human being. What did that make me?

"Tell me about your agreement with Fatso."

"Let me lick it," he begged. "Just a taste!"

"He flew out of here last Wednesday, right? Going to Cuba?" I held another chicken wing close enough that he could smell it.

"Saw him climb out of his limo and walk up the gangway of his private jet, 'Big Boy.' Now gimme, gimme, gimme! I'm going to collapse here!"

I pressed onward. "He's coming back tomorrow morning, right?"

Quivering with desire, Blobbalicious consulted his computer screen. "ETA 0630 hours. Should be here just before dawn. What do you want to buy, anyway? Why don't you just make an appointment, like everybody else does?"

Is that what he thought we wanted?

"That's none of your business," I snapped. I teased his lips with the chicken wing. "One last thing and I'll tie your snout back on."

"Oh please…oh please…," he whimpered in agony.

"This is a *surprise* party," I said. "If you warn Fatso we're waiting for him, I will personally make sure you starve to death. Am I clear?"

"Clear!" he shouted. "Now hurry!"

I retrieved his snout and tied it back on, leaving him to his gluttony. There would be time enough to cure him once Fatso was in custody. Teach him to eat air. Right now it was more important to ensure his cooperation.

In the meantime, I had a great deal to do. We had to organize Fatso's "surprise party." As I rode the conveyor belt down to the ground, my phone rang again.

"My bags are packed," Chantal said without even saying hello. "You coming home tonight or aren't you?"

On second thought, the Air Force could organize the welcoming committee.

"Why don't we have a romantic dinner?" I suggested. "I'll pick up some flowers on the way home. We can open a window. Suck down the exhaust from the highway overpass across the street. What do you say?"

She purred. "Don't forget the flowers."

As a footnote, Blobbalicious was eventually freed from his control tower prison. It took a small army of chainsaw-wielding liposuction experts to cut away the excess fat, and a team of helicopters to lift the remaining blob of flesh from the toilet seat where he'd been sitting for more than a year. Later measurements of man and blubber suggest he weighed upwards of three and a half tons.

Our civil engineers tell me that another couple hundred pounds and the control tower would have collapsed. As it is, the tower suffered serious structural damage, and has since been condemned as unfit for use.

I am pleased to report that Blobbalicious is successfully undergoing rehab in a fine Fat Camp in upstate New York, where he has discovered the joy of taco air and, I am told, has even fallen in love with a fellow camp attendee, a former Miss Obese New York. They plan to get married and have children, just as soon as they get their waists down to fourteen inches.

FOURTEEN

I BOUGHT A DOZEN RED ROSES ON THE WAY HOME. Completely illegal, of course. They were smuggled into the country by so-called coyotes, who risked their lives to cross the New Mexico desert with hundreds of long-stems strapped to their backs, and a watering can to keep the flowers cool.

But my wife and I had a lot to celebrate. She deserved a treat. Take care of Fatso, I mused, as I drove through light traffic, and the Food Mafia tumbles. Supply would disappear, Chantal would get over her withdrawal symptoms and the three of us would be a happy family at last.

I thought of Nathan and smiled. I was so proud of the kid. Just last week he'd won an award for air-eating at school. The teacher had gushed over his technique and applauded his faith. I couldn't wait to see him tonight, give him a big hug and tell him how much I loved him.

By force of habit, I swung past Green's house. Crazy, that accident. And there was something I was supposed to do. What was it? I shook my head. It would come to me. I drove the extra two blocks home, parked the Smart Car and limped up the drive.

I opened the front door, and Nathan came running to meet me. I put the roses down and threw open my arms.

"Hey there, skin and bones," I called out. "How's Daddy's favorite walking skeleton?"

His limbs, like sticks, flailed as he careened down the hallway at full speed. Five minutes passed. Ten. My arms began to ache. Finally he fell into my embrace, gasping, "Daddy, Daddy, how was your day?"

"It was air-yummy-licious," I said. I held him at arm's length. His stomach bulged like a beer belly. That was new. I frowned. "Has your mother been giving you beer?"

"No, silly," he giggled. "Beer's an addictive caloric substance. You know I'd never do *that*."

I fought back tears of joy. "I am so proud of you, son."

"Well I'm not."

Chantal stood in the former kitchen doorway, arms folded across her chest.

"Oxy," I said, in my warning tone of voice. "Not in front of the boy."

"I'll say whatever I feel like," she said. "You've brainwashed him. It's disgusting."

I ruffled Nathan's hair. It was falling out in patches. "Run along, kiddo. Go snack on some air."

When he was gone, I picked up the flowers and turned to her. "Can we not fight tonight?" I asked. "I brought these home for you."

"Flowers," she said with contempt. "Is that all?"

I backed toward the wall. "I thought you liked flowers."

She grabbed the bunch of roses and bit off a flower head.

"But—what—what are you doing?" I stammered.

"You going to report me?" she sneered, chewing the rose petals. "Put me in Fat Camp again?"

"What has gotten into you?"

"You mean what *hasn't* gotten into me," she snarled, and bit off another flower head. "Why can't you bring home the bacon like all the other ATFF agents?"

"Bacon?" I cried. "Are you crazy? You have any idea what the penalty is for possession of preserved pig flesh?"

"I don't want to *possess* it," she said, spitting flecks of rose petal in my face. "What I want is to FUCKING EAT IT!"

This was too much, even for me. I am a patient man, but I don't have to put up with that kind of abuse. And using the f-ing e-word. Sheesh.

I edged past her toward the basement door. "Have yourself a nice romantic dinner without me," I muttered. "I'm going downstairs to pray. For you."

"You mean to eat Twinkies?" she screamed.

I reeled, and grabbed the doorknob for support. How did she—

"Oh, you think I don't know about your private stash? You think I haven't tried every combination I can think of?"

I put my finger to my lips and ran to the bathroom. I lifted the lid. Was that an ancient bit of unflushed poo? A stain, perhaps? Or was it a wireless toilet cam?

"What are you talking about?" I shouted down at the water. "How dare you accuse me of that! Me! A decorated and loyal member of the ATFF!"

I slammed the lid shut. Chantal stood in the doorway.

"Have you gone mad?" she said. "You're talking to the toilet!"

"Toilets have ears," I advised her solemnly. "Be careful what you say, and where you poo."

"Now if only I had something *to* poo."

"Chantal—"

"No." She held up a hand. "Listen to me. I don't care about myself anymore. And you can keep your goddamn Twinkies. But you bring home food for Nathan or I will."

I gasped. "Are you threatening to hurt our son? To give him food? Do I have to call child services?"

"You do that, this family is over," she said. "I'm not the one killing him. You are."

"What are you talking about?" I demanded. "There's nothing wrong with him."

"You think I'm exaggerating? You think I'm being hysterical?" A rose petal stuck to her chin. She popped it into her mouth. "I took Nathan to that naturopath. The one Janine recommended."

Janine. Green's wife. Of course. That's what I forgot to do.

"That quack?"

"That *quack*, as you call him, knows a thing or two about health. Know what he said? That if Nathan doesn't eat some food and soon, he's going to die." She brandished the half-eaten bunch of roses in my face. "To *die*, love bundles!"

I rolled my eyes. "Hippie left-wing claptrap. Tell him to burn some incense, put some crystals on his chest and calm down. There's nothing wrong with Nathan that a nice, fresh meal of air won't cure."

"Right." She stormed into the kitchen and banged open a drawer. "See this, my air-eating husband?"

It was a clear plastic bag stenciled with the blue initials "UN." Inside, two squares of bread. Frills of lettuce protruded from the sides. A glimpse of pink, maybe ham. It was the sort of thing the UN included in their food drops, the ones that got through. But special forces were tasked to hunt down and destroy those shipments.

"How did you get your hands on that?"

"The only way I could," she said, and cocked her hip. "I went down to the docks and whored myself to a dozen sailors."

My whole body trembled at this news. "We had a chance," I said. "To raise our child food-free." I grabbed for the sandwich, but she held it overhead. "Why don't you give him some heroin, while you're at it? Stuff some cocaine up his nose?"

"Didn't you hear what I just said?"

I jumped for the sandwich, but couldn't reach. "You're corrupting our child. How long has this been going on?"

She shook her head. "Oh, Frolick."

"Answer me!" I roared. "How long?"

She advanced on me, jabbing her finger into my chest. "Today I sucked and fucked the entire merchant marine of a small island seafaring nation. Bareback. Multiple times. To pay for this sandwich. To keep my son alive. How does that make you feel?"

I'd forgotten to close the bathroom door, I realized. "Keep your voice down," I said. "Do you want them to hear?"

"*Let* them hear!" she shrieked. "How I had to whore myself to feed my son, because my husband tried to starve us to death!"

"This is all my fault," I said. I fell to my knees, and reached for her hands. "Give me one more chance."

Her hands fluttered in mine. "Really?" she said. "I mean, you understand?"

"Sure." I nodded. "You're a junkie. I should have gotten you treatment earlier."

She pulled away.

"Let me enroll you in Fat Camp again," I said. "Get the monkey off your back."

"I don't want to get the monkey off my back, you idiot!" she shouted. "We're supposed to eat. It's part of living. The naturopath said so!"

I gazed up at her. What had happened to the woman I fell in love with? All I could see was a withdrawal-crazed madwoman. "That's what the ferrn agro-business conglomerates want you to think," I said.

She studied me for a long moment. "You really believe that, don't you."

I got back to my feet. "Yes. I do."

"Then I feel sorry for you," she said. "A hypocrite who doesn't even realize."

"Who are you calling a hypocrite?"

She snorted with laughter. "A man who eats only air by day, but spends his evenings stuffing his face with stale Twinkies? What else would you call that?"

"Hey," I said. "It's not my fault if suicidal flying Twinkies force themselves down my throat and into my stomach. Rape is rape. I mean, come on."

Her eyes opened wide at that. Finally I'd made her see. "Is that how it is," she said.

I puffed up my chest. "Darn tootin' right."

She covered her face with her hands. When she lowered them, the sandwich was crumpled up into a ball. Her face was pale. She wiped away tears.

"Three days," she said. "No. Don't talk. Just listen. Three days. You bring us home some food. Or it's your fault if he dies. And if he dies…" She turned her back on me. "You no longer have a wife."

She turned and walked off down the hall, sandwich in hand, to our son's room.

"Chantal, wait!" I called after her.

She paused at Nathan's bedroom door. "And now I'm going to feed our son this sandwich. That I worked so hard to purchase." She tried to smooth out the crumpled slices of bread, but gave up. "You go down to your basement and eat some air, my husband. And you have a good long think about what I just said."

"Please, Chantal," I said. "Be reasonable."

"Three days," she repeated. She went into our son's room and shut the door behind her.

I felt like I'd been punched in the stomach with a three-week-old contraband burrito. Somehow I made it down the stairs. I slumped to the ground in front of the Twinkies. They towered over me like some pagan god. I groveled to my Twinkie-Baal, begging for mercy, knowing there would be none. I was a human blood sacrifice on their altar of golden pastry deviance.

A dab of cream spattered my cheek. They were attacking again. Rage blinded me, and I drew my service weapon.

"Stay back!" I shouted. "Keep your wings where I can see them!"

They responded with an all-out blitz. They wanted me to know who was master. I'd show them.

I opened fire. *Blam! Blam! Blam! Blam! Blam!*

But they flew so fast my darts only bounced off the metal walls and ceiling. Finally I winged one. It fell into a dusty corner of the vault, where it mewed pitifully. I crawled to where it lay. It was covered in bits of hair and flecks of dirt and plaster. It hopped up and down, flapping its good wing. I couldn't bear to watch it suffer. I put it out of its misery. I shoved it down my throat.

There was one dart left in my gun. I spun the cylinder and put the barrel in my mouth. My family would be better off without me. This was the only way to free myself—and them—from the Tyranny of Food. A dart in the brain would be fatal. They'd find me tomorrow morning, my brain oozing out of my nostrils onto my shirt.

"*We command thee not to do this,*" rang out the voice of Twinkie-Baal.

"Eat you," I said.

"*In time. We are the LORD YOUR GOD. Know that in heaven there is only us. Twinkies everywhere. Floating through the clouds. Playing harps. Et cetera.*"

I took the barrel from my mouth. "Et cetera? Really?"

"*Et cetera,*" boomed Twinkie-Baal.

I cried then. Long, wet, heaving sobs. Lamenting my oppression. There was no escape. No way out. I would be a slave forever, even in the afterlife. There was nothing I could do. Not even momentary relief from the hell that was life on earth.

Well, there was one thing.

I jammed the muzzle against my thigh and pulled the trigger. I caught the dart the first time.

Wham.

As the tranquilizing laxative coursed through my veins, I thought: One in six odds. Sometimes the casino pays.

FIFTEEN

COLD. WET.

I groped in my sleep for the bed covers.

Cold. Wet.

Where were the sheets? Chantal must have yanked the blankets over to her side. I lay back. I didn't complain. I didn't want to pick another fight.

Cold. Wet. Cold. Wet.

All right, already. I turned to grab the blanket from her, and woke up.

Something sharp dug into my leg. The dart. My service revolver lay next to me. I plucked out the needle and threw it to one side, where it joined a pile of identical syringes.

What time was it? I got to my feet. Cold diarrhea trickled down my leg into my shoe. Ick. I'd have to get cleaned up. Have a shower. Change of clothes. A clean trench coat. Idiot! Your watch. I must still be drugged. I pushed back my sleeve. 4 a.m.

Just enough time, if I hurried. To get to the airport and help the General capture Fatso. Too much time, in fact. Time to listen to my Twinkies parrot Chantal's words over and over again:

"I'm not the one killing him.

You are...

Three days, Frolick."

I shucked my dirty clothes and got in the shower. Was it true what she had said? That all the other ATFF agents "bring home the bacon"? There were a hundred thousand Food Enforcement officials across the country. They couldn't all be corrupt, could they? And if there were such a conspiracy, how come I knew nothing about it?

The hot water poured down my back. I hung my head.

"But what if she's right?" came the sing-song chant.

"The naturopath—is he a kook?

Or does he know the truth?

What if Nathan needs some food?"

I chuckled. Crazy talk. I reached for the soap.

But the Twinkies would not let up:

"What if air isn't enough, enough?

What if just oxygen isn't up to snuff?"

I cracked the bathroom window and took a big gulp of air. I chewed thoughtfully. But something was wrong. I swallowed more and more air, but it didn't fill me up.

Terror clawed at my soul. Was this what they meant by doubt? My digestion was destroyed. I could starve to death. Worse, I would be contagious to everyone around me until I regained my faith. What had happened to it, and how did I get it back?

The doubt gnawed at me like I was corn on the cob slathered in butter and salt. The sort of thing I used to eat when I was a food-addicted child.

"Suppose she's right," the Twinkies sang.

But this is ridiculous.

"For the sake of argument.

Suppose, suppose, suppose!"

Where would I go to get some food?

The evidence warehouse was out. Since the scandal last week, every calorie that went in or out got counted.

I could try the small-fry dealers on the street. Only problem was, they knew me on sight. *ATFF! Put the food on the ground and your hands in the air! Now!* They'd flush their stash as soon as they saw me. Chuck it down the sewer. I could not be bribed. They knew that. Even if I tried to explain my change of heart, there's no way they'd agree to sell me food.

That left the mafia big boys. But if we succeeded in nailing Fatso today, and tearing down his organization, where would I go to get food for Nathan? The kid would die. Chantal would leave me. Everything I'd worked so hard to build would fall apart.

What was the alternative? Refuse to arrest Fatso? Help him escape? How? Or warn him in some way, and risk being branded a traitor and shamed by all who knew me?

What in the name of the Prophet was I going to do?

SIXTEEN

I ARRIVED JUST IN TIME FOR THE PRESS CONFERENCE. A temporary command post had been set up at the base of the control tower. A score of dignitaries had assembled there, plus the press corps. A billion-dollar stealth tent concealed them from view. It consisted of a black canvas tarpaulin nailed to wooden supports.

"The man of the hour!" the General cried when he saw me, and hugged me to his chest. His ribbons dug into my face. I regretted teaching him this new hugging habit.

"Photo op!" Major Turdd barked, and the reporters obediently obliged.

The General beamed. "This is the man who made this glorious day possible!"

I blushed. "Just doing my job, is all."

"And modest, too." The General chuckled. "Make sure you put that in your stories, boys."

"Already got it in there, sir sir sir sir sir," Turdd said. He passed out folders to the journalists. "I wrote their stories for them. *New York Times... Washington Post...* But do feel free to change a comma here or there. Punctuation is not my strong suit."

"Wouldn't dream of it," said the *Post* stringer.

"Ditto the *Times*."

"Got a minute or two for questions," the General said. "Who's first?"

The *Times* reporter chewed on a fingernail. "Isn't it true you're a swell guy?"

"Sure is!" the General said. "Who else? What about the *Post* this morning? Hit me with a hard one."

The stringer thought for a moment. "Just how great is it to have a leader like the Prophet, anyway?"

"Pretty great, I'd say." The General smiled. "Well, that's all we have time for today, if you'll just—"

"General, I have a question," a ferrn voice said. From a European network, I forget the name. You ferrners are always watching their lying propaganda. He asked, "Isn't it true the US of Air uses snakelike toilet cams to spy on people's bottoms when they're on the toilet? And that there's a giant bunker full of poo analysis machines accessible through a back door passage in the Lincoln Memorial?"

The General frowned. "What a bunch of bullpoo. Where did you pick up that rumor?"

"Anonymous tip," the reporter replied. "Said it was time the NSA had some leaks. Said you'd know what that meant."

I knew what it meant. Green was alive. I was surprised he was conscious, much less making phone calls to Europe. I would have to visit him in the hospital, have a chat about this treasonous behavior.

The General's face turned red. I slipped out unnoticed. He could handle the wolves of the press corps on his own, I was sure. It was time for me to join the assault team. I wanted to be the first aboard Fatso's plane. Have a private conversation with the big man. Ask him his advice. Was it true you really needed to eat? Was my son going to die? If anyone knew the truth, I felt sure it would be him.

Captain Lean passed me the binoculars. "There. Do you see him?"

I scanned the purple horizon. Dawn was not far off. The jet was coming in low from the south. I grinned like the proverbial food-addicted child in a candy-dealer's den of vice.

"Well, hello, Big Boy."

The Thin Beret commander crouched next to me, huddled behind Fatso's limo. We had seized the car when it showed up, and arrested the driver. The luxurious interior was now crammed with thirty-eight of our country's thinnest commandos. The Godfather of Food was in for the surprise of his life.

"Wait." My stomach leaped. "He's turning away."

The captain took the binoculars. He swore and reached for his walkie-talkie. "Get me the General."

A tense moment ensued. Was this it? Say goodbye to the biggest collar of my career? I kept a souvenir scrapbook under my bed. I cut off the shirt collars of all the criminals I arrested and pressed them neatly between the pages. Fatso's had easily dwarfed the others, but when the charges were dropped, I had to give it back. I was looking forward to adding his to my permanent collection.

Captain Lean's walkie-talkie squawked. "It's the air traffic controller. Blobba-whatsizname. Pilot's asking for some kind of landing code."

Airmen in Mafia Waiter jackets were chucking empty boxes onto the conveyor belt. Above our heads, Blobbalicious bellowed,

"You trying to kill me? I lost five hundred pounds last night. Bring me a couple dozen cheesecakes before I starve to death!"

I grabbed the walkie-talkie. "Tell the blob that if he doesn't give out the right codes, and now, Agent Frolick will personally make sure he never eats again."

We waited for the command post to relay my message. Of course, we could have called for fighter escort and forced the plane to land. But the risk of Fatso throwing evidence out the door of the jet, evidence that might hit an honest air-eater in the mouth, right when he was having breakfast, when it might go down his throat by reflex—well, the risk was just too high to ignore. It would be far better to trick Fatso into landing.

Over the walkie-talkie I heard Blobbalicious drawl, "Uh, this is Boring Tower. Landing code is 'Food is good, Food is God.' Repeat, 'Food is good, Food is God.' Over."

A tense pause. We waited anxiously. Would it work?

Then a radio crackled: "Roger that, Boring Tower. Returning to land."

I scanned the sky once more with the binoculars. "He's coming back. Let's move."

The captain and I squeezed into the limo. We crawled over the others until we were plastered between a pair of boots, a helmet, two gun barrels and the ceiling. I craned my neck upside down to see out the window.

The jet landed with a squeal of tires. It turned off the runway and taxied to a halt. The door opened. Ground crew pushed stairs up to the aircraft. A man in a poo-colored suit appeared in the doorway. He carried a briefcase. The limo drew up at the foot of the stairs.

"On my mark," I said.

The man descended the stairs. He looked puzzled. Halfway down he stopped and looked around, as though expecting to be met by someone.

"Go!" I ordered.

Thin Berets tumbled out of the limo.

"ATFF!" I shouted. "Freeze!"

But the man broke into a trot, trying to get back up the stairs.

"Fire!" the captain ordered.

Thirty-eight darts slapped into the man's back. He slid head-first down the stairs to the ground. A pair of Thin Berets cuffed the limp, diarrhea-soaked food terrist. I led the way up the stairs, Laxafier at ready, expecting at any moment to see Fatso's great bulk appear and block the doorway.

What would I do when I saw him again? I was suddenly unsure. The man was an extremist bent on the destruction of our very way of life. How could I beg him for advice?

"But what if your way of life is wrong?" those insidious pastries cooed. *"What if eating food makes you strong?"*

We crept up the gangway, the Thin Berets behind me. It took almost half an hour, not counting frequent breaks, to make it to the door of the plane. I held up a hand. The shuffling behind me stopped. I was going in first. Alone.

Deep breath. Big air snack. One, two, and—

I surged inside, finger on the trigger. The cabin was empty. I hobbled down the aisle, sweeping each row for hidden interlopers. Past the massive in-flight food lab and the table in the shape of a pizza wedge. It was clean. All of it. Even the bed in the master bedroom was unslept-in.

I rapped on the cockpit door. The pilots waddled out. I shoved past them: lots of blinking lights. No Fatso.

"Where is he?" I demanded.

"Where's who?"

I pointed the gun at the pilot's chest. "Fatso, who else?"

The two men looked at each other. "Who's Fatso?"

My walkie-talkie crackled. "Congratulations!" the General's voice boomed. "You got him! Is he alive or dead?"

The evil mafia leader had escaped my grasp once again.

"But are you really sorry about that?" a Twinkie twittered.

I swallowed hard. "Neither, sir sir sir sir sir," I said. "He isn't here."

SEVENTEEN

THE DEADLINE HAD PASSED. 8:37 A.M. BY MY watch. The Coalition of the Fasting convened at the Thin House seven minutes ago. I had failed. Every minute that ticked by without Fatso in custody meant another poor child in the Turd World was pinching off a loaf, when they could be eating air. Like Manuel Tortilla down in Fondueras, struggling to free his people from their servitude to corn. Because of me, the Tyranny of Food would continue for another generation. School children would learn my name and revile me, cursing The Horrible Frolick for failing humanity at this all-important juncture.

"Because of you, your son will die!" a cloud of Twinkies declared cheerfully.

Unless, of course, I was wrong, and everything I thought I knew was a lie. But honestly, how likely was that? I scoffed. My doubting Twinkies retreated to a far corner of the ceiling.

The pilots knew nothing. Even their bowels were clean. They promised not to do it again, and I let them go. Now I sat across from the man in the poo-colored suit, his briefcase open on the jet's table between us.

"To: Special Agent Frolick," I read out loud. "From: Fatso.

With: love." I slapped the gift card on the table. "You mind telling me what in the food this is?"

The briefcase contained ten kilos of whole wheat flour. Street value: twenty-five million dollars.

We had searched the plane, of course. Pried open the ceiling, ripped open the hold. Nowhere for Fatso to hide. No hidden contraband. Only a single steak in the freezer, with a note absolving the pilots of ownership, and which the man in the poo-colored suit now pressed to his forehead. A large bruise had formed there, where he had face-planted into the tarmac. One arm was in a sling. It had taken all thirty-eight Thin Berets to lift him and carry him up to the plane door. It was a stirring patriotic sight. It reminded me of the flag-raising on Iwo Jima.

"Why are you asking me?" he groaned, and shifted the frozen T-bone to the other side of his forehead. "I'm just the messenger."

"I got you by the bowels," I told him. I squeezed my fist in his face. "You had enough poo up your hole to send you away for ninety days. A hundred and eighty, you don't cooperate."

He sighed. "Look. Agent Frolick. Fatso obviously knew you were waiting here for him. Right?"

I smacked my palm with my fist. Of course. Why hadn't I thought of that? Blobbalicious had warned Fatso somehow. Who else could it have been?

"So...?"

"So why did he send me?"

I put on my sternest countenance. "That's precisely what I intend to get to the bottom of."

The man dropped the bloody steak on the table. "As punishment. I screwed him on a food deal. Big mistake. He knows you're going to put me in Fat Camp."

"That doesn't explain why you were full of poo," I objected sharply.

The man's lip quivered. "He force-fed me at gunpoint. It was so…horrible. What was I supposed to do?"

"Oh you poor thing," I breathed, and clasped his hands in mine.

With a sob story like that, how could anyone remain unmoved? I let him go.

"No interruptions," I told the Thin Berets guarding the door.

I needed time to think. The question was what to do now. I turned the card over in my hands. The briefcase full of flour was a clue. I was sure of it. But what did it mean? I wished Green was here. He would know what to do.

"Take some, take some,
but be quick," my Twinkie cried.

Take what? The flour? But that's state's evidence.

"Take it, take it for your son.
Take it for yourself.
You're not the only one!"

I picked up a kilo bag. Taking it home would be illegal. I cut the bag open with a knife, moistened my pinkie and sampled the package. 100% pure, uncut powdered human misery. My stomach revolted at the taste. How could I have ever thought my son needed this?

The cabin door crashed open behind me. I banged my fist on the table. "I said, no interruptions."

The General barged into the food lab, flanked by half a dozen Thin Berets. They pointed their laxative rifles at me.

"What's going on, sir sir sir sir sir?" I asked.

He picked up the gift card and read, "From: Fatso. With:

love." He dropped the card on top of the flour. "Oh Frolick," he said. Tears welled up in his eyes. "How could you?"

I frowned. "How could I what?"

"Betray our country like this." He flung a pudgy finger at my head. "Arrest that man!"

"On what charge?" I demanded indignantly.

"The charge of treason."

YOU DOWN THERE. IN THE AUDIENCE. YES, YOU. Where do you think you're going? Hey! Stop them, Corporal.

What's she saying? She wants to *what?* Bring them down here.

Little girl, what's your name? That's a pretty name. That's a pretty dolly you have there. Now, your mommy says you have to go potty. Is that true?

Uh-huh. I see. Is it a number one or a number two?

That's what I was afraid of. Your parents should be ashamed of themselves. Giving you food. And at your age. Here. Take these. Four Prophet Packs for you and your family. Including one for your dolly. Embrace his words. Teach your dolly to embrace his words. You are so young. There is still time for you to free yourself from your addiction to food.

I know you still have to go. You're going to have to wait until we're finished broadcasting, is all. I'm sorry, ma'am, but you should have thought of that before getting your child hopped up on addictive caloric substances. If you really have to go, then do it right here on the floor in front of everyone.

That's a great idea, actually. Anyone has to do a number two, come down here to the front. Show us your shameful excretions.

The world will watch and judge you by your actions.

Grab them, Corporal. Don't let them leave. No one leaves. Lock the doors, post men at all the exits. I bring a holy message from the Prophet. You dishonor him and his name when you try to sneak out like that.

Now. Where was I.

Cap sprung me from the brig later that day. Writ of Foodeus Corpulus signed by Judge Meyer-Weiner himself. And I thought the Prophet had suspended Foodeus Corpulus three years ago.

Outside in the grey November sunlight, Cap pulled me aside. "How stupid can you be?" he demanded.

"What do you mean?"

"They think you warned Fatso!"

"But why would they think that?" I asked.

"In exchange for this?" Cap held up the briefcase. "They found you with your finger stuck in a bag of flour."

I brightened. "You taking that home for it to be destroyed?"

My boss rolled his eyes. "What is wrong with you, Frolick?" he asked. "Why can't you learn to play ball?"

"What kind?" I asked him.

"What kind *what*?"

I ticked them off on my fingers. "Basketball, baseball, football, volleyball…" I thought for a moment. "Did I say baseball?"

He covered his face with one hand. "You did."

I followed him to the car. "What are you saying, Cap? I should get more exercise?"

His Smart Car was easy to spot. As D.C. ATFF Battalion Commander, his cruiser had a six-foot-tall red siren on the roof, a beacon of revolving light that would equally serve most lighthouses.

He unlocked the passenger door and turned on me. "Get the Twinkie out of your ass, Frolick," he growled. "These people are playing for keeps. Be careful or you'll wind up like Green. Or worse."

I perked up. "How is Harry, anyway? You been to see him?"

He grunted and got in the car. "Full body cast. Eating air through a straw."

"Did he ask about me?"

The car puttered to life. "Said I'm supposed to remind you to do 'that thing.' Whatever that means."

We pulled out of the parking lot and rode in silence. When we hit the freeway, he turned on the siren. The car rocked back and forth with each revolution of the rooftop light. Soon we had the slow lane to ourselves.

"Where's the crime?" I asked.

"Just wanted a little privacy," he shouted. "Something in the glove compartment for you, by the way."

I gave a cry of joy. "My gun and badge and tape measure?"

Cap grinned. "Go on. Open it."

I popped the glove compartment. Inside lay a Twinkie. My Twinkie. The Twinkie the wardens had confiscated. The pastry sang out in recognition when it saw me.

Cap must have seen the horror on my face. "Don't worry," he said. "The windows are tinted. No one can see. You must be hungry."

I gritted my teeth against its attack. Rape me no more! I slammed the glove compartment shut. "Get it away from me!"

Cap stared out the window. "You know," he shouted. "Sometimes it's OK to have a snack."

I made a noise of disgust. "What makes you think I'd want to eat *that?*" Strange ideas people have about Twinkies.

"This isn't a test, Frolick."

"I know it's not," I said. "It's a very serious matter. I wish I knew what to do about it."

Could I ask Cap to arrest the Twinkies? But were they even subject to our laws? And then they'd take their rapist proclivities into prison with them. No. I couldn't let the other prisoners suffer like that.

He pounded the steering wheel with an open palm. "I'm telling you—no, I'm ordering you—to eat that Twinkie."

Then I saw what he was trying to do. To suspect me! Of food terrism! And telling me it wasn't a test. "It's OK," I said, and patted his knee. "You can tell Internal Affairs I passed."

He hung his head. For a moment I thought he was going to veer us off the road. "I like you, Frolick," he said at last. He didn't look at me. "You're a good man. I pulled a lot of strings to get you out of jail. Don't let me down."

"But what did I do that was so wrong?" I asked. "I don't understand."

He sighed. "I know you don't. So I'm going to give you a choice."

"What kind of choice?"

"One: you can conform. You can cooperate. You can eat. Food." He waved away my interruption. "Or two: you can go into exile. You've heard of the Underground Food Road?"

I made a rude noise. "Illegal emigrants," I said. "A conspiracy to funnel food terrists to Canafooda."

We pulled up in front of my house. Cap put his lips close to my ear. "I got friends in the Food Road. They can get you out. What do you say?"

The brown stain on his chin throbbed. He was serious, I realized. I pulled away.

"I love this country, sir," I said. "I worship the ideals she was founded on. Let me finish, sir. Please."

I passed a hand over my forehead. The siren was giving me a headache. "I will overlook this indiscretion. But if I *ever* hear of you pimping for rapist pastries again, or worse, proposing illegal emigration to a subordinate—it will be my duty to arrest you and put you in Fat Camp." I paused for breath. "Is that clear, sir?"

Cap regarded me for a moment. He killed the siren, and reached across me and opened my door.

"You're off-duty until further notice," he said. "An ordinary citizen. Nothing more."

"But what about the Prophet and the Coalition of the Fasting?" I exclaimed. "We've still got to catch Fatso."

"Drop it. You meddle in matters that don't concern you, we'll see who puts who in Fat Camp."

EIGHTEEN

BACK AND FORTH I PACED OUTSIDE THE BUNGALOW. A sign on the door read, "Dr. Full Stummick, Naturopath." Dead weeds covered the yard. Garbage spilled from a bin. Through the broken front window, a television glowed soundlessly. Rain spattered the sidewalk at my feet. Should I go in? Or should I go home?

Home meant Chantal and her incessant demands for food. A horde of Twinkies had chased me from the house, screaming, *"You're killing your son! He's going to die because of you!"* Maybe the doctor could help me cure my doubt. I had slunk into Georgetown after dark, looking for the address Green had given me.

Besides, a promise is a promise. I owed my partner. But this was no doctor's office. It was a run-down food house, no doubt full of junkies getting their fix. What was Green doing hanging out here?

This is a major criticism I have of France, by the way. I visit your cities and I have yet to see a single food house. It feels so—I don't know, ferrn. It is a mark of our great virtue—the righteousness of the United States of Air—that some people are unable to compete. Without the poor, the needy, the addicted and the insane, how would those of us who have everything be able to appreciate what we have, if not on the backs of their suffering? But don't worry. Once France bans food, you too will enjoy all the best our country has to offer.

So now, as I stared through the broken glass window of the house, trying to decide what to do, the Prophet appeared on the television screen. He wore a bandage over his nose. Looked like a press conference from earlier in the day. The running tickertape at the bottom of the screen read: "Coalition of the Fasting destroyed. Fatso at large." I hung my head. It was all my fault.

A family of four stumbled out the front door, glazed looks on their faces, hands caressing their bellies. The girl was five or six, the boy not much older.

"That was great!" the girl said, her blond curls bouncing as she skipped along the path. "Can we do that again sometime soon? Pweeze, Daddy, pweeze?"

The man spotted me blocking the path, my hands on my hips, glaring at them. He shushed his daughter.

Poisoning children from such a young age. Unbelievable. As the junkie dad passed, I hissed, "You ought to be ashamed of yourself."

"I don't know what you're talking about," he said, eyes cast down at the ground. He shepherded his children into a new Mercedes and drove off.

Some naturopath. Just another skanky parasite corrupting our young, enticing them with candy, then—*wham!* Addicted. Charge whatever he wanted after that.

Eat it. I had no gun and no badge, but I was going to turn this scumbag upside down. Make a citizen's arrest, if I had to. I strode up the path, lowered my shoulder and charged the door.

THE UNITED STATES OF AIR

I stifled a cry of pain. For a moment I thought I'd broken my arm.

"It's not locked!" a voice called out.

The doorknob turned easily. I stepped into the room. The silent TV cast flickering light over ripped sofas covered in broken glass. The carpet was blackened in places, where food addicts had made cooking fires. Broken plates covered a coffee table and spilled onto the floor. Junkie food paraphernalia. Typical.

"Soup's on!" the voice sang out from the back of the building.

Soup. Addictive caloric substances in a base of hot water. A cloud of Twinkies surrounded my head. They sang:

> Soupy-doopy dooper,
> don't be a party pooper.
> Have some soup!
> It's full of goop.
> And don't forget about your son…
> he needs to eat—
> he's not the only one.

The doubt returned. What if I was making a mistake? Were the Twinkies right? Did I really need to eat? Was it possible my whole life—the Prophet forbid—was a lie?

I shooed the Twinkies away and advanced down the dark hallway, glancing into each room as I passed. Empty. The sound of running water came from up ahead. Dishes clinked. I flattened myself against the wall and peered around the corner.

It was a food lab, all right. Spotless, compared to the front room. A huge vat simmered on the stove. A refrigerator hummed to one side. A man in a tall white chef's hat stood at the sink washing dishes. His hat scraped the ceiling. I put on my battle face. This must be "Doctor" Stummick himself.

Karate Chop Suey Attack: No. 17 on menu of Kung Yum Chop martial art tactics. Effective even without chopsticks as weapons. I employed it now. I leaped into the room, my hands harassing the air, and shouted, "ATFF! Don't move! You're under arrest!"

Stummick turned. "Chop Suey No. 17," he said. "I'm impressed, Agent Frolick." He grinned, and twirled his waxed mustachios. "Welcome to my humble soup kitchen."

I started at that, and accidentally cleaved an oxygen atom in two. "How do you know my name?"

"Agent Green has told me much about you." He laid a clean place mat and spoon on the table. "I guessed the rest."

"The rest of what?" I demanded. I karate chopped the air again. "What can you possibly know about me?"

"I know you love your wife and child. That you don't want to lose them." Stummick ladled soup from the vat into a bowl. "I know that you're hungry for the truth."

"That's right," I said. "The truth. And only the truth." I stared at the steaming bowl. Danger! Danger! Twinkies alighted on the rim of the bowl and dipped their forked little tongues into that noxious broth. "Nothing else."

The man chuckled and set the bowl on the table. "Not even for soup?" He pulled back a chair. "Please. *Bon appetit.*"

"Didn't you hear what I just said? I didn't come here for that."

He raised his eyebrows. "No? Then what did you come here for?"

"As a favor to Green. He asked me to pick up a shipment for his family. Whatever it is."

The chef indicated a burlap sack in the corner. "Rice and beans. Help yourself."

"What do I owe you?"

I had brought five thousand in used bills. It was my Twinkie money, in case of severe depopulation. I hoped it would be enough.

"Put your money away, Agent Frolick," the man said with a laugh. "I do not charge for food."

Same old strategy. Hook new clients, get them coming back for more. Wasn't going to work with me. Crazy junkie.

"In that case," I said, "I'll be on my way."

I grabbed hold of the sack and heaved, and sat down abruptly on the floor. It must have weighed five pounds. "Now what am I going to do?"

"Maybe if you eat some soup, you'll have the energy you need," the chef suggested.

I stood up. The Twinkies sang and danced around the bowl. I put my fingers in my ears, but they only sang louder. Step by lead-footed step I clomped toward the table. They were calling to me, demanding I obey.

"*There is no shame in obeying Twinkie-Baal,*" my god boomed. "*I am your master and you are my slave.*"

"No!" I shouted. "I will be a slave no more!"

I grabbed a rolling pin that lay to one side and smashed it down on the Twinkies' heads. The soup bowl exploded into fragments, splashing me with hot liquid calories.

"Take that!" I shouted. "And that! And that! And that!" The Twinkies hid themselves in the soup vat. I overturned the twenty-gallon pot, flooding the floor with hot liquid. I splashed through the deluge, hunting down every last flying Twinkie in that room until their cakey skulls oozed brains onto the sopping floor.

When I was finished, I stood there, panting, and finally let the rolling pin slide to the ground with a splash. For the first time ever, I had conquered my Twinkies. A warm glow of success filled my empty belly.

Stummick cleared his throat. I looked up. My host was a big man. A food terrist. And I just smashed up his laboratory equipment. Now what was he going to do?

"That soup was for members of *La Résistance*," he said. "To give them strength to resist their oppressors."

I cheered up. "In that case, I'm glad. They'll have a chance to eat some air."

"We are not the enemy you think we are," Stummick said. "We can help you."

I snorted. "How's that?"

"Suppose I told you there was a way to eliminate supply. Nail Fatso and decapitate the Food Mafia."

"But you're a food terrist," I objected. "Why would you want that?"

The man removed a pack of Gauloises from under one armpit. "I am not just any food terrist, *monsieur*," he said. "I am a French spy."

"Oh yeah?" I said. "Where's your stripey shirt?"

He unbuttoned his chef's smock. There they were—the telltale horizontal navy stripes.

"Gimme your phone," I said, looking around. "I'm calling the SS. Maybe it'll get me my badge back."

The man lit a cigarette. A cloud of blue smoke surrounded his head. "I don't think you heard me, Agent Frolick," he said. "I can help you catch Fatso. Then you'll get your badge back, plus a promotion."

I laughed. "You're going to help me find him?"

A Gallic shrug. *"Mais oui."*

"May we what?"

The chef/spy/naturopath blew smoke at the ceiling. He gazed at me from under hooded eyelids. "We put Fatso in business," he said. "He was an agent of ours. One of the best."

"Then you admit it!"

"But now he has gone, how you say? Rogue. Turned in many of our networks to the SS."

"Why would he do that?" I asked. "All you Frenchies want is to see us stuffing our faces."

"Fatso now is making hundreds of billions of dollars a year. More than he ever made before. Guns? Racketeering? Gambling? Prostitution? Who cares? These things are just play now, a handful of dust compared to the Food Syndicate."

"So why do you want to get rid of him?"

The man pulled a beret out from under his other armpit and swapped it for the chef's hat on his head. "Let me bare my soul to you, Agent Frolick," he said. He held a hand over his heart. "Our farmers of France are crying out for help. To sell once more their tinned *escargot* and frogs' legs in this country. What we want is to legalize food. But in order to do that, we must first eliminate supply."

"But that makes no sense!" I protested.

The cigarette flashed through the cloud of smoke. *"Au contraire, mon ami,"* he said. "We believe that when no food is left here in *Les Etats-Unis de l'Aire,* the people will rise up, and, led by our trained fighter-chefs of *La Résistance,* remove the Prophet from power and repeal the Amendment."

I listened to this speech with growing amazement, and finally laughed out loud. "That's where you're wrong," I said. "When

Fatso is gone, the people will dance in the street, hugging each other, sucking down the sweet air of liberty."

A smile tugged at the French spy's lips. "We agree to disagree, then. Do we not?"

The man had cured my doubt. I hadn't even asked him for a consultation. I felt alive again. I pounded my fist on the table. "I could not agree to disagree more. What's the plan?"

NINETEEN

S TUMMICK LIT A FRESH CIGARETTE. "TOMORROW is your, how you say? Day of Giving Thanks?"

"That unholy Thursday," I groused. "What about it?"

Maybe Fatso had something to celebrate at his Thanksgiving banquet this year. I sure didn't.

"What you do is simple," Stummick continued. "Go undercover to this feast. Sneak into the kitchen. Poison the soup. *Voilà!* No more mafia."

A makeup artist and member of *La Résistance* had joined us in the kitchen.

"Tonight you shall be Alberto Caponey Baloney of Chicago," the man told me, holding up the mask of the ugliest and fattest member of the Food Mafia. Boils sprouting hairs blistered the man's forehead. A thick scar meandered across one cheek and severed the nose in two.

"But what about the real Baloney?" I asked. "Isn't he going to be there? Rather awkward if we both show up."

The makeup artist sighed. "Alberto, I am sorry to say, suffers from high cholesterol. *Si triste, non?* His favorite food is pig dick on a stick, deep-fried in pig fat. A Chicago delicacy. His doctor has been warning him for years to cut down. Sadly, he refuses. It will come as no surprise to anyone when he is found dead due to a heart attack. Naturally, the body won't be discovered until Saturday or Sunday at the earliest. *La Résistance* will see to that."

I tried on the fat suit and mask. It itched.

"Whatever you do, don't scratch," the makeup artist warned.

"How do I walk? How do I talk? How do I hold myself?" I asked. "I've never met Baloney in person."

"With that I cannot help you, *monsieur.* You will have to, how you say? *Improviser.*"

I turned to Stummick. "These are real live human beings we're talking about," I said. "Addicts and food terrists, sure. But otherwise people just like me. How can I assassinate hundreds of my fellow creatures?"

Stummick puffed on his Gauloise. "They are guilty, are they not?"

"They are innocent until proven guilty," I scolded him. "Who am I to take the law into my own hands?"

"You're the law," he said. "You're ATFF. Remember?"

"That's true," I said. "I *am* the law." Although his argument left me unconvinced. "Why don't I call Cap, then?" I suggested. "Have the fatty wagons ready. We can round them up. Put them in Fat Camp."

"*Non! Monsieur.*" The spy stubbed out his cigarette. "You must speak of this to no one. Fatso has spies everywhere. Even in your department. One little phone call, and—*poof!* You will never see Fatso again."

Reluctantly, I agreed to his plan. In the meantime I decided to visit Judge Oscar Meyer-Weiner, ask his advice. I know, I know, Stummick said to tell no one. But if you can't trust a Food Court judge, who can you trust?

TWENTY

HE NEXT MORNING, I SLIPPED INTO THE courtroom and sat in the back—and worried. Had Meyer-Weiner heard about my suspension? What would he say? Would he still be willing to give me the advice I so desperately craved? I chewed my fingernails—and swallowed, cursing myself for my lack of faith—and waited for him to finish with the current defendant, a seventy-eight-year-old food terrist from a nearby nursing home.

"It was just a cracker," the old woman said, her voice wavering. "I was so hungry. Just a little cracker. That was all." She looked around the gallery, looking for allies, but found only accusing stares. "Does no one else feel hunger anymore?" she cried out. "Am I the only human being left who remembers what it's like to eat and feel full?"

"Counsel!" Meyer-Weiner exploded from the bench. "Control your client!"

Her lawyer stood up, an obvious air-eating virtuoso. He stroked his glistening waddle with a manicured thumbnail. "Mrs. Jenkins has been a food terrist all her life, Your Honor," he said. "At her age it is difficult for her to make the adjustment, to learn the heavenly secrets of atmospheric consumption. As

210

even a short stint in Fat Camp will likely prove fatal, we therefore throw ourselves on the mercy of the court."

"Understood," the judge said. He lifted his gavel. "In that case—"

"I do nothing of the sort," the woman said, her voice rising in a screech. "I eat, and I like to eat, I don't see anything wrong with eating, and I'm going to keep on eating just as much as I feel like. Or should I say just as much as I can get my hands on these days."

"French propaganda," Meyer-Weiner thundered. "You undermine this great nation when you repeat such obvious lies. Think of the damage you to do to our troops, who are fighting and dying in the Global War on Fat to keep this country safe."

"You ought to be ashamed of yourself, young man," she said, and wagged a finger at the judge. Meyer-Weiner was in his sixties. "That Prophet of yours, too." She shook her fist at the portrait of our Divine Leader, a massive oil canvas that hung behind the bench. The artist had rendered him with a halo and wings. "Eat air," she scoffed. "Next you'll be telling me to drink gasoline and shit petunias."

"Madam," Meyer-Weiner said, and pointed his gavel at her head. "If you do not refrain from this sort of behavior, I will be forced to—"

"I will refrain from nothing!" she shrieked. "It's about time someone gave you people a piece of her mind. You're the ones who killed my grandchildren. Jacob six and Andrea eight and Justin three and a bunch of others I can't remember now. Skeletons! That's all they were when we buried them. Bits of skin and bone delivered in a pine box from that Fat Camp of yours. And draped in a flag! As if that makes it all better! Well I got nothing left to lose. I'll scream until the Prophet himself hears me! Let me go!"

The bailiff grabbed her around the waist and lifted her off the ground.

"Guilty," the judge intoned. Smack of the gavel. "Thirty days. Sixty more for repeating French propaganda. Ninety more for blaspheming the Prophet. Get her out of here."

"Let go of me!" she hollered, and struggled in the bailiff's arms. Her lawyer followed her out, pushing his client's walker ahead of him, his jaws chewing on something almost imperceptibly.

"Next case!"

I stood up. "May it please the Food Court."

Meyer-Weiner squinted into the gallery. "Special Agent Frolick!" he said. He waved his gavel at the crowd, and gestured at me. "A true Airitarian hero. What brings you before the seat of blind lady justice?"

Oh thank the Prophet. He hadn't heard about my suspension after all. Still, I was reluctant to speak freely in front of so many people.

"Perhaps a fifteen-minute recess would be welcome by the court?"

The judge nodded. "Fifteen minutes." He banged his gavel and swung down off the bench. I followed him into chambers.

I'd known Meyer-Weiner since my days on the D.C. force. Back then the press had dubbed him Judge Hang M. High, or Hangnail for short. He liked the nickname so much he asked all his friends to call him that.

Together we'd sent thousands of marijuana users to prison for life. "Half a joint?" Hangnail used to say. "Let 'em get ass-raped for the rest of their lives and die of AIDS. They deserve no better."

"Now, now, Hangnail," I'd scold him, over a late night all-you-can-eat buffet, plates piled so high we could no longer see each other. "I find it hard to believe that the other prisoners would ever do such a thing."

"Nothing like a good back door gangbang to teach a man the true meaning of justice," he would grunt, and sneak outside to smoke a funny-smelling cigarette.

Our late-night buffets ended when the Prophet came to power and revealed the far greater menace lurking in our midst—food itself. Meyer-Weiner had the highest conviction rate of any Food Court in the country. What was even more amazing, he was just as obese now as he was when I first met him.

He flopped back into his chair and closed his eyes. "I am so tired of these goddamn food terrists I could puke," he said. "Is it really so hard not to get caught?"

"And getting harder," I said with enthusiasm.

He opened one eye. "That's the spirit. Pretend you're still on the bandwagon."

I puzzled over this. "What band? What wagon? I don't even play an instrument."

The judge chuckled and slapped his knee. "You and me are survivors, Frolick." He stood up. "Can I offer you some refreshment?"

"Vanilla air, you got it," I said. "Asparagus if you don't."

"You ought to do standup, you know that?" He opened a wall safe and took down a plate. I gazed in horror at what lay there.

"Hangnail!" I exclaimed. "Where in the name of the Prophet did you get that?"

The judge held up a knife. "I'll cut, you pick." He winked. "Sound fair?"

A small chocolate doughnut gazed up at me like the Eye of Lucifer. I struggled to my feet. "Are you offering me an addictive caloric substance?" I lowered my voice. "Here? At Food Court? In judge's chambers?"

"There's no need to whisper," he said, and took a massive bite of the doughnut. "And you can drop the act. No one can hear us. I locked the door."

I pointed at the open bathroom door and mouthed the words "Toilet tap."

He swallowed. "I'm sorry?"

"The NSA has tapped every toilet in the country. Picks up anything within earshot."

The judge stared at me for a moment, then roared with laughter. "And I thought I was paranoid." He patted me on the shoulder. "*I'm* the one who orders toilet taps installed, my friend. Not the other way around!"

"You don't believe me?" I asked. I went into the bathroom, rolled up my shirt sleeves and plunged a hand into the toilet bowl.

"Whatcha looking for, my day-old turd?" Hangnail called out from the other room. He cackled and stuffed another bite of doughnut into his mouth.

My arm disappeared into the cold water. My elbow hit bottom. There. It was moving backward, trying to avoid me. But not fast enough. I grabbed its head and pulled.

Inch by inch it emerged from the toilet bowl. Unlike the prototypes I'd seen at the NSA, shimmering and colorful, this one was encrusted in poo. Three feet long and more it came, writhing in my grip until it let go of the plumbing and I stumbled backward against the bathroom wall. From the judge's chambers came a crash.

Panting, I held the squirming thing in both hands and advanced into the room. A broken plate and a quarter doughnut lay at the judge's feet.

"My God," he said. "What is it?"

"Like I was telling you," I said. "A toilet tap. Now do you believe me?"

At the head of the snake, a small video camera twitched back and forth, looking at the two of us. A bulge like a microphone protruded from its nose.

"Shit! It's seen me!" The judge wiped chocolate from his lips. "Smash it! Do something!"

He ripped the toilet tap from my hands and swung the snake in the air. The head cracked against the edge of his desk. The mechanical creature contorted in lifelike agony. A second whack, and a third brought a crunching noise of shattered circuitry. The thing went limp in Hangnail's hands.

"This is all your fault," he growled at me, shaking the dead snake in my face.

"My fault?" I said. "Look at the poo caked to its sides. It's been watching you for months."

"It has?" The judge shuddered and cast the snake on the floor.

"Taking videos of your bowel movements," I said. "It can even read your thoughts."

"My thoughts! But how?"

"By analyzing your ass lips when you're on the potty. It's designed to detect food terrists."

Hangnail clutched his chest. "Then they know everything!"

"Exactly," I said. "That's why they call it Total Poo Awareness. Total Power."

"But now what do we do?"

My eyes widened. "That's what I came here to ask you."

He fumbled in his desk drawer. "Only one thing we can do. Emigrate."

He pulled out a passport. All passports had been confiscated years ago. I wondered how he had managed to hold on to his.

"We can't do that!" I wailed. "Then we'd become illegal emigrants!"

"They're coming for us, Frolick," he said. "We've got to get out of here now." He looked around wildly and pushed a chair against the door.

"Wait," I said. "What if there's another way?"

"Like what?"

I told him all that had happened in the last forty-eight hours, since Green and I arrived to investigate the dead pizza dealer. When I came to Full Stummick's plan to poison the Food Mafia, the judge whistled.

"So you want to make yourself the new Fatso?" He clapped me on the back. "I didn't think you had it in you."

"What are you talking about?" I asked. "The plan is to get rid of supply. Then we'll finally be free to eat air. And you won't have to go for treatment for your doughnut addiction. The whole country will be like one giant Fat Camp."

Hangnail looked at me funny. "You really believe that, don't you?"

"Of course," I said. "Don't you?"

He slumped back into his chair. "Killing the current mafia leadership won't make any difference," he said. "Other criminals will take their place. They always do."

"Not this time, Mister Cynic," I said, hands on my hips. "You sound just like that French spy, you know that?"

"Oh yeah? How's that?"

"His crazy theory—try not to laugh—is that if we knock off the mafia, and no one can get food, instead of celebrating, the people will rise up and overthrow the government. Stupid, I know."

A look of wonderment passed over Hangnail's face. "I hadn't thought of that," he said. "It's brilliant. Without the mafia, there'll be major disruptions in supply. For weeks. Maybe months. Then all this bullshit goes away. And I can end this stupid diet I'm on."

"That's the spirit!" I exclaimed. "Kick that doughnut habit once and for all, and suck down God's own air, like the rest of us." I anointed his scalp with a vial of water from the sacred drinking fountain in the men's locker room at Fat Camp. I carry one with me at all times to baptize errant sheep who return to the fold. "So what do you think I should do?"

He wiped the water from his forehead and took me by the arm. "We've got to get you out of here before they come. You're this country's last and only hope, you understand?"

I had never seen my friend like this before. "I'll do my best."

"With a single stroke, you can save our country from this madness."

"End the curse of food," I said brightly. "We agree. That's why I need your advice."

"Sure," he said. He dialed the combination to the safe. "What do you need?"

"We're talking about the extrajudicial assassination of Airitarian citizens right here in the US of Air. Who am I to set myself up as judge, jury and executioner?"

He turned and looked back at me over his shoulder. "So… what do you want from me?"

"A verdict."

At that moment a pounding shook the door. "Meyer-Weiner!" a voice shouted. It sounded familiar. "Judge Oscar Meyer-Weiner!"

"Your bailiff?" I whispered.

Hangnail's face went grey. "They're here. Quick!" He pushed me around the desk.

I resisted. "But we're talking about mass murder."

His face took on the grim aspect he wore when sentencing food smugglers to the suffocation chamber. "Special Agent Frolick," he said, using his solemn voice of justice, "I hereby sentence all members of the French Food Mafia to death. That good enough for you?"

I stroked my chin. "But what about their wives and girlfriends? Some of them are totally innocent. When I poison the soup, they'll die too."

He held up an index finger. "Guilt by association, my friend. It's in the Constitution."

"It is?"

"Sure."

"Judge Meyer-Weiner!" the voice outside shouted. "I know you're in there! You and Frolick."

I recognized the voice. It was Erpent. "The SS!"

"Hurry!" the judge hissed. "Your mission is too important." He opened the safe door, and held out his hands to boost me up.

"I'll count to three!" Erpent shouted. "And then my TWAT team will break down the door. One!"

"But their women," I insisted. "I need your verdict."

"Two!"

"Guilty," he said. "Sentence is death by poisoned soup. May they rest in peace. Now are we good?"

Something brushed softly against the door. Like a cat wanting to come inside. Probably a battering ram. Standard TWAT team uses twenty guys, swinging in shifts.

"Hey, that's not fair!" I shouted. "You didn't finish counting to three!"

"I'm lousy at math!" Erpent shouted back.

"Come on, Frolick," Hangnail said. "Let's go!"

I stood on his hands and looked in the safe. I would barely fit. "There isn't room for both of us to hide!"

"The back panel's an escape hatch," he whispered. "It takes you down a garbage chute to the rear exit. I'll be right behind you."

I pushed my way through the back panel and tumbled head-first down a narrow shaft. I cradled my head in my arms and prepared for impact.

Woompf.

I landed in a dumpster full of foam padding. I rolled out of the way, expecting the judge's substantial bulk to be right behind me. He didn't come. A faint shouting echoed down the garbage chute.

"I can't fit!" Hangnail called out. "Frolick, I'm too fat!" The sound of metal screeching and bending. "They're here! Follow the plan! It's a good plan! It's the only way! It's the—*no!*"

Noises of struggle. Silence. Another voice took its place.

"Run, little Frolick," Erpent said. "I'm coming for you."

I ran.

TWENTY-ONE

ALL AROUND ME FACES FROM WANTED POSTERS laughed and chattered, their corpulent bodies clad in tuxedos, their women in colorful silk. These were men I had sworn to arrest on sight. I tugged at my neoprene mask. We stood in line outside a Georgetown high school gym, shivering in the chill autumn air. I wouldn't be arresting them tonight. But if my mission was successful, they would soon be getting their full measure of justice.

"Don Baloney!" cried a voice at my elbow. A short man, twice as wide as he was tall, with a greasy blond ponytail. I recognized him as Hippie LePew, head of the Berkeley branch of the Syndicate. What do you say to a California gangster famous for his human sausage and breast milk pizza?

"Hippie," I said, in my best South Side twang. I took his hand. "How's it hanging out there in Cali?"

"You know me," he said. "King of the Crunchy Granola." He lowered his voice, kept my hand tight in his. "I just want you to know, you have my full support."

I nodded my head, mystified by this. "As…you do mine?"

Hippie looked at me sideways for a moment. Had I given myself away? Then he clapped me on the shoulder and laughed.

"Don Baloney, always a joker. Right? Am I right?"

The gangster turned to greet another colleague. I fingered the vial of poison in my pocket. Enough to kill every last member of the Food Mafia present here today. O Mine Prophet, I swore silently. How was I ever going to pull this off?

"Don Baloney! Yoo-hoo!" A woman in tight green silk waved a mink wrap in my face. She jiggled her waddle at me. "You remember Boise, don't you?" She giggled. "The spud plucking?"

Rapid calculation: Baloney wasn't married. No known girlfriend. Maybe he was having an affair. But she would be able to spot me as a fake. *Cut her loose.*

"Do I know you?" I asked coolly. "Have we met?"

Her jaw gaped wide. "And after all I've done for you," she whispered.

Oops?

The gym doors clanged open. Two guards with Uzis—the kind that use real bullets, totally illegal, by the way—took their places to either side. A shadow loomed behind them. It stepped forward, and the light fell across a man's face.

Fatso himself.

The line advanced until his gruesome form filled my world. Blubbery cheeks spread wide, cavernous mouth agape, shark teeth ready to engulf me. An open palm slashed at my abdomen. Would he disembowel me if he found out? He'd been known to strangle informers with their own intestines. Fingers squeezed my bicep through the fat suit. A warm hand grasped my own.

"Caponey Baloney!" the Godfather of Food cried. "How eez my-ee fayvoreet don frum Chicago?"

He waited. I was supposed to say something. Of course I was supposed to say something. But my voice! Would he recognize my voice wasn't the same as the real Baloney? M-f-word s-word g-d-word! Why hadn't Stummick thought of that? They could at least have recorded the dead man's voice before killing him. That way I could have practiced. Fatso's grin slipped.

"Yoo say nuh-seeng, my fren," he said, lowering his voice so the guards could not hear. "Pare-haps bee-cuz yoo air fatt-air zan mee, yoo seenk yoo air a bigg-air man zan mee."

Still my tongue refused to obey, and Fatso's grin turned terrible. "I haf haird many seengs frum my *agents* een Chicago, fren Baloney. How yoo deeslike how zee *organisation* eez run. How yoo seenk yoo can doo bett-air zan mee."

What had I stumbled into? *Come on. Just f-ing word say something. And attitude. You're a gangster. Attitude.*

"Vicious rumor, Don Fatso," I said. "Lies designed to drive us apart." I lifted his hand to my mouth and kissed his pinky ring. The guards hovered close by, fingers on the triggers of their Uzis. "It's true that I's a bigger man than you," I said, and patted my stomach. "But you's got more brains than me."

Fatso seemed to relax a little. "Zat eez troo."

"Besides," I said. "You know how much time it takes to get this fat? When I got time to want your job, huh? I's happy with Chicago."

"Hey! We're hungry back here!" yelled a voice behind me.

"Yeah, come on, what's the holdup?" a woman screeched.

"Quiet back zair," Fatso roared, "or I weel roast yoo ho-ell like peegs, and feed yoo to zee uzz-airs."

The line went silent.

I forced a chuckle. "That's what I love about you, Don Fatso."

"Wat eez zat, pleez?"

"Your sense of humor."

Fatso stared at me for a moment. Then he laughed. "Yoo all rite, Baloney. Tell me zumsing."

"Anything, Don Fatso."

He turned in profile. "Doo I look fat een zees?"

"No, no," I said, thinking fast. "You look great in that, boss. Skinny. As the Prophet. Skinnier." I did my best to boom a belly laugh.

"Zat eez not zo, my fren," Fatso said with a smile, "boot eet eez nice uv yoo to say so." He poked me in the gut. "Tomorrow wee begin our die-ets. But not tonite, *non?*"

I nodded. "Not tonight."

"Go find yor seet," Fatso said. "Tonite yoo seet wees me, at zee table uv honor."

I bowed at the neck, unable to bow lower down. "It is I who am honored."

With that I waddled past Fatso, between the two guards, and into the high school gymnasium. The place had been decked out like a ballroom from Versailles: gilt furniture, golden candelabra, wall tapestries, rich carpets. Here and there the gleaming parquet floor of the school's basketball court peeked through the gaps. On the stage an empty throne overlooked the hall. A table for eight stood to one side.

"Don Baloney." A skeletal-looking head waiter consulted a clipboard. "Will you follow me please, *monsieur?*"

"Show me where the food is, man," I boomed, to the delight of those already inside. "That's what we're here for, isn't it?"

"Precisely so, *monsieur.*" He eyed my girth. "This way, *s'il vous plaît.*"

He led me toward the stage. I studied the tables as we passed. The plates were larger than normal—platters, really. And in the shape of a trapezoid. I stifled a groan. Unbelievable. Such spite.

Stairs led up to the stage. The head waiter gestured for me to climb.

"Up there?" I said. The last thing I wanted was for the entire mafia to stare at me. The fewer people who saw me, the better.

"Of course, *monsieur,*" he said. "You sit at the table of honor. Did Don Fatso not inform you?"

"Oh, *that* table of honor." I laughed.

I climbed the stairs and took my seat. The other seven chairs stood empty. A vacant throne twenty feet tall and six feet wide sat next to the table. The head waiter loosened my napkin and tucked it into my shirt collar. As he did so, he whispered in my ear, "I have to say I am surprised to see you here after what happened last year."

"What happened last year?" I whispered.

"Hey Baloney! Good to see you!" shouted someone from down on the main floor. An unknown gangster waved up at me. I waved back.

The waiter straightened up. "May I wish you a spectacular *bon appetit, monsieur,*" he said. "Tonight's *dégustacion* will require all of your substantial, err, talents."

I wondered at the waiter's words. What had happened last year? Was I screwed already? The ATFF dossier on Baloney was as thin as the man was fat. What crucial piece of his bio was I lacking? I settled back in my chair and sighed. Too late now.

The others straggled in. There was Hippie LePew, and the woman from Boise, whoever she was. Spaghetti Marinara made a grand entrance. He was the Italian head of the New York mob. Then came Chew Chow, the former Chinese triad who ruled the Bay Area from a hilltop in Chinatown. The last one in before they shut the doors was Gassy the Geek. I'd heard a lot about Gassy.

From Texas. Skinniest man in the room, and owner of a bum trumpet like no one else. They said he lived on chicken blood. Bit their heads off live and poured the blood down his throat.

Ice cubes crashed at my elbow. My water glass filled. I jumped in my chair.

A young waiter stood at my side. "My apologies, *monsieur*. I will be your personal waiter this evening."

Attitude, Frolick. You're a gangster, d-word it.

"I ask for water?" I snarled.

The man stammered, "*Non, monsieur.*"

I bunched up my fists. "Then what you doing, huh?"

The waiter inclined his head. "Please do not kill me, *monsieur.*"

"Quit your blubbering," I said, as irritably as I could manage. My heart went out to him. I had hurt his feelings.

The man left the pitcher of water on the table and scurried down the stairs. I followed him with my eyes, and let an idle hand drape across my pocket. The vial of poison was still there. *Remember your errand, you idiot.* You could poison the pitcher of water, but that wasn't ideal. Only kill half a dozen people that way. Might even miss Fatso. No. Got to get into the kitchen somehow, and do it soon. Hang on. Wasn't soup usually a first course? Make that real soon.

The waiter walked along the side wall and pushed backward through a swinging door. The crash of plates and an oath in French escaped the gap before it swung shut again.

That was where I had to go. The food lab. But how was I going to get in there without getting caught? I was the fattest man in the room, even fatter than Fatso himself, and I was sitting in full view of everyone. Why couldn't Stummick and the makeup artist have chosen a less conspicuous alter ego?

The hall was packed. And still I was the only one on stage. Fatso entered, and the guards chained and padlocked the doors. The don of dons led a procession toward the throne, including Marinara, Chow and Gassy. They mounted the stairs and took their seats, except for Gassy, who approached a waist-high microphone. Fatso reclined on the jewel-encrusted throne. Rumor on the street was that the chair was made of solid platinum.

Fatso put his hand over his heart. The others did the same. Gassy dropped his pants and farted the "Star-Spangled Banner." He had some trouble with the high notes. When he was finished, he received a standing ovation.

"Today eez a day uv Sanksgeeveeng," Fatso said in a loud voice. The hall went quiet. "Zerefore let oos geef sanks."

Waiters brought each of us a magnum of French bubbly sour grape juice and a tall, narrow glass delivery device. A chorus of popping corks echoed in the hall. The magnum crunched into an ice bucket at my side. I was supposed to drink all of that?

"Let oos geef sanks," the Godfather of Food said again, and lifted his glass in a toast, "for zee Prophet."

Snickers from below. And not the candy bar kind, either. (Trust me on this one. I know the difference.)

"Do not mock," Fatso said sternly. "Weezout zee Prophet, wat bizz-nees wood wee haf?" He let the question linger. Heads nodded. "Be-cuz wee air bizz-nees-men. Men like oos bilt zees cun-tree. Wee air wat make zees cun-tree great."

More heads nodded.

"Yeer by yeer ow-air pow-air grows," he continued. "Sanks to one man. Zee Prophet. Zee *decisions* wee now make—wat food to import, wair to sell eet, and, *crucialment,* at wat price," —this drew chuckles from the audience— "zeez *decisions* air

more important zan any law zat zee Air Congress passes, or proc-
lamation from zee Zeen House, or *jugement* from zee Supreme
Food Court. Zerefore, *je dis encore, merci beaucoup, Monsieur le
Prophet.*" And so saying, he drained his glass.

The others repeated the toast and emptied their glasses. I
brought the delivery device to my lips, but could not drink.
How could I? Alcohol contains calories. The others were staring
at me. They expected me to drink. They probably expected me
to eat, as well. How was I going to survive this evening?

I opened my mouth wide and poured the sour grape juice
down my shirtfront. Fatso frowned. My waiter stepped forward
and patted me dry. At a nod from the throne, he refilled my glass.

The man on the most expensive chair in the world lifted his
champagne flute once more. "To zee Prophet," he said quietly.

I echoed the toast. Fatso drank. He looked at me. Forgive
me, Mine Prophet, I whispered, and freebased the prohibited
liquid down my throat. Bubbles burned my tongue. I forced
myself to swallow. I gagged, but managed to keep it down.

Fatso said something to Marinara on his left. The Italian
laughed. Soon the whole table was giggling. They kept glancing
at me. At Don Caponey Baloney. What did that mean?

I felt funny. Dizzy. The calories must have gone straight to
my head. I had to find some excuse not to eat. As it was, it would
take months to undo the damage from the glass of champagne.

Fatso tapped his champagne flute with a large carving knife.
"Dinn-air eez sairved!"

The soup! D-word it. I was too late. The waiters returned
from the kitchen carrying gigantic silver platters, each covered
with a domed lid. Wait a minute. That didn't look like soup.
Maybe there was still hope. My waiter put a platter down in
front of me and lifted the lid.

Flashback to Gramma's house. A roast turkey big enough for our family of eighteen, plus leftovers for a week. I stared around the room in horror. Everyone had a whole turkey. Except for Fatso, who had an entire suckling pig, an apple clenched between its crispy jaws.

"Hey Fatso," Gassy called out. "Great hors d'oeuvre, man."

Hors d'oeuvre?

The mafioso tore at the dead birds with their hands. Now what was I going to do? The mission had failed. Or was the soup course later? Either way I'd have to play along. But that meant consuming the dead flesh of a fellow creature.

I studied the glistening brown skin of the avian corpse in front of me. I tugged at a turkey leg, and it came away in my hand. Poor thing. I wiped away a tear. How much worse could things possibly get?

My waiter slid a platter of mashed potatoes onto the table next to my turkey. The other diners got the same. A pyramid of pureed spuds, ripped untimely from their earthy womb, that towered to the same height as the candelabra. In order to eat we must be so cruel. Upturned grey horns protruded from the mash. I let out a cry of grief when I realized what they were: ground up pig flesh stuffed into the animal's own small intestine. I went immediately into mourning.

"Baloney!"

Fatso tore at a pig leg with his teeth. "Wat eez zee problem? Don yoo like eet?"

"Great turkey," I said, with a neoprene grin. "Fabulous spread. Ain't got nothing like this in Chicago."

"Funny yoo say zat," he said, and swallowed. "Cuz I doo not see yoo eeting nun uv eet, *mon ami.*"

I speared a tiny fragment of breast meat, apologizing silently to that once-proud bird. At Gramma's house we had engaged in similar gluttonous acts of cruelty, and called it family values. A shudder rippled through me. Thank the Prophet this murderous, self-indulgent, unholy day had been finally banned.

"Don't think he's gonna eat nothing, boss," Gassy said, and farted again, this time the theme song to *Top Gun*.

I touched the morsel to my lips. The smell made me nauseous. To eat meant going against everything I believed in. To refuse to eat meant torture and death. The fork slipped from my hand and clattered to my plate.

"Guess I'm just not hungry," I said.

Everyone at the table stared at me. Fatso pounded the table. "Yoo heer zat?" he roared. "Baloney eez not hun-gree!" He laughed, and soon the entire hall was laughing with him.

A gunshot ended the merriment. Fatso held a gold-plated pistol overhead. He lowered the gun until it pointed at me.

"Yoo doo not eat be-cuz yoo air not hungree?" he asked. "Or be-cuz yoo seenk eet eez poisoned?"

Poison! *Change the topic, fast!*

"Of course not," I said. "Why would it be poisoned?"

"Gassy," Fatso ordered. "Gif Frolick yor bird."

A cavalry charge of a fart sounded in the hall. "Sure thing, boss."

Our waiters interchanged the turkeys. Fatso's gun did not waver.

"Now eat."

I looked down at the turkey. Another avian friend, ruthlessly murdered in cold blood to satisfy our addiction. My lips cringed.

"I can't."

Fatso's finger tightened on the trigger. "Or maybe yoo air not zee reel Baloney. Maybe yoo air sum airhead cop."

The Twinkies returned in a glorious flutter of translucent wings. They sang a new song:

Life or death.
Eat or die.
It's food, not meth—
you're a spy!

They clapped their wings together and chanted:

At-ti-tude!
At-ti-tude!
At-ti-tude!

I glared back at Fatso's gun. "Eat you," I said. I ripped a drumstick from Gassy's partially dismembered turkey and bit off the biggest piece I could fit in my mouth. I chewed it twice and swallowed. The gun followed everything I did. I grabbed the serving spoon and slopped a mound of mashed potatoes down my throat. A sausage followed. The hard lump of my lost porcine brother—may he rest in peace—galloped down my throat, bruising my innards.

I shoved more and more food into my body, defiling that air-eating temple. I kept my eyes on my plate and ate as though the fate of the world depended on it. Which, as I was later to find out, it did. My Twinkies cheered and clapped, urging me on. It was the first time I had eaten anything in more than three years. It wasn't long before nausea took hold.

Vomit filled my mouth. Oh no! I completely forgot. I could die of overdose. Like the junkies we often found in the gutter, all skin and bones, dead from gluttony. All around me the sounds of slurping and gulping. Fatso mauled his pig leg. His gun lay on the table. I swallowed the mouthful of puke.

I needed to get to a bathroom, and fast. I pushed back my chair and struggled to my feet.

Fatso glanced up. "And now I suppose yoo air going to tell oos yoo air full?"

"Leaky prostate, boss," I said. "That OK with you?"

"Use a catheter," Chew Chow said. "What I do. That way you don't miss a single course."

"Plus a colostomy bag," Marinara added. Everyone at the table groaned. "I know, I know, it sounds gross," he said. "But seriously." He gestured at the food. "Who's got time to take a dump?"

Fatso grunted and returned his attention to his dead baby pig. He chucked a half-eaten leg over his shoulder. The waiters behind him scuffled, and one came out of the fray with the gnawed bone in one hand, his white tuxedo jacket ripped at the shoulder.

The nausea boiled inside me. I edged around the table to the stairs.

Gassy wiped his lips, and farted "America the Beautiful." When the applause died, he said, "Hang on, man, I'll come with you."

"I can go potty on my own," I said. "Unless you're one of those poo-eating freaks, that is." Food withdrawal had sent some crazies in LA into a sewer treatment plant. The cops caught them with their mouths full of raw sludge.

Gassy leaned toward me, enveloping me in his stench. "Thought you said it was your prostate?"

"It's both," I growled. *Attitude. Good.* "Or do you expect me to announce my bowel movements to the entire table, the way colostomy boy here just did?"

"Whatever, man." His face lit up, a chicken-sucking Lone Star grin. "You first. I insist."

I waddled down the stairs, Gassy a half-step behind me. I had no idea where the bathroom was. At the bottom, I turned. "Why don't you go on ahead?"

It wasn't a question, but Gassy took it as one. "Us gangsters got to stick together," he said, and slapped me on the back. "Both on and off the shithole. Ain't that right?"

I resumed my slow-motion walk. I could move faster—the fat suit was quite light—but it would not look natural. Plus, if I needed to run, a sudden sprint would take them by surprise. With all the calories I'd just consumed, I'd have the artificial energy of a food-popping Olympic athlete.

Two blue doors flanked the kitchen. I headed toward them, hoping one of them was the men's room. Maybe Gassy would tire of my slow pace and jump ahead of me. But he seemed content to lag behind, farting the funeral march in a minor key.

We passed the first door. A faded men's room symbol adorned the chipped paint. I leaned against it, but it didn't move.

"Nah, man," Gassy said. "Don't you remember? We gots to use the outhouse. Like we some cracker hillbilly white trash or some shit."

Outhouse?

So that was how Fatso had evaded capture for so long. We had guessed as much, of course, but it was different to know. To dig a hole to hide your secret excretions... I shuddered. It was too shameful to contemplate.

"Come on," Gassy said. "This way." He held open the kitchen door for me.

My luck was turning. Maybe I'd get a shot at the soup after all. I straightened my bow tie, thrust my hand into my pocket and gripped the vial of poison. Then I strode past him into that pit of evil.

Now, I have busted food labs in my time, but I have never seen anything like Fatso's Thanksgiving kitchen, before or since. The turkey was a morsel compared to what was to come. Hundreds of dead, skinless cows rotated on skewers over charcoal pits dug into the concrete floor. Thousands of bottles of wine filled every free space. Wheelbarrows of bread stood in a row to one side. Punch bowls of salad covered a side table. Freezer after freezer along one wall bore the notice "Ice Cream." Nuts, cheeses, dried and fresh fruit. A table a hundred yards long, with chocolate cakes to infinity, bottles of cognac and whiskey between them.

Then I saw it. A six-foot-tall vat in the center of the room. Beneath it a massive gas burner. A sign on the cauldron read, "Soup." A wooden step stool led halfway to the top. A chef in a towering white hat reached over his head to stir the unseen broth.

"Hey man, you coming or arentcha?" Gassy laughed. "You act like you ain't never been to one of Fatso's Thanksgivings before."

I followed him through the busy food lab. Dozens of chefs were at work practicing their sinister craft. At the other end of the kitchen, Gassy pushed through a pair of heavy fire doors, and we stepped out onto the high school's playground. A red carpet stretched across the asphalt to the soccer field and climbed a flight of stairs onto the back of a flatbed truck.

That was the outhouse?

The portable feces receptacle shelter was built of marble and roofed in solid gold. Inside, chandeliers made of diamonds illuminated a two-holer. The toilet seats were studded with emeralds. Rubies the size of my fist held the toilet paper rolls in place.

"You want left or right?" Gassy asked. The room smelled of incense and rosewater, a futile attempt to disguise the stench of addicted humanity's ridiculous droppings. Without waiting for an answer, he dropped his trousers and sat down on one hole.

Vomit surged again in my throat. There was no stall, no divider. He would see me. He would hear me. "I think I'll go use the bushes."

I shut the door and sprinted across the soccer field. The fat suit jiggled as I ran. Bushes along the far fence stood in shadow. Behind me the outhouse door banged open.

"Wait up!" Gassy shouted.

My knees scraped into a patch of bramble. I stuck two fingers down my throat and retched. It all came up. Or most of it, anyway. Enough to prevent an OD. I unbuckled my belt and dropped my pants.

Shoes squelched behind me in the wet grass. "Hey, you all right?"

I straightened up and wiped my lips. I pulled my pants back up. Gassy stood at my side. "If you must know," I said, "I had the squirts." *Remember, attitude.* "And what the food do you care if I go poo in the bushes?"

"I hear you, man. This business, you can't be too paranoid."

"Paranoid's the word," I agreed.

We walked back across the soccer field to the school building. A movement caught my eye. A guard's boot crunched on the gravel rooftop. An Uzi glinted in his hand. Had he seen me? Maybe he was just making the rounds. I hoped it was the latter.

Together we filed back into the food lab. It was now or never, I realized. I had to find a way to ditch Gassy and poison the soup.

"You go on," I said. "I'm going to sneak a piece of cake."

Gassy whistled. "Don't let Fatso catch you, man," he said. "Remember what happened last year?"

"Of course I do," I snapped. *Time to double down.* "That's precisely why I'm going to have some cake."

"Wouldn't want to be you if they catch you."

I made a finger gun and jabbed it between his eyes. "I got plenty of friends down in Texas owe me a favor. You wouldn't be thinking of telling on me, now would you?"

He held his hands out wide. "No way, man. I wouldn't do that."

I dropped my thumb. "Bang."

The man flinched.

"Now get the food out of here."

Gassy returned to the banquet hall. When the doors swung shut behind him, I surveyed the room. Chefs swarmed around me, hacking at still-raw cow corpses with meat cleavers. The soup vat was unattended. Maybe they were saving it for the dessert course.

I strolled among the tables, dwarfed by food piled high to the ceiling. *Grip your lapels. The connoisseur casts a critical eye over the food lab product.* Is anyone watching? I reached out a hand to touch a cake, but stopped, fingers an inch from the frosting. *Swivel the head from side to side.* No one was looking. No one cared.

More quickly now I waddled toward the soup vat. I took the vial out of my pocket. Ten feet to go. Around a table of pies. I uncorked the vial and covered the tube with my thumb.

I circled a table of chocolates and waltzed around a coffee urn. Nothing stood in my way. No chefs nearby. I approached the bubbling cauldron. The soup gurgled and hissed above me. I double-checked the sign: "Soup." No mistake there. The top of the vat was two feet overhead, just within arm's reach. I didn't dare use the stepladder. I stood on tiptoe and sniffed loudly. *A curious diner wishes to sample the broth.* I could smell nothing.

I lifted the vial, still tight in my fist. *Thumb to forehead. Scratch an eyebrow.* In the burnished stainless steel of the vat the bustle behind me continued, distorted. *Fist to top of head. Scratch scratch scratch. Stretch arm overhead. Wrist on top of vat.* Hot. Hot hot! *Let fist drop open.* A soft plop.

Hold that position. No sudden moves. Nothing suspicious to see here. Just being nosy. My calves began to ache. *Down from tiptoe. Hands in your pockets.* Now all you have to do is turn and stroll back to the dining hall. When the soup comes around, find a way to spill it in your lap. My face was slick with sweat beneath the mask. It was hot here next to the cauldron. *On the count of three, turn and go. One. Two. Thr—*

"Don Baloney," said a voice behind me.

I turned to face this new threat. *I am in charge. I am a senior leader of the French Food Mafia. If I feel like sniffing the soup, you're g-d-word right I'm going to sniff the soup. Hands behind your back.* No wait, they don't reach. *Rest them on your stomach, then.* Don't reach that way either. *D-word it.*

It was the waiter. My waiter. The one I'd been rude to over the water. He was looking at me funny. Had he seen me drop the vial? I couldn't risk it. The mission was too important. I would have to kill the man. *Find some excuse. Find a weapon.* Chocolate cakes towered over us on either side. A serving knife lay at the base of one. It would be a simple matter of grabbing the blade and stabbing the waiter before he could cry out. I could tell Fatso the man had been insolent with me.

But what if the waiter had seen nothing? Was I prepared to murder an innocent man? I rested my fingers on the table near the knife.

"Whaddaya want?" I snarled.

"Fatso sent me to find you, Don Baloney," he said. "When Gassy came back alone, the boss wanted to know what you were up to."

"'Up to'?" I asked, and grabbed the knife. "What does it look like I'm 'up to'?" I spread my arms wide. What was that in my hand? Besides the knife. The other hand. S-word. The cork. *Make a fist and hide it. Good.* "I'm admiring this splendiferous repast of illicit viands our illustrious Godfather has seen fit to shower us with this fine Thanksgiving day."

The man ducked his head. "I don't know what that means, Don Baloney." His accent, I realized, was French.

"Then why. Are. You. Still. Here?" I pressed my gut against his skeletal chest, and scratched his ear with the tip of the knife.

He stiffened. "Fatso boss of us all. Only he ask I bring you message. He say to." His English was getting worse.

"Spit it out, man." I nicked his ear lobe with the knife. Blood trickled down his neck. "Or I'll cut off your ear and eat it for dessert."

"Come back to the table now, or no come back at all. I just messenger, *monsieur*! Please!" He stepped backward and held up his arms as though to ward off a blow.

I followed his stare. A knife overhead aimed down at his chest. I was holding the knife. I was getting too much into this role. I put the knife back on the table. Around us dishes clattered, chefs shouted in some unintelligible ferrn language. French, I suppose. The silence between us continued. I didn't believe he had seen anything. I would spare his life.

"Come on," I said, and patted him on the back. "I'll save you a turkey leg. How's that?"

The man seemed overwhelmed by this generosity. "That would be wonderful, *monsieur!*" he stammered. "Food enough for my whole family for the rest of the week!"

I waddled along beside him back to the banquet hall. "How big is your family?"

"Five kids, Don Baloney," he said. "Plus all my in-laws, cousins, parents, aunts, an uncle and my ex-stepsister's lesbian partner."

We stood before the swinging doors. I breathed a sigh of relief. The hard part was over. I had done it. I allowed myself a tiny smile. By this time tomorrow, the entire mafia leadership would be dead.

"After you," I said.

"Thank you, oh thank you." The waiter kissed my hand. Still in Turkey Leg Shared Sixteen Ways Dreamland. I felt so sorry for these food addicts. Soon they would learn what it means to eat air. The waiter pushed open the swinging doors and stepped into the hall.

I waited until the doors swung back before making my entrance. Generations of school children would study what I had done here today. The Prophet himself might give me a medal. The Congressional Medal of Air, like General O'Shitt has. There I'd stand, on the Thin House lawn—no, in the Rock Garden—the sun shining down, the Prophet in front of me, the medal in his hand, pointing a gun in my face—

Six men stood on the other side of the door. One held a pistol to my nose. It wasn't the Prophet, and he definitely didn't have a medal in his hand. Behind him, the entire hall had turned to watch.

Fatso stepped forward, still chewing on his piglet leg. "Well, Don Baloney," he said. "Wat doo yoo seenk uv ow-air Sanksgeeveeng feest?" He smiled, and ripped meat from the bone with his teeth. "Or shood I say, Special Agent Froleek uv zee ATFF?"

TWENTY-TWO

WHAT HAPPENED TO THE LIGHTS? THE French police? They're *what?* That's ridiculous. Why would the French police attack us? We're doing a show here.

A flashlight. Thank you. Corporal, get into that control booth, please. I don't care if there's French special forces rappeling down from the ceiling. Shoot them and get the lights back on.

Wow. What a mess. So that's what happens when you pump a bunch of French commandos full of Laxafier juice. Unbelievable. You Frenchies really stuff your faces, don't you? Look at the vile secretions seeping from their pants.

Wants to talk to me? Who is it? A hostage negotiator? They're not hostages, you idiot. They're the audience! All right. Fine. Translate this: I am the ambassador to France, and I am ordering him and his men to back off.

The president himself. Of France. Give me the phone. Listen, you frog-leg-chewing scum bag, I know where you pooped last Friday night. I know what it smelled like, what it consisted of and what you were thinking when you were sitting on the potty, and let me tell you, it wasn't pretty.

240

That's right. Apology accepted. In the future, remember the chain of command. You report to me. I report to the Prophet. I run this country. You are my puppet.

Sheesh. These people just don't know their place.

Excellent work, Corporal. Now that the lights are back on, please dispose of these filthy French pigs in their black ski masks, and we will continue with our show.

TWENTY-THREE

THEY RIPPED THE FAT SUIT OFF ME AND TIED me naked to a chair. A wicker chair without a seat. A plastic bucket sat underneath. They were going to torture me, I realized. Pull out my fingernails. Pluck out my eyeballs. Hack off my limbs. Fatso was famous for his creative torture techniques.

Well, I could suffer pain. I could suffer anything, knowing that the soup was poisoned. That my death was not in vain. I would be a martyr for the good ol' US of Air. For the Prophet. The People. The Future. Hope.

Fatso held up his pig leg for silence. Grease glistened on his cheeks. "And now," he said, "zee entertainment for zee evening shall *commence.*"

"Go ahead and torture me," I sneered. "You can't make me talk. My faith is strong. Happiness is Eating Air."

"Eez eet?" he asked. He turned to the audience. "Wee shall see."

Laughter shook the hall. I lifted up my voice in prayer. "O Mine Prophet," I prayed, "Forgive these poor food terrists who would impose their extremist fundamentalist beliefs on our great nation. Show them the light, the one true—"

But the words stuck in my throat. The waiter brandished the instrument of torture. I had expected a gun. A knife. Car battery clamps, an assault on my testicles. That I could live with. But this… It was too horrible for words.

"No!" I shouted, shrinking back in my seat. "Not that! Anything but that! Please!"

The waiter advanced. His face was grim. To stoop so low—it was barbaric. Inhuman. Torture beyond my wildest fears.

"You cruel monster!" I choked out.

In his hand lay a Twinkie. They had snapped off its beautiful gossamer wings. It flopped back and forth in agony.

I could smell it now. Its fear. Its pain. The waiter pressed its head against my lips. Rapist or no rapist, I could not bear to listen to the Twinkie's cries of suffering. I opened my mouth and let it wriggle onto my tongue. It panted for a moment, catching its breath, then leaped down my throat in a suicidal swan dive, and so left this world of sorrow for the Twinkie graveyard of my stomach.

"Please," I whimpered. "No more. I'll tell you anything you want to know."

"But wee all-reddy know everyseeng, Agent Froleek," Fatso said.

"See that pallet over there?" The waiter pointed. Thousands of Twinkies waited their turn.

I gasped in horror. To be forced to watch them torture innocent Twinkies—these pastries had done me no harm—was more than I could bear. But Fatso and his crew were hard, relentless men. One after another the waiter shucked the Twinkies, discarding the plastic cocoons and brutally snapping off their wings. I opened my mouth and put them out of their misery. What else could I do? It was an act of kindness. Of mercy.

"Yoo wair a phoney Caponey Baloney," Fatso said. "How doo yoo seenk I knew?"

I moaned. Twinkie guts coated my lips. "Not enough attitude?"

He swallowed another mouthful of pig flesh. "Cuz I keeled heem myself," he said. "Rite wair yoo seet now. Cut out heez asshole and shoved eet down heez throte. Hee wuz last yeer's entertainment."

Thousands of Twinkie wings fluttered overhead, drawn by their brethren's death agony.

"But if Baloney's been dead for a year," I said, "why did the Resistance—"

The flying Twinkies cut me off. *"Betrayed, Betrayed! You've been betrayed!"*

"Stop singing!" I hissed at them.

"Your hear that, boss?" Gassy said. "He wants a song." He farted "The Battle Hymn of the Republic."

Fatso chuckled. "Full Stummick works for mee. Hee eez my head chef."

"A French spy? Work for you?" I shook my head. "I don't believe it."

A man in a ten-foot-tall white hat strode from the kitchen. "Frolick!" he cried. "You made it! Will you not enjoy this bountiful banquet I have prepared for us?"

Was Stummick playing a double game? Maybe Fatso didn't know about our plot.

I opened my mouth to reply, but two more injured Twinkies fought to rape my esophagus. I helped them kill themselves, then said to Fatso, "How can you live with yourself? Torturing innocent people like this." Because Twinkies are people too.

"Inno-sent?" Fatso said. "I am not zee wun hoo poy-zunned zee soop."

Found out! Now there was no hope. I slumped in my chair. My death would be for naught.

"Good thing it wasn't really soup," Full Stummick said. He held up the sign from the vat and turned it around. The other side read, "Dirty Dishes."

Fatso hooted with laughter. "I hate zee soop. Always haf."

The mission was a failure. I was a failure. Because of me the world was doomed to slavery and addiction. I wanted to die. I hoped they'd kill me soon.

"Show him the video!" someone called out from below.

The cry was repeated. "The video! The video!"

Fatso gave a nod. A projector screen was lowered onto the stage. He turned to me. "Zees eez my favoreet part."

View from a pinhole camera in someone's lapel. In the distance, the Thin House. The camera panned left and right. LaOmelette Park. Near where we found the body of Jacques Crusteau. A man in a trench coat approached. No tape measure, but thin enough to work for the Skinny Service.

"You order a pizza?" said a gruff French voice from above.

The buyer wore a fedora pulled low over his eyes. A grey scarf hid his face. "Yes," he said, and reached for the pizza.

The seller drew back. "First let's see the money."

"Right here." A chrome pizza wheel glittered in one hand.

"No you don't. No money, no pizza."

"I'm sorry," the man said. "But I don't have the money." The voice was strangely familiar.

"What the food?" the man said. "They told me you were a qualified buyer. Look, I'm outta here. What are you doing? *Merde, ne peut pas—*"

The pizza wheel slashed through the air. Blood splattered the lens. A gurgling sound. A view of the trees. The dying man clawed at his assailant's face. The scarf came away in his hands. The image on the projector screen froze. My soul froze too.

It was the Prophet himself.

"But how?" I managed.

Fatso shrugged. "He eez boot a man. *Non?*"

The video resumed. The Prophet opened the pizza box and crammed slice after slice into his mouth until it was all gone. But the seller wasn't dead. He lunged up, and for a moment the view was in darkness. A scream from above.

The vendor fell back. A bloody hole filled the space where the Prophet's nose had been. He lifted the pizza wheel and slashed again and again at the pizza dealer until the man stopped moving. A siren sounded in the distance. The Prophet looked up. He stuck two fingers down his throat and vomited on the body. A half-chewed circle of pepperoni covered the lens. Violent kicks turned the body over onto its stomach. The video ended.

I rallied. "How do I know this isn't a fake?"

"Why do yoo seenk eet eez zo hard to arrest oos?" Fatso asked. "And wen wee doo get arrested, why doo wee always, how yoo say, get off? Wee haf a *collection* uv videos like zees, *mon ami.*"

He was right. It all made sense. It was too much. The world was upside down. The Prophet—a food terrist? Everything I believed in—wrong? The room began to spin. The flying Twinkies swirled about my head. They sang:

> *Left is right and up is down,*
> *black is white, a smile's a frown,*
>
> *short is tall and happy's sad,*
> *inside outside, turned around,*

fat is thin and thin is fat—
you're a fool, whaddaya think of that?

"No!" I screamed, and everything went black.

TWENTY-FOUR

I WENT INSANE. I KNOW THAT NOW.

It's…it's hard to talk about in front of so many people. All you ferrners out there watching.

For a brief span of time, I actually believed the Prophet was a food terrist. I am ashamed to say it, but I let doubt overwhelm me.

Let this be a warning unto you: just because all the evidence proves you're wrong, doesn't mean you are. This is why faith is so important.

I woke to the sounds of laughter. The banquet was in full swing. The waiter pushed a Twinkie into my mouth. I chewed and swallowed. That's odd, I thought. No Twinkie song. No wings. Just little bits of yellow cake dough stuffed with cream.

It felt good to have food in my stomach. I couldn't believe I had been so stupid. Starving myself for all these years. I was lucky to be alive. Of course you have to eat food. How could I ever think otherwise?

The waiter pushed another Twinkie at my lips, but I turned my head away.

"Could I have some real food, please?" I ventured timidly.

"Wat, like sum vanilla air?" Fatso mocked.

I flushed. "No," I said. I glanced at the others' plates. "Maybe some turkey with cranberry sauce and stuffing and yams and salad and bread and butter and maybe even some pumpkin pie with ice cream for dessert if that would be alright with you?"

Gassy whooped. "You broke him, Fatso!"

The mafia leader looked at me from under hooded eyes. "Breeng een zee food."

They did. Piles of it. Everything I asked for and more. I began to eat. Slowly at first, then faster and faster until my hands were a blur from plate to mouth and back again. I had three years of starvation to make up for. My body clamored for calories.

"To Agent Froleek!" Fatso cried, champagne flute held aloft. "Heez first good meel een yeerz!"

"To Frolick!" the guests shouted, and drained their glasses.

The feast continued until dawn. When I finished the turkey in front of me, they brought me another. And another. And another. Then they brought in an entire cow corpse, and I ate that too. My stomach stretched painfully, but still I kept eating. I was grateful for the bucket under my chair. My waiter changed it several times.

One by one the guests departed, groaning, hands on their bellies, until only Fatso and I were left. The Godfather of Food offered me a box of after dinner mints. I stuffed a handful of the wafers into my mouth.

"Zo," Fatso said. "Now yoo air a slave to food. Yoo like?"

"If this is slavery, baby," I said, "I'm lovin' it." And reached for more mints.

"Excellent." He snapped his fingers. "Bring monsieur his clothes."

The waiter untied me and handed me a trench coat. One of my own, from my own closet. How did they get a hold of that? I tried it on. It no longer fit.

"So when does the feast begin tomorrow?" I asked.

Fatso smiled. "It duzzn't. Wee air going home, and zo air yoo."

Home! The kid! Chantal! I had completely forgotten about them. I had to get some food for them before they both starved to death. To think she had to whore herself because I insisted she eat air. I had so much to make up for. I eyed the leftovers on the table.

"Could I get a doggie bag then?"

Fatso chuckled. *"Non, monsieur. No doggee bag for yoo."*

"But...but..." I looked around in desperation. "What am I supposed to do? How am I supposed to get food for my family?"

The Godfather of Food stood up. Food stains flecked his tuxedo. He grinned. "Wat fameelee?"

"Why? What have you done with them?"

"Wen wee dropped by-ee to peeck up yor cloze, yor wife wanted to know wair yoo wair."

Pigging out on Thanksgiving turkey. "You didn't."

He lifted his fat shoulders, let them fall with a jiggle. "I expect she's haf-way to Canafooda by now. Zat eez wair she sed she wuz go-eeng, anyway." He nodded to a pair of guards. "Now get heem out uv heer."

They dragged me down a hallway and chucked me out the back door into a dark alley. Dumpsters overflowed with garbage. Rats swarmed around my ankles.

I picked myself up off the ground. Fatso stood in the doorway. He held a cell phone to his ear.

"Eez zees zee I-SEE-FAT hotline? Yes, I want to report a food *terriste."* He gave our address in Georgetown.

He was calling me in. Me. A food terrist. They would hunt me down and put me in Fat Camp. I could starve to death.

"It's a lie!" I shouted. "Don't listen to him!"

But Fatso had already hung up. "Eet wuz…a playzh-air, Agent Froleek." He bowed at the waist. "I am shoor Fat Camp weel kyoor yoo of yor…addeection to food." He winked. "Enjoy eating air. *Bon appetit.*"

He slammed the door shut in my face. "You can't do this to me!" I shouted. I pounded the door with my fists. "I'm a loyal and decorated officer of the ATFF!"

But the door stayed shut. It started to rain. Now what was I going to do? Fatso's torture had been worse than I imagined. He had turned me into a food terrist.

No. That wasn't it. I should be grateful to the man. He had helped me see the truth. I had been betrayed. Lied to. Swindled. Bamboozled. Hoodwinked. Because of the Prophet I had lost everything. "Food is a drug? All you need is air?" How could I have been so stupid?

I made a solemn vow then. The guilty would pay. For the first and only time in my life, I would kill. The Prophet must die.

I was going to kill him myself.

TWENTY-FIVE

A LIGHT FROM ABOVE BLINDED ME. A HELICOPTER chop-chopped overhead.

"This is the SS," a megaphone boomed. "Come out with your hands on your belly. You will be treated fairly."

I couldn't let them catch me. They were hypocrites, all of them. I saw that now. And the Prophet was a dangerous lunatic. I had to stop him.

A Laxafier dart shattered at my feet. I sprinted out of the alley, weighed down by my engorged stomach. A jeep full of cannibals peeled around the corner. Be treated fairly, my ass. I pressed myself flat against the wall, but the helicopter came around and picked me out with its spotlight.

The cannibals gave a cheer. "Soo-shee!" they shouted. "Soo-soo-soo-shee!"

Blowtorches sizzled in their hands. I couldn't outrun the Sushi Gang, much less the helicopter. Maybe I could lose them on a side street, or duck through an abandoned building. I faked right and ran left, down a wide boulevard. Dead trees lined the street on both sides.

Tires squealed behind me. "Tastes better when they're sweaty," a cannibal shouted. "Like salty popcorn!" The spotlight circled around me. The chopper followed overhead.

"We can save you from addiction!" the SS megaphone thundered. "Get the monkey off your back!"

"Fuck your monkey!" I shouted. I gave them the finger, and dodged a Laxafier dart in return.

I passed a crumbling wreck of a supermarket. Most of its roof was still intact. I leaped through a broken window and huddled behind a checkout counter. The spotlight disappeared. The cannibals piled out of the jeep. I turned and jogged down an aisle toward the back. If I could find the rear exit, maybe I could escape.

Concrete slabs from the ceiling blocked the way. The cannibals were coming. I could hear them. Behind me. *Hide. Quick.* I lay myself flat on an empty bottom shelf. In the darkness they might not see me.

They got closer. "Who won the toss for his eyes?" one shouted.

Farther away, a voice shouted back, "Dude, I got dibs on his ribs!"

They must be searching every aisle, I realized. They reconvened just feet from where I hid.

"He isn't here, boss," one whined.

"Oh, he's here," said a voice. "I can smell him." A loud snuffling sound. "We don't find him, we'll set the place on fire."

"Bar-be-cue!" the cannibals roared.

They spread out again and resumed their search. I climbed out of my hiding place. I had no plans to be anyone's chargrilled dinner. I followed the cannibal ahead of me. He crept along the aisle toward the front. Maybe I could distract him somehow, get past him into the street. He disappeared around the corner. *Almost there. A few more feet, then run for it.*

A knife pressed against my throat. Hot breath tickled my ear. I went still.

"It's sushi time...," whispered a voice. It was the sushi boss himself.

Time to bluff. "Let me go," I commanded. "I'm a special agent for the ATFF."

"Not anymore," the man cackled. "You're public enemy number one and a half. There's even a price on your head." He shaved the stubble from my neck with his knife. "Thankfully they don't care what happens to the body."

So this was it. Game over. I swallowed hard. "You going to eat me now?"

"Not all at once. Piece by little piece." He cackled again. "Any last words before I cut out your tongue for an appetizer?"

Rage boiled inside me like a spicy Kundilini curry. I had been lied to all my life, and now I would never get revenge. "Yeah," I said. "My only regret is I'll never get a chance to kill the Prophet, and expose that hypocritical piece of shit to the world."

A gagging noise made me turn. The sushi boss's throat gaped open in a bloody grin. He fell to the ground with a thump.

"Frolick," said a familiar voice. "Get out of here. Go!"

I peered into the blackness. It was Hot 'N' Juicy, the coroner. He towed an oxygen tank and IV stand behind him.

"Doc!" I said. "What are you doing here? Are you examining a murder? 'Cause I think you just caused one."

"Hey boss," called out a cannibal from a couple of aisles over. "Nothing here. What about you over there?"

Juicy snuffled loudly around the plastic tubes in his nose. He pitched his voice low. "Not a piece o' skin to munch these parts. Wincha go look in aisle seven?"

I gasped. "Are you with the gang?"

"No time to explain," he hissed. "I heard what you said. About killing the Prophet." He pressed a gun into my hands. "Take this. Use it. Go!"

The way to the window was clear, but I struggled to make sense of what was happening. "I don't understand."

He put his hand on my shoulder. "I am being punished for my sins, Frolick. It's no more than I deserve."

"What sins?"

"They caught me with a special ham. Left me out for the cannibals. I convinced them not to eat me, 'cause I'm a doctor."

The chop-chop of the helicopter moved sideways. Light flooded through a gap in the ceiling. Three cannibals stood nearby. They whooped when they saw us.

"Yeah, baby! Dinner is served!"

Two of the cannibals came at us from behind. Only one blocked the way to the street. Juicy's scalpel flicked across the man's throat, and the way was clear.

He gave my shoulder a final squeeze. "You deserve better than this. Now go! I'll hold them off!"

I leaped through the window and turned back. The other two cannibals circled him warily.

"See the change you wish to be in the world!" he shouted.

Those were his last words. The two cannibals tackled my friend and cut off his head with a machete.

I fled into the night.

TWENTY-SIX

I F I SUCCEEDED IN KILLING THE PROPHET, THE SS would no doubt return the favor. I decided to visit Green in the hospital. He was my friend. I wanted to say goodbye.

I snuck in through the janitor's entrance just before dawn. Green was encased in a full body cast, all four limbs in traction. I could just make out his eyes and lips under the plaster. I arranged a bunch of dead twigs in a vase at his bedside—I hadn't dared buy flowers, what with the price on my head and all—and drew back the curtains.

He blinked in the morning sunlight. "I must be dead. Is that Frolick?"

"Not dead," I said. "And look at what I brought you." I held up a kilo bag of rice.

His eyes widened. "Frolick? With food? Now I know I'm dead."

I laughed. "The most amazing thing happened to me, Harry. An epiphany! Do you realize you need to eat—food, I mean—to stay alive? I know! Crazy, isn't it? Who would have thunk?"

A chuckle came from inside the cast. "You been to the naturopath, then? He get you the rice?"

My brow darkened. "Don't get me started on that lowlife."

"Lowlife or not, he's good for a fix." The body cast wiggled. "Did you pick up the food for my family like I asked?"

"Sure," I said. "Went by just now to drop it off." I had left it at Stummick's house for safekeeping. He had since disappeared, leaving the food behind. "Only they weren't at home. I found a note."

"A note? What'd it say?"

"Gone to Canafooda, looks like. With Chantal and Nathan. Economy class tickets on the Underground Food Road. Left on the 5:23 express this morning."

He sank back against his pillow. "Oh thank goodness," he said. He blinked twice. "You going too?"

My face took on a solemn aspect. "No, Harry," I said gravely. "I'm going to kill the Prophet."

We were silent a moment. "I see," he said. "What makes you think you can pull it off?"

I struck a bodybuilding pose. "I can out-fight, out-run and out-think anyone in the Skinny Service. After what I ate last night?" I hacked the air with my hands. "They don't stand a chance against my calorie-fueled karate moves."

"But the whole country is looking for you," he said. "I saw it on television. You have any idea what the reward is for your capture?"

"A hamburger, fries and a coke," I said. "I know. They're desperate, huh? Pity I can't turn myself in."

From the hallway came the sounds of boots limping along the hall. Green tensed.

"It's a trap," he hissed. "They're coming for you!"

"Sure it's not your doctor?"

"I heard the guards talking. There are Thin Berets everywhere."

The bootsteps got louder. "Don't worry," I said. "Super Frolick is here to save the day." I put my fists on my hips. "When I'm finished, we'll get you some food. How does that sound?"

"It's too late," he said. "Promise me something, Frolick."

The bootsteps halted outside the door.

"Anything, Harry."

"Forget about the Prophet. Go to Canafooda. Be with your family. It isn't worth it."

I thought of Chantal whoring herself for a sandwich. How could I ever look her in the eyes again? I set my jaw in grim defiance. "I'm sorry, Harry. I can't promise you that. That lying sack of poo destroyed my life. Destroyed this country. He deserves to die."

The door inched slowly open. A platoon of heavily armed Thin Berets stood in the hallway.

I grinned. "Excuse me for a moment, will you?" This was going to be fun.

For the next three and a half minutes, I was a superhero. I moved so fast they couldn't keep me in their sights. The poor commandos were so thin, so weak from lack of food, I simply took their weapons from them one by one and knocked them to the floor, where they lay on their backs like helpless cockroaches, burdened by fifty pounds of gear.

I winked at Harry. "More coming, I'm sure. Better get moving." But Harry said nothing. "Harry? You alright?" Still nothing. I stepped over a dozen flailing limbs and made my way to his bedside. His eyes were open, but unmoving. I put my hand over his mouth. No breath.

Special Agent Harry Green of the ATFF, my partner, was dead.

More bootsteps limped down the hall. There was no time to mourn. Wiping away tears, I strode down the hallway to the service elevator, brushing Thin Berets aside with a flick of my wrists. I pushed the down button and waited.

Come on. What was taking so long?

The doors finally opened. Twenty fat men wearing camouflage and floppy berets the size of Mexican sombreros slouched out of the elevator. I tried my karate moves, but my lethal attacks just bounced off their substantial padding. They laughed. Not a man among them weighed less than five hundred pounds.

"Who *are* you people?" I asked, in growing horror.

"We're a new Top Secret unit," their leader said. He doffed his cap and bowed, or tried to. "We're super-special forces. They call us the Fat Berets."

"But—but how?" I spluttered. "You didn't get that big just from eating air."

"Who says we didn't?" said another. And they all laughed. "Now come along quietly or we'll be forced to sit on you."

TWENTY-SEVEN

Y TRIAL LASTED FIFTEEN MINUTES. IF YOU can call it a trial. Judge Meyer-Weiner presided. Pretended not to know me, the bastard. Agent Erpent testified against me. Explained how I had "sabotaged" his investigation. Cap put in a thirty-second appearance. Was I, in his professional, expert opinion, a dangerous food terrist? Yes, I was.

"Guilty! Indefinite detention, Fat Camp."

"What do you mean, indefinite?" I protested. "That's against the Amendment!"

"For as long as the Prophet and the National Thinness Council deem you a threat to our national security. Next case!"

Meyer-Weiner didn't even look at me. He must have talked to save his fat hide. Hell, for all I knew he was on Fatso's payroll. Him and Erpent both. Not that it mattered. He had won and I had lost.

They put me in chains and covered my head with a hood. I stood in line with other prisoners. We boarded a bus. Hours passed. The warmth of the weak sun faded. Then we were there.

"Welcome to the final stage of human evolution," our guard said with a laugh, and whipped off our hoods.

It was the same Fat Camp I attended three years ago. But

it looked different now. They had replaced the crude wooden sign over the gate with a marble archway. Same words, though: "Enter Slaves. Depart Free Men."

The camp was surrounded by countryside, dead and brown as far as the eye could see. No one lived out here anymore. It was the perfect location for a Fat Camp, I had to admit. Even if I managed to escape, which seemed unlikely, where would I go? The only passing traffic were military patrols.

The bus crunched up the gravel drive. On either side of the road, backhoes dug great pits in the earth. Bulldozers pushed piles of firewood into the freshly excavated holes.

Firewood? I squinted through the dirty pane. Firewood doesn't have feet. Thousands of them, naked wet toes in the freezing drizzle. And heads and arms and torsos. The bodies fell into the pit. The bulldozer retreated to bury a second stack.

What was going on? This wasn't the Fat Camp I remembered, of campfire singalongs, hushed eager enthusiasm for the Prophet's latest broadcast, and Mexican night on Thursdays. Things had changed.

We came to a razor-wire checkpoint—also new. A machine gun guarded the gate, facing inward toward the camp. What an idiot the camp commandant was, I thought. How on earth could they protect us from marauding cannibals if the machine gun was pointed in the wrong direction?

Another surprise waited for me inside the gates. Hundreds of walking skeletons stared up at us as we drove into camp. Shreds of clothing hung from their limbs, exposing wrinkled flabs of skin, hallmark of the formerly obese. Men. Women. Children. All old before their time, giant heads atop their twig-like bodies. The children sat in the mud, listlessly eating dirt.

Then I saw them. Both of them. There, in the middle of the crowd. Chantal! Nathan! But what were they doing here? I thought they'd gone to Canafooda. This was terrible. They looked so skinny. What was I going to do? It was my fault they were here. I lunged at the window, pulling at my restraints, and called out their names. She looked up. She spat and turned her back on me.

Probably had a bad taste in her mouth. Or maybe she mistook me for someone else. With the glare on the dirty glass, it must be difficult for them to see me inside the bus.

Soldiers armed with rifles—the kind that use real bullets, and fixed with bayonets—herded us off the bus and into the barracks, the very same I'd slept in three years ago. Only now there were more bunk beds, stacked seven high and so crowded together I could barely slip between them.

The other prisoners avoided me. Strange. Then I realized: I knew everyone in that room. A former high school PE teacher, an old girlfriend, the guy who works at the gas station I always use. Even my old elementary school best friend. What was his name again?

There was no time to solve this puzzle. Three women in brightly colored leotards and leg warmers cartwheeled into the room.

"U-S-A! U-S-A!" they shouted. "We're number one! Whoo!"

"Who are you?" asked the old man in the bunk above mine. He used to cut my hair when I was twelve.

"We're your slimming consultants!" said a girl in fuchsia tights and an orange Lycra top. She high-kicked.

"Let's shed those ugly unwanted pounds!" said a second girl, and did a back flip.

"Remember, we're here to help!" the third one said, and they formed an impromptu human pyramid.

"Now come on, gang!" the first one said, leaping from the backs of her sisters. "Let's get over to the gym and get you started! We've got some exciting activities for you here at Fat Camp 34792! Let's show some pride in that number! 34792! Whoo!"

Three tumbling blurs of spandex led us from the barracks across the yard to a great glass dome. That was new too. Soldiers scanned our social security bar codes and we passed inside.

The dome was full of treadmills and stairmasters and weight machines. Thousands of them. And every one occupied by a struggling skeleton. Around the outside edge of the dome lay exercise areas covered with mats. People I knew danced and bobbed and waved their arms in the air to aerobics music.

Our slimming consultants led us to an unoccupied exercise area. The three ladies clapped and did the splits in unison. A bored-looking soldier with a bayoneted rifle lounged against the wall, munching on a candy bar.

"All right, gang!" shouted one of the girls, this one in aquamarine and puce. "Let's show those guys over at Camp 56924 we've got more spirit than they do!"

She pushed a button on a boombox and a thumping rhythm shook the floor. They gyrated through a rapid series of aerobics steps. We did our best to keep up, but our shuffling was not what they considered "spirit." It had been three days since my Thanksgiving feast, and my super powers were waning. The others were in much worse shape. The old man next to me, my bunkmate and former barber, tripped on a tricky move and fell to the ground. He lay there panting.

Two of the perky slimming consultants danced over and pulled on his arms. "Get up, get up!" they cried. "We've got to help you burn that fat!"

"What fat?" he wheezed. "I'm as skinny as it gets."

"Don't be silly," said a consultant. "You're an ugly fat old monster like everyone else here. The journey to eating air begins with losing weight."

"You can't eat air," the man snapped. "What are you? Crazy? Or just stupid?"

The two consultants sighed. The music stopped. They motioned to the soldier, who finished his candy bar and sauntered over. Together they looked down at the old man.

"I'm here to defend your freedom," the soldier said, and unslung his rifle. "Do you want to be a slave?"

"What good is freedom if you're hungry?" the old man retorted.

The soldier stabbed the man through the heart with his bayonet. The old man's body arched. The soldier twisted the blade. The old man fell back. Blood pooled on the mat.

Two of the slimming consultants high-kicked. "Live Free or Die!" they whooped. The third consultant, dressed all in red, stood to one side, her arms crossed.

The music resumed. "Let's put some bounce in it this time!" one shouted, climbing an invisible ladder. "Shed those unwanted and unsightly pounds!"

We resumed our dancing, this time with bounce.

Three hours later, they let us outside for our evening "air meal." Hundreds of people milled around. I knew them all. I approached my old sixth-grade teacher, but he edged away from me. I tried to talk to my postwoman but she limped toward the exercise dome as soon as she saw me coming. I wanted to ask them if they'd seen Chantal and Nathan, but no one wanted to speak to me. I was surrounded by a bubble of air as I walked through the crowd.

"Not the most popular rat in the sewer, are you?" said a voice behind me.

It was Mr. Burgher VIII. He wore a bandage around his neck.

"Rat Boy!" I exclaimed. "At last a friendly face. What are you doing here? And what happened to your neck?"

"Because of you, I've just had an esophageal bypass."

"A what?"

"You know," he said. "Like a gastric bypass, only they clamp your esophagus shut so you can't swallow."

"But why would they do that?" I asked. "I'm surprised they even caught you in the first place. Didn't the arresting officer appreciate your cockroach mousse?"

He lowered his voice. "Skinny Service. They're doing a purge. Anyone who's ever known one Jason Frolick, formerly of the ATFF."

I gasped. "But why?"

Rat Boy shook his head. "You really have to ask?"

"If I don't ask, how am I ever going to know?"

"Because of that stupid murder you insisted on investigating," he hissed. "You couldn't leave well enough alone? As if we don't all know who the murderer was."

"You mean the Proph—"

"Ssh!" He clamped a hand over my mouth. "See that building over there?"

It was white with a red crossed knife and fork painted on one side. I nodded.

"That's the hospital. You think esophageal bypass is bad? I hear they're working on even worse experiments."

A new trio of leg-warmer-clad slimming consultants pranced outside. "Come on, gang!" they shouted. "It isn't time for bed yet! Let's shake some booty and burn some calories! Whoo!"

Six hours of aerobics later, they somersaulted us back to the barracks. I could barely stay on my feet.

"Just a short day today," gushed a blonde in lavender and peach Lycra. "Tomorrow we'll get you started on a real workout! Go the Power of Air!"

We had half an hour to curfew and lights out. I hurried outside. I had to find my family.

I found them standing in line next to a dump truck. I wrapped my arms around them both and kissed them. "Thank goodness you're all right."

Chantal's face was a rippling mass of hatred. I drew back. "What's wrong?" I asked.

"What do you *think* is wrong?" she said, and hefted Nathan in her arms. His head flopped against her shoulder.

I put my hand to his forehead. He was cold to the touch. "Is he sick?" I asked. I took off my jacket and covered him.

"He isn't sick, you moron!" she said. "He's dead! Our son is dead because of you!"

Dead! I put two fingers to his throat. No pulse. I lifted his eyelids. Nothing. "But how did this happen?" I asked. "I thought you'd gone to Canafooda."

"We did," she sobbed. "But Fat Berets crossed the border and kidnapped us."

"They can't do that!" I exclaimed.

"They told the Canafoodians we were wanted food terrists."

She pushed tears around on her face. "And now I'm standing in line to bury our son, whose body is about to be dumped into an unmarked mass grave."

I hung my head. "This is all my fault."

"Yes," she said. "It is. And my only consolation is that we'll both be joining him soon."

The line advanced. We straggled forward.

I studied the razor-wire fence. Guard towers spaced at hundred-yard intervals. Soldiers patrolled the outer perimeter.

"What if there were a way out of here? A way to escape?"

"There is no escape," she said. "Don't you get it? They will hunt you down wherever you go in the world, and shove their air-eating bullshit down your throat. And besides," she sneered, "isn't this what you always wanted? 'Happiness is Eating Air'?"

I fumbled for words. "I'm not the same man," I said. "I see now the error of my ways."

"Bit too late for that," she snarled.

I was losing her. I took Nathan from her arms and cradled his corpse against my chest. "There must be somewhere we can go. A place to hide. If I can get us out of here, will you come with me? We could try again. Maybe even have another child."

She spat in my face. "I would rather die than live another minute with you. Give him to me." She yanked our son's body from me and turned to face the front of the line. Nothing more I said had any effect. She had turned to stone.

I returned to the barracks. I felt so ashamed. My only child was dead and all I could think of was how hungry I was. One of the inmates was selling contraband. I took off my wedding ring. It didn't look like I was going to need it again anytime soon.

"What can I get for this?" I asked.

"Dime bag of flour." He slapped it on the table and took my ring. "Next!"

"Hang on," I said. "Is that it? The ring is all I have. What am I going to do for food tomorrow?"

"Not my problem. Next!"

The inmates behind me pushed me aside. I huddled in a dark corner and poured the flour into my mouth. I choked. It had been cut eighty percent with chalk dust.

I lay down on my bunk and closed my eyes. The lights went out. Perhaps in sleep there would be some release from sorrow. I was drifting off when a voice growled in my ear, "Well if it isn't Agent Frolick."

I opened my eyes. Sergeant Thinn stared down at me. He looked distinctly underweight.

"What's the matter, Thinny?" I asked. "No zero-calorie burgers when you need them?"

He grabbed me by the shirt and shook me. The other cops were there too. The ones from the park. "It's your fault we're in here," Thinn spat. "You and that dead pizza dealer. You couldn't leave well enough alone, could you?"

I shrugged. "Sorry."

"Sorry's not good enough," Thinn said. He unbuckled his belt. "Tie him down, boys."

"What are you doing?" I shouted. "Help! Somebody, please!"

The others turned to watch, but no one intervened. Thinn crouched over my face and went poo-poo in my mouth. I tried to spit it out but they forced my mouth shut and pinched my nostrils together. I swallowed.

"You puke that up," Thinn said, "you'll be licking it off the floor until it's clean."

The other cops followed Thinn's lead. When they were finished, they invited everyone else in the barracks to do the same. One by one every man, woman and child I had ever known took their vengeance on me, crouching and grunting over my face until they had pumped the contents of their bowels into my stomach.

When I woke up, a group of slimming consultants in matching pastel leotards leaned over my bed. One clucked her tongue.

"Food terrist in our midst," she said.

"Terrible," said a second.

"Don't worry," said a third. "We're going to fix you up so you never have cravings to eat shit again."

"Cravings?" I said. I lifted my head. I was still bound to the bunk. "They tied me down and forced me to eat their poo!"

"So sad."

"In denial."

"Blames everyone but himself for his troubles."

I struggled against my bonds. "You think I wanted them to do this to me?"

A medic appeared at my side, a syringe in one hand. It pricked my arm. I blacked out.

When I woke the second time, a surgeon in scrubs peered down at me. I blinked in the bright light. My belly was exposed to the open air.

"He's awake," the doctor said.

An anesthesia mask descended toward my face. I shook my head from side to side. My arms and legs were strapped to the operating table.

"What is this place?" I asked.

The doctor blinked. "You are about to undergo experimental surgery to remove your entire digestive tract, from esophagus to anus. You will never be able to threaten our national security again."

I gasped. "But if you do that, I'll die!"

"Not necessarily. A new school of thought says air-eating actually takes place in the lungs, not the stomach." He chuckled and reached for a scalpel. "With enough faith, you could outlive me."

"Faith in what?" I asked. "Eating air? Are you serious?"

The doctor patted my shoulder. "Pray to the Prophet for strength." He forced the gas mask over my nose and mouth.

Without warning, his head slumped down over my chest. Brains oozed out of his nose. He slid to the ground. In his place stood the slimming consultant from yesterday, the one all in red. She held a Laxafier in her hand. She undid the straps that held me to the table.

"Who are you?" I asked. "What's going on?"

She pulled me to my feet. "No time to explain. Can you walk?"

I tried my legs. "Sure."

"Then let's move."

She led me through a maze of dark corridors. She shot two orderlies along the way. We left them lying in puddles of their own feces and made our way out the back door. We stumbled into the open air just as the alarm sounded.

"Now we've got to run," she said.

Across the barren mud we trotted, to a space between the guard towers. She picked up a pair of wire cutters and metal gloves and snipped away at the razor fence.

"Will you please tell me what is going on?" I asked.

"The Prophet ordered me to rescue you," she said, and pushed aside a mass of fencing.

"The Prophet? But why?"

The way was clear. She motioned me through the gap. I did not move.

She sighed. "Agent Erpent of the SS is the one responsible for this outrage." She waved a hand at the Fat Camp behind us. "He's plotting to get rid of the Prophet."

"Get rid of him? Why?"

"We have to go," she said, pushing me forward. "I'll explain later."

"There they are!" shouted a voice. Bullets zinged overhead. I ducked through the gap and crawled to freedom. The consultant was right behind me. I stood up and turned to help her to her feet. A bullet struck her in the back and flung her to the ground.

"Go," she gasped. "The Prophet needs you. He said you're the only one who can save him."

"But that makes no sense," I protested. "I swore to kill him."

But she was dead. Bullets filled the air like flies at a picnic. I turned and ran.

TWENTY-SEVEN AND NINETY-EIGHT ONE-HUNDREDTHS

I STOOD IN THE SHADOWS OF LAOMELETTE PARK, A pizza on my shoulder, a Laxafier in my pocket, and waited for the Prophet to arrive. The smell of the pizza made my stomach growl, but I ignored it. Soon my hunger would not matter. Soon nothing would matter. The Prophet would die for his crimes, and I would find peace.

My week of waiting had finally paid off. When the dealer showed up at two in the morning, I knocked him out and took his pizza. I left him bound and gagged in a nearby alley. No one else needed to die because of me.

Getting the Laxafier had been trickier. They were watching my house, I was sure of it. Instead I used what little strength I had left to assault a lone ATFF agent in the middle of a Girl Scout cookie bust, and stole his weapon. The Girl Scouts did the rest.

A figure flitted across the park. Was that him? I squinted. There. It moved again. It *was* him. It had to be. He merged with the shadow of a nearby tree.

"Foood! Foood!" an owl hooted.

Odd. There were no more owls left. The Air Force's herbicide

272

spraying program had destroyed their habitat. The remaining birds had migrated south to Mexico.

"Foood! Foood!" the owl hooted again.

A signal. Of course! Why hadn't I thought of that before? I should have interrogated the dealer before knocking him out. I would have to improvise.

"Yeah, yeah. I'm coming," I said.

I strode from the shadow with more confidence than I felt. I kept my hands where he could see them, one at my side, the other holding the pizza. I came to a halt in the same spot where Jacques Crusteau had died.

"Now where's the money?"

The man edged forward into the light. He wore a trench coat and fedora with a scarf around his face, but his voice was impossible to disguise.

"What's the code word?"

"Eat the code word," I said. "I don't see no briefcase. How you gonna pay me?"

A muffled chuckle came from behind the scarf. "Don't worry. I'll pay you." A chrome pizza wheel glinted in his hand.

I threw the pizza on the ground and drew my Laxafier. "You're going to pay, alright," I said. "For lying to the Airitarian people. Or should I say, the *American* people." I aimed at his head. I was going to blow his brains out, then turn the gun on myself.

The pizza wheel slipped from his hand. He took off the scarf and fedora. The gaunt face of the Prophet gazed back at me. His nose was still covered in bandages.

"Oh thank goodness it's you," he said.

"What do you mean by that?"

"You're here to kill me, right? So do it!"

My grip on the trigger loosened. "Wait. You *want* me to kill you?"

"Why do you think I had them let you go?"

"You *what?*"

He fell to his knees and wrung his hands. "What are you waiting for? Kill me! Now's your chance!"

I faltered. "But why would you want me to kill you?"

"Because I'm an addict," he sobbed. "I'm a food terrist. A murderer. I'm a fat disgusting worthless piece of shit!"

I had expected anything but this. "You're not, actually," I said. "Fat, I mean."

He grabbed fistfuls of stomach fat through his trench coat. "What do you call this? And this? And this?"

"Um. Loose skin?"

"I am such a hypocrite," he said. "Telling everyone to eat air. When I can't even do it myself."

I snapped my fingers in his face. "Hello? No one can eat air."

"That's not true. You remember that scientific study I ordered last year?"

"The Hunger and Appetite Commission. Sure."

"Our country's top scientists proved that human beings can subsist—flourish, even—on an air-only diet."

The gun fell to my side. "A scientific study? With real live scientists?"

The hum of Twinkie wings descended from the heavens. Millions of them. The flying pastries settled like locusts on everything in view—dead trees, dead grass, even the Prophet's head. And they were all singing the same song:

The world is fat and so are you.
Whose fault is that? I would be too!

Slim the others first—
it's their fault, see?
When their disgusting bellies burst,
then you'll be free!

"Oh no," I whispered in horror. "Not again. We've got to do something about this."

"I know we do," the Prophet sobbed.

I thought quickly. My persecutors had returned. They attacked because my faith was weak. But why was that? Why was my faith weak? The Twinkies said it themselves: because of those unbelieving fat ferrners, especially the French. Only one man had the power to help me. The Prophet himself. How could I make him understand?

"Real live scientists," I said, marveling. "So we *can* eat air."

"Don't you see?" The Prophet pounded his palm with his fist. "I'm not worthy to lead this great nation of ours."

I knelt down at his side and dried his tears. "It's not your fault," I said.

"Of course it is. Whose else could it be?" He reached for the pizza.

I slapped the box shut. "It's like you always say. 'See the change you wish to be.'"

"Wha-what do you mean?"

"How can you be free when you're surrounded by fat people?"

"I know all that," he said. "Why do you think we passed the Amendment? Look at what good it did."

"Not us," I said. "Them! It's their fault! The ferrners' fault!" I lashed the air with my arm in the general direction of France. "Don't you see? They conspire against us, keeping us down, preventing us from reaching our true potential as atmospheric munchers!"

His face furrowed in concentration. "You may be right."

"I know I'm right."

"But it doesn't matter anymore," he sobbed. "The mafia and the SS are blackmailing me. All because of my weakness, humanity is doomed. Please! Just kill me now!"

"But you've got to lead us! Don't you realize what this means? You're the only one who can end our slavery to addictive caloric substances! Release us from the evil jackboot Tyranny of Food!"

"No, no," he moaned. "I'm not worthy. I'm scum. I'm so fat I can't even stand to look at myself in the mirror. Why won't you put me out of my misery?"

The Twinkies whispered in my ear. They told me what to say next. I grabbed him by the shoulders. "What if I knew of a way to get you off the hook with the mafia and the SS?"

"Like what?" he said. "I tried to capture Fatso. You saw how that turned out."

I crossed my arms. "They've got tapes. Right?"

"And they'll expose me to the world if I don't obey them."

I crossed my arms. "And who has a kill switch to the Internet in his office?"

"I do. But—"

"Who controls the media? Who puts television newscasters in Fat Camp for distributing French propaganda? Who deports ferrn journalists for asking hardball questions?"

"I do. What are you getting at?"

I shrugged. "They've got their tapes. Let them keep them. Who will ever see them?"

"Well," he said. "I suppose the ferrn TV stations might show the videos."

"Duh!" I said. "To other ferrners! And who cares what they think?"

"The Coalition of the Fasting depends on the support of ferrn governments."

"Who needs them?" I scoffed. "We're the most powerful country on the planet. We don't need their help."

He nodded and wiped his tears. "Good point. But what about Erpent?"

I grinned. "You let me worry about him. I've got a plan."

The Prophet got to his feet. "Thank you," he said.

"No," I replied. Tears welled in my eyes. "Thank *you*, Mine Prophet."

"Come with me," he said. "If you're right, we've got a lot of work ahead of us."

I stood up. "Where are we going?"

"The Thin House, where else?"

The holy of holies! To enter that sacred shrine, with my Supreme Leader at my side… I shuddered in anticipation.

"And don't forget the pizza!" he called over his shoulder. "We can use it to test our faith."

The Twinkies rose up in a golden cloud and followed us across the street. We passed through the outer gates and strolled in the shadows of the Rock Garden. The Prophet walked in silence, contemplating his own greatness, no doubt. I dared not disturb his reflections.

"Do you like ranch dressing with your pizza?" he asked abruptly.

Such profundity of thought! "I was always a hot sauce man, to be honest with you," I said, and added quickly, "although of course I don't eat pizza anymore."

"Neither do I," he said, with a magnetic grin.

We entered that temple of wisdom, truth and justice, and proceeded toward the West Wing and the fabled Trapezoidal Office. The home of good government—to see it with my own eyes! The same room where both Abraham Lincoln and the Prophet signed their respective Emancipation Proclamations!

But the way to the inner sanctum was blocked by Erpent and two Fat Berets. Erpent hurled an accusing finger at me and shouted, "Arrest that man!"

"Hold," the Prophet snapped. "This man is my guest."

The Fat Berets paused.

"Mine Prophet," Erpent said, with a stiff bow of his head. "Former Special Agent Frolick is an escaped food terrist. He is a danger to you and our national security."

I thought of my wife and child, dead in Fat Camp. The purge that took all my friends and family from me. "You're the threat," I growled. "People are starving to death in Fat Camp because of you."

Erpent crossed his arms. "Is it my fault they can't eat air?"

Twinkies swirled about my head, chanting their haunting melody in my ear. Then I understood.

"You're right," I said. "It's not your fault. It's my fault." I hung my head. "My doubt infected all those people. That's why they couldn't eat air."

"No," the Prophet said. "It's not your fault. It's the ferrners' fault. Remember?"

The Twinkie chorus swelled and broke into symphonic overture. I gasped. The final piece of the puzzle fell into place. "Of course." I put on my stern face. "I can't wait to get my hands on those French food terrists. And you." I turned to Erpent. "Shame on you. How dare you engage in favoritism."

He raised his eyebrows. "Favoritism?"

"My family and friends enjoyed the finest facilities Fat Camp has to offer." I threw out my arms. "But every citizen of our great land deserves that experience!"

Erpent cleared his throat. "What do you propose?"

"You must build more Fat Camps," I said fervently. "Hire more judges. More slimming consultants. Buy more leg warmers. So that everyone can learn to eat air."

Erpent glanced at the Prophet.

"He has a point, you know."

"Very well, Mine Prophet," the SS agent sneered. He saluted with a limp hand and muttered, "Go the Power of Air." He turned to go.

"One more thing," I said.

Erpent was no longer smiling. "What is it?"

I pulled out my Laxafier. "I want you to experience the joys of Fat Camp, too," I said. "Maybe then you'll be a nicer person." And shot him in the leg.

He collapsed on the carpet in a puddle of his own excrement.

The Prophet patted me on the back. "Good work."

I tingled with pride at this unlooked-for commendation. My feet left the floor and I floated up toward the ceiling.

"Get him on the next box car leaving town," the Prophet ordered the Fat Berets. "One of you wake up the Joint Chiefs. Yes, I know it's two in the morning. I'm calling an emergency meeting of the National Thinness Council."

The Fat Berets gave a smart salute, about-faced and marched off, dragging Erpent between them.

The Prophet looked at me strangely. Could he tell my head was touching the ceiling, surrounded by swarms of flying Twinkies?

He grinned. "Come on. Through here."

I followed him into his office. I gazed in awe at the triangular tables that filled the nooks and crannies of that irregular quadrilateral. Here I was, a pizza on my shoulder, the Prophet at my side, standing in the Trapezoidal Office itself!

He stepped around behind his desk. He reached into a drawer and took out a bottle of ranch dressing and one of hot sauce. "That looks pretty heavy," he said. "Why don't you put it down?"

"Did you want to test your faith?"

He winked at me. "It crossed my mind."

I put the pizza down on the Trapezoidal Desk. "Maybe we should throw it away."

"Maybe we should," he agreed.

Never underestimate the power of unbelievers to damage your own faith. It had been a week since I had last eaten. So when the Prophet opened the box and offered me a slice, French doubt wafted across the Atlantic Ocean, sending my Twinkies into a frenzy. They violated me with those triangular portions of cheesy, gooey, crispy crust 'za. By the time the National Thinness Council showed up, the Prophet and I were both in tears, and the pizza was gone.

"The ferrners made us do it," I said. "You realize this makes us both food terrists?"

He came back from the bathroom wiping vomit from his lips. "Don't you worry," he said. "We'll get those French evildoers."

The double doors swung open, and there was no more time for idle chit-chat. In waddled a dozen of the strongest believers I had ever met. Every single one had an eleven-inch waist, just one inch more than the Prophet himself. And what an inch it was! First came the Joint Chiefs of Stick, in all their beribboned glory. They had to duck to bring their rank balloons into the room. The balloons bobbed against each other, threatening to explode on the sharp points of the chandelier.

"General O'Shitt!" I exclaimed, counting the stars on the blimps that rose from his shoulders. "You made it to twenty-six stars, I see!"

The NSA commander beamed. "All thanks to you, my skinny friend," he said. "And why stop at twenty-six? New ranks have been created. I'm on track to make a hundred stars by the end of the year."

The other generals and admirals scowled at this. They obviously had not the wit to dream so boldly.

Following them were four of the Cupboard members. I recognized them from televised news conferences: the Typist of State, the Typist of Defense, the Typist of Offense and the Typist of Special Teams. All believers of superhuman faith, as their tape measures proved.

The furniture creaked as the assembled lowered themselves into their chairs, and the Prophet began.

"Gentlemen," he said, "we are faced with our country's greatest crisis. The survival of this nation—our values—our way of life—is at stake. Food terrists threaten to destroy us with their addictive caloric substances. I asked you here this morning to announce my plan to deal with this menace."

"What sort of plan, Mine Prophet?" O'Shitt asked.

The Prophet turned his charismatic eyes of power on the General. "A plan to humble our greatest and most fearsome enemy," he said.

"Cuba?"

He shook his head.

"Canafooda?"

"No. France."

The assembled thrilled at the mention of our great arch-enemy, the cradle of food terrism.

"About time," growled an admiral with ribbons glued to his forehead. "Mothereating French with their wine and their cheese. Stubbornest enemy I've seen since the Micronesian Police Action last year."

"Yes," said the Typist of State. "We have exhausted all diplomatic channels to convince them to crack down on their food terrist training camps called 'cooking schools.' The French have even persuaded the UN to relocate to Geneva, just because the Receptionist-General claimed he was starving to death in New York." She turned to us, pleading. "I mean, come on! The man's African. You would think he would know how to eat air by now."

The Prophet nodded solemnly. "General O'Shitt. Military options? What about we nuke 'em?"

O'Shitt folded his hands together on his stomach. Or tried to. "We of the Joint Chiefs believe you should give diplomacy another chance."

"Oh please!" the Typist of State said. "What's the point of having this superb nuclear arsenal you're always talking about if we can't use it? Especially against harmless countries like France that can't fight back."

O'Shitt cleared his throat. "May I remind the Typist that the French have nukes too?"

"Do they?" State said. "Well, I'm sure a first strike can knock out their primitive nuclear facilities before they can get a missile off the ground."

The Typists of Offense and Special Teams were on their feet. "Mine Prophet, I must protest!" protested Offense. "We only have ten thousand or so nuclear warheads. If we use a couple dozen on France, we open ourselves to attack from countries like Lesotho, Equatorial Guinea and Bhutan!"

The Prophet held out a hand for silence. "We have a new secret weapon I intend to deploy. More powerful than any nuke."

"A new weapon? The first I've heard of it." Offense turned to Special Teams. "Or is it one of yours?"

"Not mine," said Special Teams.

The Prophet stood up and came around the desk. "What do you think, Special Agent Frolick?"

I shuffled my feet and stared at the floor. These dictation-takers of wisdom wanted my advice? "I guess the French would rather eat air than get nuked," I said at last.

He grinned. "I was hoping you'd say that." He put his arm around my shoulder. "Gentlemen," he announced, "meet our new secret weapon."

I pulled away. *"Me?"*

The Prophet looked me in the eye. He spoke with passion. "Go to France," he said. "Be our ambassador. Teach them the one true way."

"But how?" I asked. "I thought that diplomatic channels were exhausted."

"They're tired, yes. But not quite pooped." He turned me to face the probing stares of the Cupboard. "We need to put a human face on our struggle to eat air. Help them understand the innocent lives they are destroying with their addiction to food."

"But what do I say?"

He patted me on the shoulder. "Explain to them your battle with addictive caloric substances. The loss of your wife. Your child. Your friends. Completely uncensored. Make them sympathize with you."

The Typist of State raised a finger in the air. "And then we nuke 'em?"

"No!" the Prophet said. "Or not yet, anyway."

State persisted. "He explains our demands then, right?"

"What demands?" I asked.

She ticked them off on her fat fingers. "Cessation of food terrist training camps. Outlaw the possession and consumption of addictive caloric substances. Airborne herbicide spraying to destroy grow-ops in the countryside. Construction of Fat Camps to re-educate the entire population. Teach them how to eat air."

I glanced around the room. Utter silence. "And if I fail?"

The Prophet pointed to a young Air Force officer in a corner of the Trapezoid. I had not noticed him until now. "If you fail, Stan here's got the football. Get the nukes out, make ourselves some French toast. Ain't that right, boys?"

The others jutted out their multiple chins. They were staunch. Resolute. Defiant in the face of this French threat. How could I refuse?

I straightened my back, flung out my arm in salute and shouted, "Yes, Mine Prophet!"

Our Dear Leader took my hand in his and shook it. "You're our only hope, son," he said. "Go the Power of Air."

TWENTY-EIGHT

I T IS HARD, EATING AIR. SOMETIMES YOU FEEL SO empty inside. That's why you need faith. Or your doubt will consume you, and you'll wind up like these men here, dressed in French army uniforms and pointing their guns at me.

This is why I came to France. To share my faith with you. So that you can learn to eat air too.

I have been here in the capital city of your food-terrist-loving nation for two weeks now. And the horrors I have seen! Worse than anything I ever imagined. Why, just yesterday I was sitting in one of your bistro food labs, refreshing myself with a glass of water—you know, the kind with the bubbles of air in it?—when the waiter, out of the blue, brought me a five-course meal of addictive caloric substances and a bottle of fermented grape juice! There I was, surrounded by infidels. My faith grew weak. My Twinkies attacked. How could I resist?

This is not your fault, I realize. The oppressive regime of France has one goal only: to keep you down. To keep you in ignorance of the truth.

My heart goes out to you. All of you. You've been slaves to food for so long, you have no idea what it's like to be free. But do not fear. We, the United States of Air, are here to help you.

285

To free you from this oppression. We are your liberators from the Tyranny of Food! Put down your guns, and welcome us with open arms. Our only desire is what is best for the people of France. It is our compassion that moves us. Our hunger for peace.

Food terrism, however, is difficult to root out of a society like France, where the preparation and consumption of your drug of choice have been raised to an art form. Therefore let me be clear: we will do whatever it takes to set you free. If necessary, we will even liberate you the same way we liberated the people of Micronesia last year: with nuclear weapons.

It is, truly, better to be dead than a slave.

That's it. Put down your guns. Group hug! Come on, group hug! Well, maybe later then.

There will be those, of course, who complain that we shouldn't bother France. Why should we care what you eat? How is that a threat to us?

But these are ignorant people. French food terrism threatens every freedom-loving nation in the world. How can we eat air if you don't too? Your doubt damages our faith. That is why, if you fail to comply with our demands, we will be forced to nuke your country until nothing is left but a twisted, molten cinder.

What's that noise? Not again. Who left the door open? How did those flying Twinkies get in here? Why can't you leave me in peace? I'm sorry, what's that? You have forty-eight hours to decide. Now shoo! Get away! Shoo!

ACKNOWLEDGMENTS

Behind every great man, they say, stands a hat rack propping him up. So it is with me.

Thanks go first to Alison Dasho *née* Janssen, whose uncanny sense of story cured this novelty of several outrageous infelicities.

My fellow expatriate, Derek Murphy in Taiwan, is responsible for the wonderful cover image—and for talking me out of the one I wanted to use.

Alison Rayner delighted me—and hopefully you—with her interior design.

Jill Mueller, whose nitpicking ways have earned her a berth in the Picker of Nits Hall of Fame in Louse Louse, Westchester County, New York, read proof.

A platoon of beta readers commented on various drafts. They were: Neal in Cali, Katy in an oil camp, Harold "El Padre" Munn, Laura in Kelowna, Steven S. in Melbourne, Rusty Y. in Sydney, Andy "flexi-buhl" Croome, Richard in Mompox, Gillian "Second Youth" Bridge, and Mark on the island. Special thanks to members of the James Bay gang—you guys helped more than you know.

Finalemente, y más importante que todo, besos y abrazos para mi conejita y ladybug girl. Te amo y te amo.

www.ingramcontent.com/pod-product-compliance
Lightning Source LLC
Chambersburg PA
CBHW031255170626
46807CB00001B/164

* 9 7 8 0 9 8 8 0 0 6 9 3 5 *